JUNIPER ASH

A. E. OGLESBY

Published by: A. E. Oglesby
Cover Design by: Spencer Lingafelter
Editing by: Harry Althoff

ISBN: 978-0-692-52923-2
10 9 8 7 6 5 4 3 2 1
First Edition

For Mary Homan

ROLLIN

The blade of my knife presses against the black man's throat and I watch with nervous trepidation as a trickle of crimson leaks from him.

"Please, mah friend, ah—"

I press the blade against him harder and hear a strangled cry squeeze from him. Blood runs in a river, staining the white bandana that hangs from his neck. He had approached me at my fire with a confident "Howdy!" I returned the greeting with the dark spell of a knife.

Many strangers have been lured by the seductive whisper of my fire, and many have been driven away by the seductive glint of my knife.

The man's eyes flick from my hand in front of him to the other that sits on my belt, where a gun lies hidden beneath my shirt. If he's easy, it'll stay there.

"All ah wanted was to share yer fire, ah swear it—"

I don't speak. Death is a simple friend when silence lurks behind in the shadows.

Fear crawls in the whites of his eyes, clutching the dark irises like a lifeline as the Grim Reaper hovers above. A beautiful life is so fragile. We're both men here, eye to eye, but one of us is real, and one of us is fake.

Words sputter from his mouth. I close my ears, my eyes, so I don't hear or see or feel anything but the cool wood of the knife handle. I have to. He's only a clone. The League said I had to kill anyone I came across, no matter what they said or did, because that's what I had to do if I wanted her back. *He's only a clone.* The thought doesn't make it easier. Of all the clones I've come across in the past couple of weeks, I haven't been able to kill a single one. I've threatened them, pushed my knife against their throats or pressed the barrel of my gun to their head, but no courage could force my fingers to make that last lethal twitch.

He walked up simply enough, but his footsteps were silent and barely left an imprint in the rubble. A flashlight dangled in his hands, casting a circular spotlight on his worn, brown shoes.

He had squinted at me, his eyes unaccustomed to the roaring flame of my fire, but nonetheless, there was a smile drawn across his face as wide as the distance between me and my home. His clothes were filthy with dirt and worn from frequent use. Though disheveled, his clothes were those of an affluent man. Southern hospitality dripped from his voice. His skin shone a dark chocolate in the firelight as a golden cross that hung from his neck flickered softly.

That's when I had pounced, as a human should on its clone. His screams echoed through the dismal world. *He's only a clone.*

"Ah can help yuh!" his words cut through my trance. "If yuh wants to get into Chicago, ah can help yuh, ah swear it, please—"

"What do you mean?" I whisper, my voice betraying my hand, the knife firm against his throat, the blood tickling my knuckles.

"Let me go and ah'll help yuh, ah swear by the Lord and all things holy. Yuh ain't gettin' in no other way."

My hand pulls away from his neck slightly, an itch attacking my ankle. "There are other ways to get into the city."

"Yuh ain't been there, ah can see it!" he pleads, his eyes sparking with hope. "Yuh know nothin', ah—"

My blade pulls away and his wound runs thick with blood. I turn away from this man below me, the man whom other men told me to kill, and it burns inside of me, a desire for an end…

How many corpses have I left behind me by now? An equal number to the nightmares I have when I sleep. I see their faces every night, haunting, relenting…is this the justice the League always preached?

An itch attacks my ankle again and my hand twitches to scratch it, but I keep it where it is, steady on the knife handle. I'm poised to kill, to take a life and further damn another.

I feel it before I realize it. A slimy appendage crawls around my ankle and I'm yanked away from the man and the world tilts—*thud*—air flies from my lungs—a gunshot explodes and I can't hear—a whine drills in my ears and the world flies in twisted colors around me—the smell of gunpowder hits my nose as the grip loosens—darkness falls but I fight and gasp and breathe and the sky returns and my eyes open and—

"Now, ain't yuh glad I stopped by yer fire after all?" the man says with the same smile, my revolver relaxed at his waist. Smoke twists through the air.

Every word flies from my head until I'm left with an empty mind and no mouth and nothing. There's nothing. My brain whirls and whizzes but it doesn't understand and neither do I.

He throws his hand out, hauling me up to my feet when my hands won't work and the slither slides off my ankle. I was supposed to be safe. The slithers don't come up here.

He tosses my gun to me and a slip it back into its holder on my waist. I open my mouth to say something but nothing comes out but exasperated air and confusion and fear—

The man starts laughing. "Yuh look like a star-struck little teeny-bopper! Yuh think ah wouldn't help yuh if ah saw a slither gettin' at yuh?"

I resist the urge to collapse back onto the ground. The slither's carcass awaits me in the dirt, and I don't feel too fond of getting close to it again. Only a slimy limb lies on the ground; the majority of the body rests underground. The slithers like to sneak up on you and stick you with poison, but I don't think it had me long enough to poison me.

"But I…I was about to—"

"Kill me?" he asks, his eyebrows raising as a chuckle escapes his loose lips. "Ah don't blame yuh, mah friend. Ah was on that dark path not too long ago, and saving yuh was yer first step toward the light and mah first step toward salvation."

I eye the cross dangling on his neck. He's one of the old believers. I didn't know there were any more out there. He presses his bandana into his wound, soaking it with blood. Soon, there's no white to see at all.

A gust of wind smacks into us and sends the fire into a wild dance. Dirt shoots into our faces. The man erupts in a frenzy of coughs as I press my mouth into my sleeve, stifling my own. I pull my own bandana over my face as I reach into my backpack for my water bottle.

Once the wind passes, I take a long swig from the water bottle to clear my throat. The man watches me as he struggles to clear his throat of dust. Pain festers in his eyes as he holds his throat, keeping the bandana against his wound instead of on his mouth. I pass the water to him. He accepts graciously.

"Thank yuh kindly," he smiles after quenching his thirst, seating himself by the fire and stretching his hands out to warm them. "Ah ain't had a drop in hours."

He returns the bottle and I place it beside me, sitting next to the man. Only a third remains.

"Mah name's Buddy, if yuh care to know," he perks up.

"Rollin," I say while staring into the fire.

We stay silent, watching the flames dance through the dark night, both of us knowledgeable of a silent agreement. Neither of us will go cold tonight.

He reaches into a backpack on his back and pulls out a leather-bound book. Across the front, white letters sprawl across the black landscape. It's a Bible, worn and well-read. He mutters something under his breath, which

I assume is a prayer of some sort. I leave the man to it. One hand is on his Bible and one is pressing the wound on his neck; between them, they hold a sin and a saint. He doesn't seem too concerned over his wound so neither am I.

It's been four weeks since I began traveling, and Buddy is the first person I've come across in that time whom I've known for more than a few minutes. I was strong in the beginning, willing to trudge through this ghost land, but I've grown tired. I can handle the walking. It's the loneliness that haunts me.

I pick up the remains of the meal I was eating before Buddy interrupted. Half a can of beans is as good as it gets when food and morals run low. The wind picks up again, sending dirt into my eyes. I huddle closer to the fire, hiding my face in my jacket. Night makes a soul weary.

Once the wind stops, I lift my gaze to the skyscrapers of Chicago. I've been camping on an outcropping of rock, far enough away the creatures wouldn't get me, or so I thought. A destroyed building shields me from the gate to Chicago, where guards stand at watch. A lone wall of the building stands, flyers fluttering weakly against the wall as rubble lies like fallen tears around the base. Unintelligible shouts echo from the distance.

The skyscrapers don't hold my interest for long. I've seen New York's skyline plenty, and all it reminded me of was my ultimate mission. I gaze at the landscape instead. Devastation lies before me. Buildings have reduced to rubble, roads have eroded to pebbles, and the railroad tracks have been ripped apart like forgotten puzzle pieces. I've seen similar terrain on my long journey, but never before was there so much destruction.

It wasn't always this way. Twenty years ago, this town thrived. People laughed, going about their errands as the virgin soil encased their virgin footsteps. The businesspeople climbed onto the train, paper masks strapped to their faces. Disease and debris was rampant but the world was created by God, they claimed, and what was meant to be would follow its course. There's a reason only a few old believers exist anymore.

I sigh, watching the chill take my breath. The past was damned, but the future is so far into hell it's hard to see the end.

"Yuh tryin' to get in those gates yonder?" Buddy says, breaking the silence.

I nod warily.

"Ah am too," he scratches his head. "What brings yuh to Chicago?"

I fold my arms, staring at this stranger by my fire. Questions of intention bring a new dimension. Usually, travelers aren't going anywhere. They drift.

"I'm looking for someone," I say hesitantly, glancing behind me. The guards shout mindlessly. Gunshots erupt. I ignore them.

"Family?"

"No," I grumble. "Just someone important."

"Ah sure hope the best," he grins again. "Have yuh been travelin' far?"

"Only from St. Louis," I lie.

The road from New York to Chicago is a long, dangerous journey. The League told me to keep to my own business.

Don't speak of New York. Don't speak of the mission. Don't speak to anyone. Don't let anyone live.

"There ain't much left there no more."

"There isn't much of anything anywhere," I mutter. "Where are you traveling from?"

Buddy's smile vanishes. "Somewhere that didn't have nothin' left fer me no more."

This is why the League told me not to talk to travelers. *Don't give trust willingly. Don't give anything willingly. Don't let anyone live.*

I turn my attention back to my dinner. I spoon beans into my mouth, swallowing quickly. I pretend it's the chocolate bars we would get as treats sometimes at the League. Another spoonful. Warm food fresh from the oven…spoonful.

"Ah want to help yuh, Rolin," Buddy whispers. "Ah want to help yuh find her."

Cold fingers grip my spin and dance across my nerves. He said *her*. I never said her name. Is it an innocent guess or a slip of the tongue?

"Why?" I stare at him, flattening my fears.

"Ah need to. Ah've sinned. Ah've crossed the Lord and ah need to do good."

Pain festers in his eyes. He clutches the Bible; his fingernails indent the soft leather cover.

He senses my hesitation. "Please, Rollin. Ah need to repent mah sins. If ah help yuh get into the city, if ah help yuh find her, maybe the Lord will forgive me. Ah need to help yuh as well, mah friend. Yer goin' toward the darkness and only the Lord can bring yuh back."

The League told me to follow their rules verbatim. They trusted me with this task—to come to Chicago, find Mira, and bring her back. Every Leaguer was sent away, everyone except me. I was the last resort.

"I'm a sinner, Buddy, but there's not a god in this world that will change that," I say darkly. "What did you do?"

"Ah killed someone," he whispers, evils clutching his voice. "Ah had a choice. It was mah life or his. Ah chose the selfish path. Ah did not choose the Lord's path. Let a sinner begin his path toward the light. Ah'm a resident of Chicago. Ah can help yuh."

I pause at this. He's a resident.

"I was about to kill you, Buddy. Why do you want to help me?"

"But yuh didn't!" he exclaims, nearly jumping to his feet. "That shows that our Lord wants yuh to repent yer sins as he wants me to."

"Where are you traveling from?" I ask, feeling my guard falling.

"Louisville, Kentucky"

"Why'd you leave Chicago?"

People don't often leave Chicago. Even fewer people return.

"Ah had to receive a parcel fer a friend."

"You're putting yourself in danger," I explain. "It's not wise."

"Mah mama raised me one way and ah've a hankerin' it's the reason ah'm still alive. Ah figured ah'd keep mahself to that."

I open my mouth to rebut him, to tell him he's going to get himself killed and his mama was foolish, but I stop.

"Ah want to help yuh find her, Rollin," he clasps his hands together. "Yuh'll be piddlin' around if yuh know nothin'. Ah reckon yuh ain't got a clue what a Privilege is."

He's right; I don't.

The League's affirmations sneak through my head: *Don't trust strangers. Don't trust anybody. Don't let anyone live.*

Every traveler must be killed, for the safety of the mission and for the mission itself. Kill all the clones. The more deaths, the better, in their eyes. I thought I could do it, since they *are* clones, but when my first victim stared at me helplessly under my knife, I couldn't go through with it.

But Buddy saved my life when I was about to take his. Without him, I could be dead. And he's a resident of Chicago, too. It'd be a crime against the mission not to accept his help. Then again, it's a crime already that I let him live.

"Okay," I whisper, as though the League wouldn't hear me if I did so. "Take me into the city."

Buddy can repent his sins by helping me and I can create sins by letting him.

Dawn glows like a dying ember on the horizon. I pack up my scarce belongings. We decide to get an early start; the gate is minutes away.

"Chicago ain't hard to slip into at dawn," Buddy explains. "Only the Oddities crawl 'bout."

A hush settles on the wasteland as the wind picks up. I pull the bandana around my nose and curl into my jacket. A chill pricks at my skin.

"Ah'm gonna start explainin' but don't yuh go lookin' at me," he begins. "Those damn Binocs will be at us 'fore we get a chance to run."

I do as he says, looking forward at the skyscrapers instead of him. Their black faces absorb the growing sunlight. Darkness radiates like an infectious disease.

"They'll be askin' fer mah name at the gate. Ah reckon yuh 'member some of the old world. Pretend yer my slave. It ain't fit, ah know, but it's how it goes."

The dark giants glower at me. I pull my head down, pressing my hand against my forehead. Heat radiates from it. I close my eyes for a moment.

I clench my teeth, pushing back against the dizziness, the headache. The world spins haphazardly around me.

"Ah wonder how yer gal got past those gates."

I keep my head down as we approach the gates. It isn't hard. I stumble on the loose rubble. Buddy doesn't notice. My heart flutters as the sun hits my neck.

The feet of three guards appear before me. The barrels of automatic guns swing by their shiny black shoes.

"State name, purpose of visit, and type," the middle guard orders.

"My name is Buddy Gavins. I am a resident of Chicago and a Privilege. This is my Oddity," Buddy motions to me, standing proudly. Any trace of the southern accent he had before has disappeared. My head lifts slightly.

Who the hell *is* Buddy?

The middle guard looks to the man on his right. He nods his head slowly but stares at me with a snarl.

Buddy strikes my face. I fall to the ground, holding my tender cheek. I stay there, clutch the rubble, and heave the contents of my stomach. I lie beside the waste as darkness bleeds into my vision, the world spinning like a top around me.

"I'll get you shipped to the suburbs, Oddity," Buddy growls in the voice of a stranger.

I keep my head down, staring at the rocks. Is this where you are, Mira?

"Drop your weapons and enter the gate," another guard yells.

Buddy snatches my gun and tosses it to the ground. A thunderous sound hits my eardrums as the massive gates are opened. Buddy snatches me by the arm, dragging me as we go. Without him, I doubt I could walk.

"Oddity scum," the middle guard growls, spitting as I pass.

The gates open to a short hallway, illuminated by a single bulb. At the end, a set of doors await. Buddy has an arm around me as I clutch onto him with clenched fingers. Whispers escape his lips as he holds his cross underneath white knuckles. The gates shut behind us and the doors in front of us open.

Immense skyscrapers glare at me like blank giants. They reflect the early morning sun with such intensity that pain burns in the back of my eyes. As much as I want to curl up, as much as I can barely stand, I make myself look. This is what I've worked for. This is where she is.

Though the sun hangs in the sky, the city before me rots in darkness. The skyscrapers cut off the natural light and cast the people in shadows. The streets are just large enough to squeeze one car through, and the sidewalks aren't much better. People march shoulder to shoulder, two people abreast. It's hard to tell the difference between them. They all wear the same jacket with a green stripe on the left arm. Hoods cover their faces and their bodies leave no hint of distinction.

A bundle of fabric huddles in an alleyway. I wouldn't know it's a person if I didn't see the scrawny hand reaching out from the blankets. What the person is begging for—money, food, or god knows what else—is a mystery.

The city is a machine. The crowd moves toward the center of the city. It originates from the left of me, where a brick wall breaks the monotony of the city. People squeeze through a singular archway; hundreds more surely wait behind them to pass. It never ends. They must be the Oddities, the ones Buddy mentioned earlier.

The strangest facet of the city is the absence of noise. The crowd doesn't speak. The bundled fabric in the alley doesn't speak. They all march, familiar with the drum of their lives. The stench is a different story; if there were anything left in my stomach, I would retch.

Within another alleyway, bodies are stacked, their pale hands stretching toward the Oddities that march past. I look away from them quickly, feeling the dizziness wash over me again. I lean on Buddy more heavily, the dark nightmare swirling around me.

"Calamity for sale," a scrawny man behind a booth yells. "Wash your worries away with one gulp!"

People have started to notice us. Some slow in the march, angering the people behind them who push them forward. They soon follow their eyes. A buzz of muttering drifts from the crowd.

"C'mon," Buddy murmurs to me. "Don't yuh look at them."

I try to listen to him, I really do, but the darkness attacks me. People stare. Their eyes trace us as we distance ourselves from the gate. Confusion lies like a heavy storm in their eyes.

We walk a block together before he finally throws me into an alley. People pass by, but not many look in on us. Buddy pulls me behind a dumpster.

"Ah'm sorry," he whispers, "but that's how ah had to act. Ah didn't mean to lay a hurtin' on yuh."

I don't speak. I collapse beside the dumpster, pull my hand through my hair, and try to put things in order—try to put myself in order. Dizziness hits me and I can't—

Buddy has been rummaging in the dumpster. He pulls out a jacket and tosses it to me. "Put this on."

I struggle to put the new jacket on over the one I currently wear. Every move sends my vision into a hurricane. The new jacket is thin as paper and rough as gravel. The wind bites at me more with it on rather than off. A forest-green stripe glints an ugly sneer on my arm.

"Yer an Oddity, Rollin. Welcome to Chicago."

ROLLIN

Yer an Oddity, Rollin. Welcome to Chicago.

The seven words echo endlessly inside my head, making my head whirl.

"Yuh okay, Rollin?" Buddy peers at me.

I press my lips together to avoid the urge to hurl again. I lean against the brick wall and close my eyes. Hot bleach begins to burn my ankle and I squeeze my mouth closed, trying to stifle the scream that's ready to burst from my body.

"The slither…poison," I pant helplessly.

My muscles are ripping themselves apart as I try, dammit I try, to keep myself together but it scratches, burns more—darkness clutches the edge of my vision, grabs and scratches and pulls me under—

My jean leg is yanked up. I pull against the darkness and force my eyes open to two men hovering over me, Buddy and a stranger. Southern and Chicago accents mix all together and I don't know.

The conversation drifts through my ears and I barely am able to listen to any of it. Something about me and poison and Buddy asking for something called Clam and the jingle of bottles all filter through my mind.

The pain is like a thousand burning suns all attacking my ankle and I try to breathe slowly and ignore it but none of it works.

The man hovering above me holds two small bottles. He has a jacket like mine and a snug black hat and beady insect eyes and a snarl but then the man is gone and the bottle is there, pressed against my lips.

A cry like a dying animal is strangled from me and then there's Buddy, lines pulled at his face and dark, midnight chocolate skin turns a shade darker. Liquid rushes through my lips, milky with a hint of coconut, and I swallow it eagerly, whatever it is, as long as it helps the pain.

I clench my teeth to see if it helps but it only makes the liquid bubble from my lips and only the darkness answers my calls. An entirety lasts and stretches across this hellish alleyway —footsteps clap against the bricks surrounding me. The last of the liquid drains from the bottle.

My ankle melts away…the pain is a distant nightmare…what'd he give me? A calm ocean waves rolls in…washing away the pain…the bleach on my ankle…I stare up at Buddy, my friend, my stranger southern friend and…it's gone, all of it.

The nightmare has been replaced with a galaxy of summer days and lightning bugs and juniper berries and…it's wonderful.

Warm arms encase me and bring me from the hard pavement, and oh, it's my friend! His name is Buddy and he's been so wonderful and he's talking to me about something, but the skyscraper, that skyscraper in front of me is so beautiful and—the sky! The blue sky shines above me and I don't know what darkness I was talking about earlier because the sunshine cascades on my face, bathing me in its warmth…like a giant lemon drop…

What was *in* that bottle? Is Buddy a genie? Is being in this city my wish? Maybe Buddy isn't a genie, but a wizard! I'm sure he can make magic potions and fly and turn it from day to night.

People crowd around me—like a wolf pack! I bet we'd be a super wolf pack. Maybe we could meet up tonight, go to a party or see the sights, though they'd probably have to show *me* since I don't know where I'm going but I'm glad to be here, you know? This city is so wonderful.

I tell Buddy that, tell him how wonderful everything is and how I want to be a citizen of Chicago—what are they called? Chicagonites? Chicagors? Chicagalapagos? I double over with laughter because, okay, that last one *was* a joke but that's okay—

Chicagoans? *That's* what they're called? Man, this Buddy is a character. He sure knows how to be wonderful. I wonder if I'm wonderful….

Where'd his accent go? Wasn't Buddy all 'yuh mamma ain't taught yuh none that yuh ain't gonna folla'? Didn't he say that? Something like 'm-m-m these grits ain't gonna get better, no they ain't'?

I open my mouth to ask him, but then we've turned into a building, twisting down the hallway as lights shine from above and everything is covered in rainbow lights cascading a glow of happiness and there's an elevator where a red light shoots out and flashes over Buddy's face and up we go!

Bing!—then we rush down a hallway with metal floors and walls and ceiling and lamps and—Buddy must run a lot because *man*, he is fast!

We race by tens of hundreds of thousands of metal doors and they all fly by, one by one like a swarm of metal insects taking flight—Buddy takes a sharp right to a door that's metal like everything else here and another rainbow catches my eye—

Click—the door swings open. How'd he do that? He didn't even have a key! I turn to ask Buddy but he's already inside, searching under a blue couch yelling at me to sit on the couch—where'd his accent go? Didn't he have a southern accent?

I step in the apartment and the walls are all opaque, changing colors all through the rainbow. And the view! Oh, the view. Beyond the opaque walls and blue couch and Buddy mumbling there is the city. Buddy orders me to come over—there's a black, metal box in his hands. What does this wizard have in store for me now? I'm sure whatever it is, it will be wonderful.

He digs in the black box, muttering—"Where are you?"—I'm right here, Buddy!

A massive needle—what's he doing with that? Oh, there's little men, falling out of airplanes above! They float down, parachuting to the ground. What's that tickle in my thigh? The needle buries into my fat, but what about the men, the parachuting men!

Then the needle is gone and Buddy makes it disappear because he's a wizard and everything is so wonderful. Why didn't I come sooner?

Buddy lies me down at the couch, pulling the soft blue blankets over me and I watch the walls continue with the rainbow—red and orange and yellow and green and blue and indigo and violet—Buddy hands me a glass of water and it runs down my throat in an icy waterfall.

I give the empty glass to him, lying down, my eyes close, the couch sinks me in, a cloud taking me away....

Where'd Buddy's southern accent go? He was so wonderful with it. My jeans roll up as tender fingers press against my ankle—was it hurting earlier? I can't remember...

Rollin?

He's calling—who is? I can't remember. What was I thinking? Some time ago my eyes closed and my brain stopped working and my muscles froze and my eyes couldn't stand to look at so much *wonderful* all the time and he started muttering so it was easier to slip away and away...

Rollin...

I can't hear him. I'm gone...*I'm wonderfully gone. I'm racing in the clouds away and up and the skyscrapers, oh, they look so wonderful from here. I'm the giant now and they're peasants and I turn around and I fly some more because it's so wonderful and I'm in Chicago, I'm one of them—a Chicagoan! Why didn't I come sooner? I could have been a Chicagoan and could fly and dance and be so happy and never have to be sad or angry or in pain and I'd always be happy.*

Forever.

I turn to someone flying next to me, trying to tell them that I once thought someone from Chicago was called a Chicagalapagos or Chicagor or Chicagonite but nothing comes out of my mouth so I keep flying.

All of us flying together above the city.

Forever.

NOVA

I drift into consciousness hazily. Oh, how I want to go back…why can't I go back? I don't remember where I was or what I was doing, but somehow I remember it being…wonderful. The most wonderful place I've ever been.

Reality is a harsher drug than the one I slip into so frequently. Micah's bedroom is dark; light flees from evil places, naturally. It isn't Micah who is evil, it's this room with its gray walls and black curtains and stuffy air and cluttered floor where you can never find anything and the smell, like—

"Nova?" a voice calls me from my side.

I roll over and his eyes, sparkling green emeralds, reflect back at me, the lone color in this sea of pressing darkness. I press my lips against his because I know he expects it from me. He returns vigorously. I comb my fingers through his rich black-brown hair. The scent of cologne fumigates the air and the black night flies from my mind for a moment.

I shove his chest, his hands crawling on my body. "Micah, you know we can't."

"Why not? Our clothes are off, we have time to spare…" he trails off, a mischievous twinkle in his eyes.

He presses closer to me, pushing himself on me as those emerald eyes close and the light is gone. I stop resisting. It's easier that way. My hand flings out to the table next to me, searching blindly for that little bottle. My fingers chase lemon drop wrappers and half-smoked cigars until finally it hits the chilled bottle. It'll take me away. It'll take me far away, to daytime, where the sun shines through the clouds and the air smells of warm Clam cookies and cold Clam shakes.

Fingers snake around my wrist. He snatches the tiny bottle from my fingers. It's so small, so unbearably small and the daylight and smells of summertime wash away and his cologne takes over again, that sweet, rich smell. I shrivel under his gaze and collapse beneath his fingers. His next touch won't be so gentle.

"You want this right *now*?" he snarls.

"No, Micah, I just—"

He clutches my jaw. "Then what, Nova? What is it?"

I pry his fingers from my jaw and pull them to my chest. "It's amazing without Clam, but it's *unbelievable* when I'm on it."

The lust in his eyes shows that he wants to believe it, the dark red lust that flames as brightly as his love for me does. His shoulders relax, his fingers uncurl, and his eyes melt into green beauties once more. The bottle twists through the air until it hits the ground, the milky substance bleeding onto the carpet. He pushes against me once more, that hunger pressing onto me, until the twinkle of my phone interrupts.

"Go ahead," Micah grumbles, rolling back over. "Answer it."

I hurry to find my phone in the abyss of garbage and dirty laundry on the floor. My purse appears as a red flame, lonely in a sea of ashes. I dig through it and feel the cool metal of my phone. I flip it open and instantly hear Ivy's voice chirping in my ear.

"Nova, where are you? I've been waiting years for you here! Hello?"

"Calm down, Ivy. I'm at…Micah's."

"Micah?! You can't be serious," she growls in a hushed whisper. "Not after…last time."

"Yeah, well," I glance at Micah, who gives me a demonic glare, "Things happened."

"Things don't just happen, Nova."

"But—"

"Whatever, I don't care. Can you hurry? Meet me at Sip and Sleep as soon as possible. Some Oddities keep ogling me through the window and it's giving me the creeps. Some of them are girls too, Nova. I didn't even know Oddities were into that. I thought—"

"I'll be there in a flash," I cut in, shutting my phone.

I pull myself from his covers, searching for my clothes in the sea. I find them quickly enough, only after discovering foreign lacy pink panties and a matching bra. I ignore them. It's easier to pretend I never found them than to pretend I don't care for Micah's midnight women. I pull my dress on, struggling to slide the leather across my slick skin.

"Oh, you look so good in leather," Micah sings, desire rolling a hurricane in his eyes. "Please stay with me, baby. Let me have you once more."

His hands reach for me, his lips beg for my kiss, and his arms yearn to hold me, not the woman in lacy pink. Only me.

His hands tear off the leather with the speed and strength of a starving animal. The wind from the fan above tickles my bare skin as he throws me onto the bed. The rough wool digs into my skin, but I ignore it. He loses himself in me, devouring me as though I'm a Calamity milkshake at Sip and Sleep—Ivy! Oh, what excuse can I give her now?

By the time he has finished, twenty minutes have passed. I find my clothes again, hurriedly dress, and sprint downstairs while calling my car, barely fleeing the pleas of Micah's manhood calling out to me once more.

"Hello? Driver? Get over here *now*."

My Oddity—the roach—is waiting promptly outside in my sleek black car. A white stripe runs down the side of the windshield, marking it as a Privy car. As I exit the building, a siren sounds, signaling to the Oddities to stop and let me pass. If they don't, they will get arrested and sent to the suburbs. I run through my path, roaches packed on either side. Some stare at me with jealousy while others, the more docile ones, avert their eyes.

My roach holds the door open as I bound into my car. The door slams behind me and it climbs into the driver's seat. Outside, the horde of Oddity roaches resumes their scurrying along the sidewalks.

"Sip and Sleep," I order.

It remains silent as it blends into the minimal traffic.

It isn't supposed to talk to me; I listed that and several other preferences on my roach quality list. This roach has been with me for a while now and is very docile. I hope it stays around. Others haven't adhered to my preferences as well.

We arrive at Sip and Sleep minutes later. The siren rings through the air. My roach jumps from the car, opens my door, and waits until I have safely crossed my Privilege path before disappearing into the car. The door chimes dully, announcing my timely arrival.

I spot Ivy in our usual spot among the orange couches in the far corner. Two melted Calamity shakes and an infuriated pair of eyes greet me. Her usually straight, black hair is curled into tiny pin-curls today, and her typical colorful attire is now black and revealing. I hurry toward her, sweat beading on my forehead. I wipe it away in disgust. Privies don't sweat. What's wrong with me?

I collapse into the cushions, ready to devour my Clam shake and drift away from the world, but knowing Ivy, that won't happen soon. Her anger radiates like a furnace.

"You left me waiting for forty-five minutes," Ivy growls. "Those Oddities outside almost broke the windows. Their stares, Nova…"

"Oddity! Bring us new shakes," I shout to the front counter, where one waits. I hope it's a docile one.

Sharply, a red-haired Oddity sweeps in, replaces our shakes with fresh ones and hurries away in its green striped apron. I wonder how many Clam doses are in this shake. Ivy and I used to fly away with only one dose, but now, after so many flights, it takes several to put us down.

"I can't apologize," I turn away from her. "Micah wanted—"

"That's what it is now, isn't it? Micah wanted this, Micah wanted that. Do I come in second to Micah now?"

"Ivy—"

"Forget it, Nova," she says, clutching her new Clam shake. "I don't know why you're so fascinated with him. He's only here for a few more weeks."

Pounding erupts against the windows. We glance over to see a group of roaches ogling us. Some of the female ones lick their lips at us.

"Oddity! Close those blinds," I call to it before turning to Ivy. "It pretends like it doesn't hear me, I swear!"

"Don't call them 'it,' Nova," Ivy attempts to be stern. "They're people, you know. We wouldn't get our Calamity shakes without her."

"Oh, stop it," I shove her playfully. "Oddities aren't people. They're roaches!"

Silence settles a frost on us. Ivy sips her shake.

I scowl as the Oddities continue to beat the glass into submission. "Were they doing this the whole time I was gone?"

"Yes, but don't worry. I called my Oddity and he sent a Warden."

"Oh, those Wardens don't help. They're glorified roaches, that's what they are."

"Yes, well…at least he'll get them to go away. I'm surprised the Binocs hadn't spotted it first."

"I'm glad there are some Privies running this town, but why would any Privy *want* to work?"

"It beats me," Ivy sips her shake, chuckling. "I couldn't imagine going to a job every day."

A commotion comes from outside as a Warden approaches the Oddities. He flattens them against the windows as he slaps cuffs on their wrists. Tonight, they'll be shipped to the production lines in the suburbs, where all the unruly Oddities are kept. Oh, the suburbs will beat them into submission.

I take my first sip of the Clam shake in celebration. Endorphins flush my system. I smile, giggling hazily. "Did you get the Smile-A-While shakes again?"

"I knew we were gonna need them," Ivy laughs, taking a gigantic gulp herself.

"Aw, I'm sorry, Ivy. Micah is so wonderful! He asked me to stay and I couldn't refuse."

"Nova, stop!" Ivy slaps my shoulder, gulping down a quarter of the shake. "I don't know how you get away from him. If it were me, I wouldn't be able to keep my hands off him! He's so…wonderful."

Half the shakes are gone.

"Don't you think!"

"Totally."

"He's a—"

"—dreamboat, an absolutely—"

"—wonderful dreamboat!"

Three-fourths have disappeared.

"You're so wonderful, Ivy. You're my best friend."

"You're *my* best friend!"

I stare at Ivy, my wonderful, best friend. Micah hates her because she's Asian.

The shakes have vanished; only the carcasses, two lone glasses, remain.

"Hey, I got an idea. Why don't I have a party this Saturday. It'll be wonderful, so absolutely wonderful!"

"Well, you'll have to order in to get an extra large, wonderful case of Calamity for everyone!"

Ivy sinks into the cushions. That Oddity sweeps towards us and picks up our glasses. It glances at us a second, fury flaming in its icy blue eyes. Nope, not a docile one. It slips something out of its pocket and places it on the table before slinking away into the kitchen—lemon drops. I always like it when Sip and Sleep gives lemon drops to us...

"Can Micah come?" I ask, staring at the lemon drops. My mouth waters.

"Oh, yes," Ivy giggles. "He's wonderful! Why couldn't he come?"

I sink into the cushions, my head rolling back. The metal lamps shine their rosy light at us.

"Nova?" Ivy chimes.

"Mmh?"

"Did you ever notice how wonderful this store is? The opaque walls, fading through the rainbow, the cushions always so soft, and the most wonderful smell like—"

"—Clam cookies," I grin, drifting into my subconscious.

"Yes...the most wonderful Calamity cookies..."

Then we're gone, *so wonderfully gone. I fly away from Sip and Sleep with Ivy zooming next to me. Oh, I'd forgotten that we get to fly! I love flying. It's so wonderful. We zip through the skyscrapers, scale the walls, fly with everyone in Chicago because we're one, all together, but only right now. None of this will ever be the same.*

Ivy and I fly, twirling in spirals as we laugh and laugh because it's so wonderful up here. It's so blissfully wonderful.

Something skits across the periphery of my vision. My head floats towards it, hazily, wonderfully...what was I doing? I can't remember.

I turn towards Ivy, but someone behind her is waving towards me. It's an Oddity. How...wonderful? What is it doing up here, where the Privies play?

Ivy shakes me gently, pointing towards the clouds. I race her, floating to the

16

monstrous marshmallows and bouncing on them. What was I thinking before? Oh, I can't remember. I'm having such a wonderful time! I throw my arms into the air, take one last leap, and cascade into the Chicago sky. Skyscrapers glisten about me.

Up here, I'm the giant. There isn't anything more wonderful than that.

ROLLIN

I bolt awake, leaping from the soft cushions I was resting on as the foreign world smacks me in the face. Where did Buddy go? Now I'm in this apartment and I don't know how I got here or where I am.

A door—I bolt toward it, tugging on the door handle but I can't get it and the cold metal chills my hand and oh god, I failed the League, I failed Mira, I failed the mission and the colonies—

"Rollin?" a southern voice drifts to me and I turn and see Buddy and I run and hug him because maybe I didn't fail. Maybe I didn't do so bad. Maybe I'm all right after all.

He chuckles. "Gosh, Rollin. Ah didn't know yuh to be a friendly fella."

"I'm just glad to see a familiar face, that's all," I say, pulling away quickly. "Where am I? What happened, Buddy? I can't remember anything after—"

"Rollin," he laughs again, "don't yuh worry. Yer in mah apartment. It's normal if yuh can't 'member nothin'."

"Normal?"

"Calamity sure does a doozy."

"Calamity? Buddy, what are you talking about?"

He sighs, leading me to the gray couch I was sleeping on before. I wrack my brain for memories between the alleyway and now, but all I find is a black hole.

"That slither poisoned yuh out there. Ah didn't think it did neither, but it got a hold of yuh," he pauses a moment, folding his hands over. "Ah ain't seen someone scream as much as yuh did in that alleyway."

The memory trickles back slowly. I was on the asphalt clutching my ankle, and the pain—my nerves twitch at the memory.

"Ah needed to get yuh the antidote, but ah couldn't pull yuh through

Chicago with that ankle killin' yuh. Ah gave yuh some Calamity, or Clam, as the people call it. It's a euphoric drug. One bottle takes away all negative emotions fer most: fear, sadness, pain, worry, grief, and anger, to name a few. 'Em that have been here a while gotta take a couple 'fore they fly away."

"Was it in a little bottle?" I ask, the image drifting through my head.

"Yessir," he says, "and ah bet yer wonderin' why yuh can't 'member nothin'."

I nod in agreement. I twist my ankle. Pain rolls through it.

"Calamity does a number of things while yer under its spell, but nobody 'members what. It causes severe amnesia. When yuh wake up afterwards, yuh don't 'member nothin' of what happened while yuh was on it. One thing is fer sure: it felt *good*."

I stare at the apartment around me, taking all the information in. Metal walls greet me on all sides except one, where a massive window expands the length of the wall. The apartment itself is very somber; everything inside is gray.

"Take a lemon drop, Rollin," Buddy gestures to the candy dish on the coffee table. "It helps some with the confusion. They're made fer post-Calamity side effects. It don't help none with the amnesia, though—that's permanent."

I take his suggestion and begin sucking on a lemon drop. "What happened afterward?"

"Oh, yes, ah was tellin' yuh a story," he laughs. "Ah took yuh to a pal of mine. Yuh two sure hit it off. Y'all was like Calamity and cookies, ah swear! Yuh don't 'member him though. He's like a witch doctor; he got everythin' yuh'd need. He found an antidote fer yuh and ah took yuh back up here to mah apartment. Yer all fine now…yuh took a nice nap, yuh did. That pain in yer ankle will fade, don't yuh worry none."

"Thank you, Buddy," I say. "I owe you one…I just don't understand why you'd risk so much by brining me in."

He pats my back with a grin. "Yuh don't owe me nothin', Rollin! Ah'm only goin' down the Lord's path and repentin' mah sins, that's what ah be doin'. Yer the one doin' *me* a favor. Ah ain't riskin' much neither. The Privies here can get away with murder, if yuh can believe it. One more roach won't hurt none. 'Side, this apartment was gettin' lonely! It ain't seen a face in a couple of months."

"How did you keep it if you've been away for so long?"

"Every Privy gets their own apartment here. Don't matter if yuh use it or not, the city don't care."

I stare at my hands again so my eyes won't deceive me and tell the truth. Honesty is in the eyes. I can't look at him. I can't watch that smile anymore. It's unbearable, unnerving. It takes a strong man to look in the eyes of his victim, and I'm not one of those men.

I escape to the windows and watch the machine of Chicago function effortlessly on the streets. My escape does not last long; Buddy soon joins me.

"Yuh see those people on that sidewalk yonder? Those are Oddities, 'roaches,' we call 'em. There are tens of thousands of 'em crawlin' in this city. They live in the other side of town, across that wall yuh saw when yuh came in. They spend their time here, in the Privy sector, where most of their jobs are. They all hafta wear those jackets. The green stripe marks 'em as an Oddity. If they're caught without it, which happens more then yuh think, they're sent inta the suburbs, to the production lines.

"The people in cars are Privileges. They don't go on the sidewalks—never. They have Oddities who drive 'em 'round, Oddities who hold doors open fer 'em, Oddities to do their biddin' cuz they're privileged and them Oddities ain't got the sense God gave a billygoat.

"Yer an Oddity, Rollin. It's the only way ah could get yuh in undetected. The city don't care how many roaches scurry on the street; it's the Privies they care 'bout. When ah said mah name at the gate, they was runnin' the Privilege directory fer mah name. They'd've skin us alive ah wasn't there!"

I think of the gates. Though I didn't realize it then, I was suffering from the poison. I couldn't walk straight. I couldn't think right. I couldn't do anything. Buddy stopped being southern for a second there. He talked and acted nothing like himself. He was a different man.

Outside, the sidewalks continue their steady stream of people. Buddy and I watch them like television show. It's surreal. Someone in the crowd stops moving and steps away from the horde of people. He wears a black cap tight around his head and his eyes drill a hole through the window. Beside me, Buddy tenses up; his fists clench in his pockets.

"Yuh want another lemon drop, Rollin?" Buddy strolls to the coffee table.

"Uh, sure," I turn to him and accept the candy.

I collapse on the couch. I don't think I can do this. I hold my head in my hands, trying to keep everything in but it doesn't work. It never does anymore.

Buddy heads to the kitchen. "Yuh hungry? Ah can call fer some fixin's."

My stomach growls. "Yes, please."

Buddy's southern voice drifts away as he leaves the living room.

What am I doing here? Is this where you're hiding, Mira?

I glance over the half wall and watch Buddy chatter away.

"Ah got some pizza. Yuh ever had any in St. Louis?"

"No," I mutter. "Never had it before."

"Well," Buddy grins, "Yer in fer a treat. Pizza is 'bout the one thing Chicago kept from the olden days. It's got a thick crust, almost like a pie, with all sorta ingredients on top. They call it deep dish. In the olden days, New York got a variation called thin crust, but there's a reason that ain't 'round no more."

I stare at Buddy. I try to see what he's hiding because there's something there, beyond his religion and southern accent and pledge to repent his sins. There's something else.

"How do you know so much about the old world?" I ask.

"Mah mama," he smiles fondly, heading to the kitchen. "She told me all 'bout how it used to be. Ah'd sit with her while she knitted, cinnamon driftin' thru the air, and she'd tell me all 'bout the old world."

I bite my lip. It's not real. None of this is *real*. The first day I came to the League, they told us how the clones function. Five years ago, the clones led a revolt against us to take the cities they rebuilt as their own. The clones' memories were wiped and replaced with the memories of the people they were cloned of. Now all the clones—Buddy included—walk around their cities thinking they are human and that their memories are real.

Buddy's mama isn't real. She never was for him. She's somebody else's memory, somebody in Europe, waiting for the clones to be exterminated so they can return to their homeland—America—where a rebuilt empire is waiting for them.

That's what I'm here for.

The League's mission is to kill the clones.

All of them.

"How the lemon drops treatin' yuh?" Buddy asks.

"Wonderful," I grin, snapping out of my trance. "Just wonderful."

My mission is to find Mira, who was originally sent here to exterminate all the clones. I'm not supposed to finish her job, but I will have to eventually. All the other cities have been infiltrated and the clones—gone. All of them, all except Chicago. When I find her, we'll finish it together. I am and will be responsible for their deaths—especially Buddy's.

Buddy saunters into the living room. "Where'd yuh get those nasty scars on yer leg?"

"What?"

"The scars on yer leg," he laughs. "Ah saw them when ah gave yuh the antidote."

"I fell into a fire a couple of years ago."

This makes Buddy laugh. "Yuh *fell* inta a fire? Have too much whiskey, now?"

"No, no...nothing like that. I got my toe caught on a tree root and fell. Hurt like hell," I murmur, turning away from Buddy.

He keeps laughing, holding his stomach like he can't keep the damn laughter from exploding out of him. I'm not stupid enough to trip over a tree root; I'm stupid enough to trust the scientists. Before I left the League for Chicago, they trained me on how to use my equipment. One of these training sessions didn't go so well.

A hand is at my shoulder, holding me steady. "Yuh okay, fella?"

"Don't worry," I look at him. "I'm only hungry. Nothing a good meal can't fix."

A bell rings. Buddy springs to his feet to receive the pizza. I don't see the Oddity that must have given it to him; I only hear muffled conversation, a slight beep, and a click of the door closing.

The most heavenly smell drifts to me. Buddy appears before me, a hot, steaming pizza in his hands. He places it on the coffee table in front of us and hands me a piece, along with silverware and a plate. I devour the delicacy as I devour my guilt.

"Yuh got a plan yet?"

"What?"

He grabs himself a piece. "Findin' her. Yer special someone."

"No...I've been too worried about getting in here to think about that."

That makes him laugh—again. "Ah can imagine."

We eat in silence for a while. I try not to look at him.

"Ah might be able to help yuh get started there, Rollin."

"What do you mean?"

He grins while chewing his pizza. "Ah have some connections with the Binocs in the city. Yuh 'member that fella yuh met? Nah, of course yuh don't! Well, he was a Binoc. Ah didn't tell him yer situation of course, but ah can get yuh a job at his post. Yuh'll be able to look fer her all over the city."

No, he can't. Please, Buddy, stop.

"I'm sorry, Buddy..." I turn to him. "I don't understand."

"Binocs're like guardian angels fer the Privies. They sit top most of those towers and watch the city. They watch fer Privies in trouble, unruly roaches, and anythin' that ain't usual. Yuh can see why it'd be perfect fer findin' yer gal."

I shut my eyes, shielding myself from his face, dark in features but bright in hope. He's one of them. All of them are, Privilege or Oddity.

"Buddy, if you could do that for me..."

"Don't think twice 'bout it. Ah'm repentin' my sins, 'member? Ah only hope yuh don't forget 'bout me when yer traipsin' 'bout the skyscrapers."

I laugh with him, reaching for another slice of pizza. I can't do this.

"Yuh can start tomorrow, if yuh'd like. Yuh'll need a good night's sleep 'fore old Marco takes yuh under his wings. He's a rascal, he is!"

Sunlight drifts through the windows, cascading Buddy in a blinding halo and I can't, I can't—

Eventually, I'll have to kill him. He's done so much for me, and I will have to murder him one day.

NOVA

"Micah, please. I don't want to, I can't—"

Fists fly. Tears fall. Courage crumbles.

My senses turn off. I refuse to feel pain. If I do, he wins. Yells erupt, splintering my ears, but I stop. I can't.

I'm in the corner now, on the ground, curled in a ball to shield my face from the abuse. People will start to question if bruises appear on my face. Micah knows this too; rarely will he hit my face, but accidents have happened.

He continues to yell, to kick, to punch. When will he stop? When will this stop?

I close my mind. I drift into my subconscious, away from Micah, from his apartment, from the blood and bruises and—

It stops. Footsteps echo against yells, the door slams, a cacophony in creation.

He's gone.

I wipe away the tears, the blood, the remorse. This is the fifth time it has happened. Each time it gets worse. Each time he apologizes. Each time I forgive him.

Ivy calls me weak. I don't disagree with her. I disagree with myself for letting it happen.

I'm still huddled in my arms, my shield, when the door creaks open. I don't emerge from my cave. I'm a roach and I deserve my dark prison.

"Nova?" a voice calls, sweet as Clam cookies. No anger. No fists. No pain.

I open my mouth to speak, but only a squeak escapes. Arms encircle me. Kisses graze the bruises. Apologies are mutter and I can't, I can't forgive him, not again, not after—

23

"I love you," he murmurs, his lips on my ear.

Ivy was right. I am a roach. Here I am, beheaded, but I survive. If a roach can keep living, why can't I?

Micah wraps me in his arms, settling me in his warm bed with his soft covers and I let him because I'm headless and he loves me and I love him. It was a mistake. It won't happen again. He *loves* me. The punches hurt, but not near as much as it would be to never see him again. Besides, it was my fault. I should've convinced Ivy to let Micah come.

"Nova," he's beside me in the bed, "I promise it won't happen again. I'm drunk, baby. I didn't have my Calamity today." He promises.

"I'll ask Ivy again if you can go to her party," I turn to him.

After Ivy and I woke up yesterday at Sip and Sleep, she decided that yes, she was going to have a party on Saturday, and no, Micah couldn't come.

Micah didn't like that.

I stretch out my arms. Pain sparks on my nerves. I stop moving. Bruises are already beginning to blossom like spring flowers across my entire body. My head and shoulder hurt from when he slammed me into the wall. I wish I could go to the Privilege clinic, but they always ask too many questions. If I say it's post-Calamity side effects, they offer me a lemon drop. If I refuse, they get suspicious. It's better to wear long sleeves and pretend it's a fashion statement.

"Micah?" I ask like a child. He's always in a giving mood afterwards.

"Hmm?"

"Do you have Clam? I'm feeling lousy."

"Mmm—why would that be, baby?"

I tread carefully. "The pain, sweetheart. It hurts. We both can have some."

He finds the tiny bottles, portals of escape. We swallow the milky Clam, bottle after bottle. We lie in his bed wordless until it takes us.

Then we're gone. *We're wonderfully gone.*

ROLLIN

Sleeping is hard when guilt hovers like a guillotine ready to fall. It's midnight now. I said goodnight to Buddy nearly four hours ago. We will meet Marco in three hours on top of the Jones Tower, or what Buddy *insists* is the Sears Tower. Buddy said it used to be one of the greatest skyscrapers in the world, and though they've changed the name several times, it will always be the Sears Tower.

I lie in one of Buddy's spare bedrooms. Buddy said good night to me a couple of hours ago. I try to sleep, but fail in every sense. How could I sleep? I lie awake, stare at the ceiling and listen. Cars honk. Sirens echo. People shout, but they're not people. They're clones.

Or that's what I keep telling myself. They're just the same as me, but seeing them as actual people will only make the eventual genocide that much harder. I have to do it. They chose me. The colonies are depending on me.

Maybe I don't have to do it. Maybe I can lie here for the rest of my life and never have to move. The League will forget about me and Mira and Chicago and everything can go on as normal and no one has to die. Chicago can go on as usual. There wouldn't be a mass genocide. But, that would be a perfect world, and in that world, Mira would be here lying next to me, laughing about how I looked when I ate deep-dish pizza.

When I was back in New York, I knew we were killing people, but it seemed so far away. It was so far away. I never watched the ignorant people pass by knowing they only had weeks left to live.

I can imagine the Oddities waking up in a couple of hours, as I will be. They'll sip their third cup of Calamity coffee because the world is awful and they might as well drown their sorrows away. They'll look up into the poisoned sky and say: "Maybe today's the day I'll be something more than a roach," but it won't be. It never is for them because they're Oddities and later they'll be found dead in an alleyway but no one will care because it's an Oddity and they're roaches. They can never be more than that.

That's what Buddy told me. It's how this world works. The Oddities go to work partially intoxicated from their Clam coffee. The people in this city have grown so accustomed to it, they need a *lot* to knock them out. Anyone can get Clam, it's the manner they use it that matters.

The League didn't tell me it was going to be this difficult. They didn't tell me much about Chicago, because I wouldn't have gone if they did. They told me it was the worst city of them all. They told me it'd be harder getting out than it would be getting in. They told me I had a good chance of dying, like many of the other Leaguers had, but I was okay with that because I had to find Mira and I couldn't leave her there and what did I get myself into—

No. I have to do this. I need to find Mira and infiltrate the system. They aren't people. They are clones.

Then, the people—the real, living, breathing people—can come back to America. That is my mission, and I can't fail. No matter what, I can't fail.

I remember my childhood. I didn't know who my parents were. I traveled a lot between cities, but there was an elderly woman who took care of me once. I called her nana. It was years ago when I last saw her, but I still remember her face. She usually didn't take in orphans, but I was Hispanic, like her. She had brown, leathery skin with the rosiest cheeks and crispiest blue eyes. When she would fall, I was afraid she'd shatter. She was the sweetest woman who always squeezed fresh orange juice in the morning. It was my favorite, and she always made sure I had some.

Some days, nana would teach me Spanish while making me a quesadilla. She always stressed the importance of heritage. I'd bite into the crunchy, cheese-filled tortilla while muttering botched Spanish. She sweated each word I learned with a different, traditional Spanish dessert, or the ones that she had the ingredients to make.

I wonder how she is or if she thinks about me. I wonder how baby Maggie is growing. She was an orphan, like me. She was only two when I left. I doubt she remembers me.

I think back to my time in the Calamity haze. It's less painful than thinking about my old life. I can't remember what I did or whom I met or what I saw or heard or *anything*, but I remember feeling. It was wonderful. If a flash of pain or confusion or anger, I forgot about it. At some point I fell asleep and it was even better and...I want to go back.

No. I can't. Buddy had some Calamity before he slept and my god, he seemed so blissfully unaware of the world around him. He was like a child; his imagination ran free and his ignorance flew high.

He wouldn't let me have any. I asked, but he denied. He said the addiction is a double-edged sword; life is punishing and dreams are rewarding. He didn't want me to succumb to similar struggles.

My stomach grumbles absently. Tired of lying awake, I soon find myself in the kitchen. There isn't much there; his fridge is empty, his cabinets bare, and his waste basket clean. If Buddy were a stranger to me, I'd think the poor man was starving.

Most likely, he doesn't buy groceries. Maybe no Privilege buys groceries. I can't see a reason why they would. As Buddy explained to me last night, Privileges have an on-call kitchen staff. Their food is charged to their room, which they pay for at the end of the month to the residency councilor. I didn't quite understand what he meant by a residency councilor, but I was too tired to ask.

It matters little, since Privileges can have whatever they want. It matters to the Oddities that they pay. If an Oddity doesn't receive enough money, death is its future.

I press a button on the wall and it begins blinking red. A robotic voice responds dully. I order the same as Buddy did before: deep-dish, Chicago-style pizza. *It'll be a couple of minutes*, it responds. *Please be attentive.*

The voice disappears and I'm left in silence once more. Buddy's snores drift in from the other room.

It's shocking how well the clones are living on their own. The colonies cut off all resources to the clone societies years ago. Once the clones finished rebuilding their empire, the clones were deemed unnecessary. Energy has been scarce. It was the first thing the colonies cut off. Once the clone revolts began, all resources and aid was taken from the clones.

We thought they'd taper off. We thought they'd die without us, but they didn't. Clones were sent into the suburbs to produce goods, grow food, and die.

Those degenerates we thought were so brainless became the bane of our existence.

A doorbell interrupts my train of thought. I make my way toward the metal door and open it to a young girl no older than fourteen. Her face is bold but her body turns inward, receding in on itself. She holds a cardboard box, wet with steam. I inhale the scent and close my eyes for a moment. My mouth waters at the smell.

"Payment," she says numbly.

I snap out of my trance. "Uh, can you charge it to the room?"

She doesn't bat an eye. "You are aware of the surcharge?"

"Yes, that's fine," I say, staring at this mysterious Oddity girl.

She wears an Oddity jacket similar to mine. I had taken it off before I went to bed. Now, all I wear is a white tank top and my boxers. Realizing this, I grin shyly and accept the pizza.

The girl stares at me a moment longer. Her brunette hair is tied lazily in a bun. Thick streaks of grease ruin the beautiful hue. Heavy bags lie under her eyes, stealing the youthful glow her face once had. Her head cocks slightly, her tired, brown eyes narrowing.

"Can I help you with anything else, Mr. Gavins?"

"No, no. I don't need any more food," I respond quickly, but I can't pull my eyes away from her. She notices.

She wraps her arms around her, trying to be brave, attempting to look into my eyes. "Mr. Gavins, there are other services I can offer."

This breaks my gaze, snaps my trance, and oh my god, she's a girl, a *young* girl and how could I and how could *she* and—

"Please," she whispers suddenly, sensing my apprehension. "I need the money."

I step back, further into the apartment, but I still hold the door open, my eyes locked on this girl. She's only a girl.

"I've had other men, Mr. Gavins," she pleads. "I understand the rules."

The *rules*? What rules are these? The pizza's aroma drifts to me once more and I gag, my stomach heaving.

I throw the pizza back at her. "Take the pizza. Eat it, throw it away, say I didn't answer the door—I don't care."

"Mr. Gavins, please, I'm begging—"

"Stop," I step back, "you don't know what you're doing."

"I am fully aware of what I'm doing," she responds, stepping forward. Bravery glimmers hopelessly in her eyes.

"Charge whatever you want to the room," I shout. "Please, just *leave*."

This stops her. "Are you sure I can't do *anything* for you, Mr. Gavins?"

"Promise me something."

"What?" she asks, confusion replacing her dim bravery.

"I want a promise from you."

She doesn't answer. Shock brings her adolescent eyes wide apart, staring at me with wonderment. She clutches the pizza in her arms, hot sauce dripping through the cracks and down her arms. She doesn't seem to notice.

"Never offer yourself to a man for payment again."

I close the door on her, still standing there in shock. She was a girl. I smelt dread on her even before I opened the door. She had planned to do that, I'm sure of it. Whoever opened that door was going to be offered the same as I was.

I press myself against the closed door, and I swear, she doesn't move.

Her breath beats at the door. I hear it through the cold metal for minutes. She doesn't move. I don't think she can. Ten minutes have passed before I catch the soft patter of her feet shuffling down the hallway. The cardboard box crinkles as she rips it open.

The League told us that the clones don't age. Thousands of people were cloned years ago, and while the humans have grown, the clones have remained exactly as they were. They can't reproduce. They can't change. They are frozen in time. The girl at my door probably has been prostituting since the clone revolt. There's not many ways for young women to make money otherwise.

I collapse on the couch in the living room. The smell of hot pizza lingers in the air. I've lost my appetite.

I need to find Mira soon. We need to leave. I can't endure this society much longer. I'm doubtful if Mira has lasted this long. The months she has lived here are no comparison to the time I've spent here.

Mira—her image lingers in my mind. It's been so long since I heard her laugh. It was like bells ringing subtly on Christmas morning. My chest aches. Memories return after so many days of holding them back. We would sneak to each other's rooms deep in the night. We'd have deep conversations about life and death, clones and humans—anything that occurred to us. I was closer to her than to any other person.

Relationships of any kind—romantic or platonic—were forbidden between Leaguers. We would soon be torn apart. Every one of us.

We were the last two remaining. She was sent to go and I was left to stay. Days, weeks, months passed and we heard no word from Mira. That's where my mission began. Has Mira seen what I have?

My thoughts fly back to the Oddity girl. What if I had agreed? Her soft voice and and false bravery fly back to my mind.

A crash explodes from inside the apartment. I jump, my heart pulling from my chest. I hear Buddy's loud snores pause, then begin again. He must have knocked over something in his sleep. Has he ever accepted young girls like her? From what I know of him, I couldn't imagine Buddy doing anything of the sort, but then again, I didn't imagine the girl doing anything either.

Hours pass. I don't sleep. Three o'clock seems like it will never come around, but soon, I hear something. It's the slightest scuffling of footsteps coming down the hallway. I barely notice it, but it's there, trying to be unnoticeable but failing. It's the sound of a cardboard box being set outside the door and hesitant footsteps trailing away.

NOVA

The Oddity stares at me blankly. Suspicion lies like ice in its eyes.

"You don't remember what happened?" it asks.

"No," I repeat. "It happened while I was under Calamity. I don't remember anything."

It doesn't buy my story. Something lingers in its mannerisms. It clutches the bandages in its hands, reluctant to give them up.

"Give them to me, roach!" I yell, startling it.

It throws them across the table, almost hitting the dish of lemon drops. I snatch them and turn away from it quickly. The Privilege Clinic is always unwilling to give any first aid materials. They're scarce enough as it is, but if you push them hard enough, they will give. They always do.

I find a bench far enough away from the intrusive roach. I begin wrapping the wounds Micah left. Bruises still scatter my body from a few nights ago, but now cuts adorn the bruises. Last night, I knocked over a candle and the spilt wax ruined his favorite leather jacket. Micah thought the broken glass was the best punishment. His glass of whiskey was on the nightstand, as well as three other empty glasses. I guess using his own body to hurt me had become boring...

It's not his fault. I shouldn't have knocked over that candle. If I had been more careful, it wouldn't have happened. I wouldn't be here.

I haven't told Ivy, and I don't plan on it. She would tell me to leave him, to report him to the Binocs and never see him again. I can't do that. I love Micah and I know he loves me. He *does*, they just don't see it like I do...

I wrap the bandages around the glass wounds. I picked the glass shards out last night, but the cuts still remain, stinging horribly with every flex of my arm. Once I finish wrapping them up, I'll take some Clam. That'll take me away.

"Excuse me, Ms. Aster," a voice sounds from behind me. "Do you need assistance?"

I turn to it, the same roach who handed me the bandages, and glare at it. Does it take me for a good Samaritan?

I set the bandages down and fish my phone out of my purse, the roach staring at me all the while. I dial the simple four-digit number.

4...3...2...1...

"Yes, an Oddity is harassing me. Please send a Warden."

A look of death cascades over the Oddity's face. Nothing spooks a roach more than an exterminator.

I pick up my bandages and return to my work. The next time I look up, the roach has vanished. Surely, it has fled the building. Fleeing is its only possible escape. No one wants to go to the suburbs, but they scarcely have a choice.

I have nearly finished. Only one cut on my leg remains. I begin wrapping it quickly, eager to take some Clam, when the door jingles. A Warden steps through the door, his jacket gleaming with a blue stripe.

"Excuse me, miss," he steps toward me. "I heard there was an Oddity complaint."

"Yes, there was," I sigh, "but it fled."

He stares at me numbly. "That is unfortunate."

I cut the last bandage and approach the Warden. "*Unfortunate*, Warden?"

Sweat beads from his forehead. "Yes, ma'am. It's rather unfortunate."

"No, it isn't. It would be unfortunate if you couldn't find it. Now go!"

The Warden bolts from the Privilege Clinic and to his car outside. Tires screech as the car disappears around the corner. The roaches on the sidewalk stop and gawk. I scowl at them.

Talk like a Privilege, walk like a Privilege, act like a Privilege, but whatever happens, never be like an Oddity. Micah told me that once. His hatred has rubbed off on me, and it has begun to show. I never liked them much anyway.

I have stumbled through the potholes of Chicago like this. I have drowned in a fermenting pool of ethanol like this. I have let the memories fly away like this. I have let my life slip away like this. I have been a Privilege like this, and I will die like this.

There was a time before Calamity came to Chicago. I was still friends with Ivy then. I had an odd habit of watching films from the olden days. It was always about good versus evil, and the good always won and evil never did. It was the way it always was. Ivy didn't care much for these movies. She'd always pour coffee into her mouth and say, "You're stranger than an Oddity, Nova." Then I'd give her the chortle she wanted and immerse myself in a drug different than the one I treasure now.

This was before Calamity. This was before Micah. Things were much different back then, but somehow the same. The environment changed, the society changed, but the people didn't. We were always like this, somewhere inside.

The ring of my phone twinkles through the air.

I flip it open. "Hello?"

"Nova! I am totally swamped for this party tomorrow night. Can you do me a favor? Can you pick me up some Clam? I'm sure you can find someone who has enough."

There are more Clam dealers in this city the rest of us combined.

"Of course, yeah," I mutter unenthusiastically.

"Great!" she squeals. "I've got to go. There is still so much to do!"

Ivy has a reputation for throwing the best parties. Anyone who considers themselves a Privy will try to be there. Ivy has a hard time keeping people out, even when her apartment can't hold any more.

I grab my purse, my cuts flashing in pain as I do so. *Micah, my love, why did you have to go so far? I love you, I do, but you hurt me....*

He did apologize afterward. He told me he loved me and that I was the most beautiful girl he had ever laid eyes on. His arms wrapped around me and he kissed the wounds. My blood was on his lips, but he didn't seem to mind. Love makes men crazy.

His eyes reflected back at me. There was light in there, as much as Ivy denies it. I wonder if he can see that light. It shines like iridescent planets yet to be found, inhabited with the strangeness of distant life and spectacular panorama of it. At that moment, I gazed into his eyes and saw little green men skipping across the soft sea of his irises. His light brown skin shimmered in the pale sunlight streaming through the curtains.

Ivy can't see this. She only sees the bruises, the cuts, and the pain. There is so much more to Micah. He is my love, and I am his. I couldn't leave him if I tried.

I dial the number for my roach to pick me up. My car arrives shortly. The sirens wail and the roaches stop on either side of the sidewalk for me to pass. We're in the central part of the Privy district, the northern side of the wall. I climb into my car and see a bald head wavering in the front seat.

"Who are you? Where is my Oddity?" I ask.

"I am your Oddity," it replies numbly.

"No, where did my other Oddity go? It was here this morning."

"I am your Oddity," it repeats. "I have been assigned to you because the previous Oddity was sent to the suburbs."

"What did it do? I demand you tell me."

"He was apart of an anarchist organization," it says monotonously. "I am your new Oddity."

I sigh. "Alright, fine. Take me to a Clam shop. I need a large batch."

It drives away silently, weaving through the roaches crossing the streets.

I hear a *thump* and a groan, but the car continues along. I can't expect him to avoid them all.

We cruise through Chicago. Only a few minutes pass when the Oddity stops before a tiny store. In massive letters, the lurid drug is written above the door. The siren wails, and I exit the car quickly.

The door sings as I enter. Several other Privies, marked by the absence of green-striped jackets, are browsing in the store. They leave carrying cases of Clam. I make my way to the counter.

A roach sits behind the counter, a dish of lemon drops full to the brim before him. Tall and wiry, it's built like a scoundrel with a smile that deceives the rest. A black cap is snug around its bony face with small beady eyes that stare out at me. I've never seen this roach here before.

"Can I help you, miss?" a gruff voice comes from the strange Oddity.

"I need five large cases," I snap. "Make it quick, roach."

Its smile melts into a scowl as it disappears behind the curtain. My luck has run out lately. I haven't had any docile roaches today. Even my new roach in the car was strangely unresponsive. It seemed reluctant to give any answers to me. I may need to replace it.

One by one, the roach brings out each case of Clam. The bottles inside chime a dizzy tune. By the end, five large cases of Calamity sit before me.

"Payment please, miss," the Oddity says to me.

I fish in my purse for my payment card. White bars lie all along the metal. I hand it to him and he swipes it absently in the machine. Most likely, he charged me far more than what it was worth, but it matters little to me.

He hands me my payment card back and I order him to bring the cases to my car. He listens to me and does so, one by one, the muscles in his neck straining against the weight. The roaches on the sidewalk don't clear a path for him as they do for me. They stare at him as he shoves through them, venom in their snarls.

I stand by the side of the door, snacking on the free Calamity cookie samples. They melt in my mouth and begin taking the pain away. I close my eyes and savor the cinnamon taste.

"You shouldn't eat that, you know," a voice chimes from beside me.

My eyes flash open to a roach beside me. The green-striped jacket glints an ugly sheen in its eyes. I look away in disgust.

"Go away, Oddity," I growl.

It doesn't move. It only stares at me longer, its eyes unblinking. "Calamity will kill you. It will kill all of us."

"Do you have ears, roach? Leave now or I'll call a Warden on you."

The Oddity smacks the cookie out of my hand. I strike its cheek venomously. It barely flinches.

"That's it, roach. You're going to the suburbs," I scream, taking the plate of cookies and throwing them on top of it.

It begins cackling, its laughter unhinged. "You're going to die. You're all going to die!"

I flip my phone open and dial that four-digit number for the second time today.

4...3...2...1...

The Warden comes briskly and drags the crazy roach away.

"You're going to die! All of you!" it continues to scream.

I hug myself, trying desperately to get the psychotic Oddity's screams out of my head. It doesn't work. I shudder, the image of the cackling roach burning a memory in my mind.

Thankfully, the Clam begins to take a stronger effect. I hope I don't remember any of this, but I don't think the cookies have enough Clam in them to do that. Oh please, I want to go far away. Why can't I go?

"Another Calamity cookie, miss?" the gruff voice drifts to me. "Here's a fresh batch."

I take a cookie from the platter the roach is holding. He places it on the same table the previous platter was on before. I bite into the cookie. Warm chocolate melts in my mouth along with the sweet taste of Clam. I close my eyes and savor it.

"The Calamity is in your car, miss," the Oddity says. "Everything is ready for your departure."

I say nothing to him. I grab the platter off the table and begin toward the door. The siren begins to wail as I exit the store. I bite into another cookie as I watch the Warden car pull away.

"You're all going to die!" the roach screams out of the car, cackling as they go.

I watch as another Warden handcuffs a roach against the windows of the shop. It's pressed into a car, a roach jacket thrown over it. Another one caught without its jacket on. Another went sent to the suburbs. Another one dead, or close enough to it.

I step into my car, the cases in the passenger's seat in front of me.

"Where to, miss?"

"I don't care," I mutter. "Anywhere but here."

The car pulls away from the curb, the platter of cookies resting on my lap.

I grab another cookie and eat it. Soon I'll be gone.

ROLLIN

"Do you want some Clam, Rollin? I got a whole batch here," Marco asks, holding out a tiny bottle.

Buddy intervenes, pushing Marco's hand back. "No, no. He ain't one of us, mah friend."

Marco's eyes raise, but he says nothing in response. The bottles twinkle as he places the box on the ground. He's a bald man, with scraps of hair around his chin that barely make up a beard. He dresses in all denim, head to toe. Buddy told me not to comment on it. It's a sensitive topic, apparently.

I pull my jacket tight around me, huddling in the thin fabric. The wind runs swifter up here than it does below.

"Cold?" Marco turns to me. "Don't worry. You'll get used to it soon enough."

We stand atop of the Sears Tower. The mess of Chicago lies under me; a swarm of Oddities crawl about the sidewalks as only a few cars twist through the streets. I am a giant up here.

"The roaches are out already," Marco mutters, sipping spiked coffee through tight lips.

Chicago lies before us. The Sears Tower is close to the lake and is in the heart of the Privy district. A mix of residential and commercial buildings fill the skyscrapers around us. Buddy's is just a block north, where the lake nearly brushes against the foundations of the building.

Opposite of the lake lies the Oddity district. A brick wall can be seen through the cracks of the skyscrapers. It stretches from one end of the city to the other. Weak mortar causes the bricks to fall, some hitting unfortunate roaches below. Through varying archways, Oddities crawl in and out. Some are returning home after work and some are rushing to

35

begin. Only three roads cross through the wall. Privileges barely go into the Oddity district, Buddy explained. The only reason some do is to visit the whorehouses not allowed in the Privilege district.

The lights of Chicago flicker weakly, like dying fireflies in the approaching autumn wind. Only the lights deemed necessary are lit. The Oddity district is bathed in darkness; no light escapes its impenetrable black wall. The city of Chicago resembles the hemispheres of the earth, half in light and half in darkness.

We stand sheltered under a shoddy metal roof. Half walls lie in a square around us. There is no glass to separate us from the wind; I could leap from the tower now, if I wanted to.

There's a ladder in the middle of the enclosure that extends a hundred feet into the abyss of the skyscraper below. It was a long, perilous journey to the top, but we made it.

Two cheap folding lawn chairs and a dinosaur-age television fill the rest of the small space. Piles of lemon drop wrappers litter the ground.

Dawn stretches on the horizon like a lazy cat. Amber reflects against the black faces of the skyscrapers. I yawn, blinking away the sleep from my eyes. I never did fall asleep last night.

"You a traveler, Rollin?" Marco turns to me. "There aren't many travelers around here."

I don't look at him. "I'm as much of a traveler as you are."

He keeps quiet once more. Buddy lurks behind us, kicking pebbles down the ladder chute. I shook him awake this morning out of his post-Calamity haze. We would have been late if I hadn't. He took a lemon drop and was well enough to go on, he said. Neither of us have had breakfast.

"Buddy says you're a nice roach," Marco grunts, spitting through the window.

"I'm as nice a man as you are," I strain a smile.

Marco spins toward Buddy, his coffee spilling over the rim. "He's a wild one! What'd you send me here, Buddy?"

"Ah told yuh, Marco. Rollin ain't from 'round here. He ain't used to our customs."

Marco turns back toward the sunrise. "Don't sweat, Buddy. I'm only playing. Some like them docile, but I prefer them with a little spirit."

Buddy continues to kick pebbles down the chute. The wind cuts through our thin layers, but I'm the only one who shivers.

I met Marco while I was under Calamity. According to Buddy, we were good friends. It must have been the drugs. I couldn't imagine feeling any different about him then than I do now. The sun isn't fully up and he's half-intoxicated, rude, and obnoxious. I don't look forward to spending the day with him.

I watch the sunrise numbly. Shades of red and orange cascade across the gray sky, blanketing the city in an ironically cheery hue.

My mind flickers back to this morning. As we were leaving, Buddy found the cardboard box outside the door. It lay there like an animal carcass brought by a housecat. He kicked it suspiciously; crumbs scattered across the metal floor. All the pizza was gone.

"Buddy?" I asked as he stared at the pizza box.

He nodded, searching down the hallway. The stench of lemon drops drifted to my nose.

"Do Oddity women often prostitute themselves?"

He gave me a quizzical look. "Why do yuh ask?"

"I ordered that pizza last night and this girl—she was just a *girl*, Buddy—she offered herself."

Blackness spread across his face. "These are dark times, mah friend. Ain't seen a time darker."

That was all he said of it.

After that, he went back into the apartment and poured half a bottle of Calamity into his coffee before returning to the hallway. He sipped it carelessly, the same look haunting his face, and continued down the hallway without another word.

"You don't have to stay, Buddy," Marco shouts over his shoulder. "We're not going to be doing much. I have to teach this roach how to be a Binoc."

"Ah want to make sure everythin' is good 'fore ah set off," Buddy squeezes between Marco and I, folding his arms over the ledge. "'Sides, the view sure is a beauty. Ah can see all the way to the suburbs, ah swear it."

"I don't know why you'd want to," Marco laughs nervously, drowning the last of his coffee. "It's all dark and devil over there."

"And without it, yuh wouldn't have none 'a that Clam or coffee or even damn lemon drops, fer that matter."

Marco waves him off. "You sound like one of those roaches down there, Buddy. You're getting more like them each day!"

Buddy laughs. "Ah'm only knowledgeable, that's all."

"Knowledgeable of nothing," Marco scoffs.

I expect Buddy to smack him for the way he's talking to him, but he only smiles, gazing back out into the suburbs. "Ah always forget this view. It sure is a beauty, ain't it, Rollin?"

I nod in agreement, sipping my coffee.

"Every time it's different. One day, ah won't even recognize this city, ah swear it."

"I don't think that'd be a shame," I laugh, watching the sun, a melted lemon drop, sit on the horizon.

Two days ago, I was eating beans by my fire when a southern stranger came by, asking me if I could share it. Then I put a knife against his throat.

Now, I'm sitting on top of the Sears Tower with him and a man harsher than sun on snow. Time is a curious stranger.

Buddy is happy, though, I know it. There's a twinkle in his eyes and a spring in his steps. He's repenting his sins by letting another create them.

I try not to think about it now, but it gets harder each time he opens his mouth. He's a good man and he shouldn't have to die. If I could save one person, it would be him. He's about the last good human left on this forsaken earth.

Buddy kneels before the half wall, his eyes at level with the edge, and folds his hands in front of him. I hear Marco begin chuckling beside him, but Buddy doesn't pay him any attention. He sits in silence for a while before he begins.

"Dear God," Buddy whispers to himself, clutching his cross tightly under white knuckles. "Thank yuh fer this day. Thank yuh fer mah good friends and thank yuh fer this blessed earth. Lord, ah ask yuh to bless mah friend Rollin in his journey. He knows not the path, but ah know yuh will show him. Lord, please forgive me fer mah sins. Ah know not what ah do and ah beg fer yer light in mah dark life. Amen."

Buddy kisses the cross softly, tucking it safely away in his shirt. He turns to me and extends his hand. "Ah wish yuh the best of luck, Rollin, but ah best be goin'. Ah'll meet back here 'round noon fer lunch."

I shake his hand, smiling. "Thank you, Buddy."

He laughs lightheartedly and begins his descent down the chute. Two brown hands soon disappear, rung by rung, into the black abyss. Footsteps fade softly away into the early dawn. Only the sound of Chicago accompanies our dull silence.

"Rollin, can I ask you something?" Marco turns to me suddenly.

I nod silently.

"Are you a man of God?"

I ponder on the question a moment, waiting a few seconds to respond. "No, I stopped believing in any god long ago."

Marco looks toward the dark Oddity sector. "I'm not a man of God either. I never understood Buddy's insane obsession with the myth, but he's my friend, and I respect him enough to let him follow his beliefs."

"It's worked well enough for me," I mutter.

Marco's head reels back, laughter exploding from him. "That's why he's helping you? Is Buddy 'repenting his sins' again? God damn that fool. He doesn't have a dark stitch in his heart."

I keep a smile back, sipping my coffee to drown the laughter. Marco is different when Buddy isn't around.

"I swear, Rollin, his 'sins' aren't more than child's play. He feels a sin is anything slightly unholy. He's helped more people based on repenting his sins than he has made sins at all."

"You've known him long?"

He crushes his coffee cup. "Too long, if you ask me."

We sit in silence for a few moments before he swivels away from the horizon suddenly, throwing his crushed cup behind him.

"One day, I'm going to leap from this tower and not have a single regret while I'm doing it," Marco collapses on a cheap, folding lawn chair, "and I won't be sinning when I do it."

I follow him and sit myself in the chair next to him. I chug the rest of my coffee and place the cup under my chair.

"You must think I'm crazy, don't you?" he says, staring off into nowhere. "I'm a Privy, for god's sake, and I'm sitting up here making sure the brats don't overdose on Clam and lie rotting in an alleyway."

I stay silent, kicking my cup down the chute. It bounces against the rungs of the ladder and against the wall for a few seconds before the noise disappears into the dark midnight.

"I'm not crazy, Rollin," he whispers. "I'm being punished. The Privileges think I'm a god sitting up here, willing to work even though I'm a Privilege, but it's not like that. They're making me."

"What'd you do?"

"In the eyes of the government," he gives a half-hearted laugh, "I sinned."

"You sinned?"

"Did Buddy ever tell you how things work around here? How this crazed city even functions?"

"No," I mutter, reflecting on his words, "I guess I've been too wrapped up in not dying to think of the logistics."

"It's interesting, to say the least," he begins. "Five years ago, this city wasn't like this. There wasn't a wall dividing the city, nor were there Oddities and Privileges. It was a city, running as well as any city can. Some people ran the government. I don't know the specifics; I wasn't too into politics back then. I used to be a mechanic, but now that job has gone to some Oddity in the south.

"Anyway, things slowly began to change. There wasn't a specific day that everything went crazy. At first, we noticed little things. Newspapers weren't being delivered. Policemen didn't patrol the streets. When there was a fire, no firefighter would come. Stores started closing. People were pushed from their homes for no reasons. Many fled the city, only to be the first trapped in the suburbs.

"The wall's construction began at the same time as the beginning of the class separation. All those on the north side of the wall were deemed Privileges and all those on the south were Oddities. Luckily, I was working on the north side when the law was passed, though I lived on the south side. After this happened, the rumors began to fly around.

"People talked of somebody new in the government who was changing everything. Nobody knew who it was, but everyone knew this person had come. All the other government leaders were cast out into the suburbs. Everyone I know started calling this person 'the Exterminator' for his unfair treatment of the roaches. The newly-dubbed Privileges nicknamed the Oddities 'roaches' earlier, since they lived in the southern side of the city where—even before the Exterminator took over—little energy was given, meaning it was constantly dark.

"Ever since then, I've been a Privilege. The Exterminator has a council under him that runs much of the city. There is a Privilege councilor, an Oddity councilor, a Binoc councilor, a Warden councilor…you get the picture. We report to them and they report to the Exterminator. At least, that's what they say. It sounds crazy, I know, but it's the truth. No one knows the exact details, but we noticed the changes.

"As for me, well, I was always a mechanic at heart. Privileges, by law, were not allowed to have jobs. During the first couple of months, I still secretly worked as a mechanic. The Privilege councilor didn't like that. Myself and several others who couldn't give up their former jobs were given 'prestigious' jobs in the community. I was declared a Binoc, though I don't see what's so glorious about being a babysitter. Others were made into doctors, government monkeys, or the councilor's little pets. These jobs couldn't be trusted to the Oddities, I guess.

"It's been this way ever since. Clam was introduced not long after everything changed, and the rest was history. The city was hooked. The Oddities served the Privileges, and if they didn't, they'd be shipped out to the suburbs to produce the goods for Chicago. But soon, too many of them started dying and…"

He lips stop and he keeps quiet. I look at him to continue, but he only stares at the ground. His face seems to have grown dark with the memories.

"I've already said too much," he whispers, reaching for a wrinkled brown bag under his chair.

He pulls it into his lap as tiny bottles jingle a melancholy tune. He takes two from the bag.

"If I'm going to be sitting up here all day with you, the least we can do is fly away for a bit. What do you say? You want some Clam?"

Buddy's words twist through my head: *It's a double-edged sword, Rollin. Life is punishin' and dreams are rewardin'.*

I accept the bottle from Marco, eyeing the milky liquid inside. It won't hurt to have one more, will it?

"Oh, come on," Marco chuckles. "Now that Daddy's gone, it'll be our little secret. I promise."

He promises, and it wouldn't be the first time I've trusted the promise of a stranger.

"Don't you remember it feeling good? Like the best thing in the world? Haven't you longed to go back?"

I have, and oh god, it felt so good. It was the best thing in the world.

I stare out at the lemon drop sun. It melts above the horizon now, shining the city of Chicago in its morning glory.

As the last of the sunrise fades away, I hand Marco the bottle back, politely declining. Buddy was right. I have a mission to do here, and an addiction will only postpone it.

Marco calls me a baby and other profanities. He swallows both bottles of Calamity and two more from the brown bag. He chuckles, the Calamity rushing through his veins. He hurls the bottles out of the window and to the streets below. I don't hear them hit the ground.

Marco slips into a slump, his head rolling back on the edge of the chair. In a minute, he's gone. He must have overdosed. I've never seen anyone take two bottles before, let alone *four*. Buddy said that people here have grown accustomed to it, and more doses are required for them to 'fly away'.

I stare out into the horizon, black skyscrapers glaring back at me. Up here, they're no longer giants.

I am.

NOVA

The sirens wail as Micah's roach holds the door open for me. I climb out of the car, yanking my black dress down as it crawls up my thighs. Micah follows closely behind with his hands on my waist. He steadies himself as he climbs from the car. Micah had an early start on the party.

Ivy's apartment building stands proudly before us. My gaze lifts up as thumping music drifts to my ears. Pulsating rainbow lights fall briefly on the dark city as we push toward the door.

"Come on, hurry up!" a roach screams from the crowd around us.

"Who said that?" Micah wails around, searching the crowd for the accuser.

No roach dares to retort. They stare at us with their yellow eyes, watching, waiting. Micah spits at their feet. The stench of booze ferments the air surrounding him. Silence marches with us until the front doors of the apartment building close.

As soon as the metal doors shut, we are cast into near-darkness. Only a single dull yellow light illuminates the hallway. It flickers, casting Micah's face in shadows.

He turns to me, pushing my shoulders against the wall as he lips find my throat. His rough kisses scratch my neck. His body presses against me.

"Micah, Micah, *please*," I whisper to no avail. "We have to go. They're expecting us."

"They can expect us for a bit longer," he growls, his hands finding the zipper of my dress.

"But—"

"Nova?" a full voice shouts from down the hallway.

I push Micah off me harshly. He stumbles backwards, alcohol swarming a dizzy torrent in his eyes. Ivy's infuriated face stares back at us. Betrayal

42

stings like poison in her eyes.

"We were coming up, Ivy," I laugh.

"I'm sure," she responds, her voice icy.

She stands there, the dim light casting her long shadow to us. The black shadow of her head touches our feet. Tension lays a thick fog over us.

"Did that roach ever bring over the Clam I got you?" I ask, twisting my fingers.

"Yes, he did," she mutters, walking toward us. "People are enjoying it upstairs. Why don't you two join us?"

"Yes, let's join them, Micah," I grab his hand.

Ivy's glare could cut me open. As Micah and I pass, she gasps. Her hand clutches my shoulder, stopping me. She grabs my dress, staring at the luxurious silk. Wrinkles cascade across the felt where Micah had clutched it with his fingers.

"Oh, your dress, Nova! Here, let me help you fix it," Ivy says, her voice riddled with false concern. "It'll only be a moment, Micah. Go on without us."

He strains a smile as he steps onto the elevator. It whisks him upward and out of earshot. Immediately, Ivy rips her hand away from my dress and snatches my arm, her eyes venomous. Her fingernails cut into my skin.

"What the hell is he doing here?" She screams at me, her fingers digging into my tender wounds.

I snatch my arm away for her, spots of red popping from the scabs. "He's my guest."

"A guest I said you couldn't invite," she says. "He better be gone before I get up there, Nova."

"Then don't expect me to meet you at Sip and Sleep tomorrow," I growl. Anger simmers dangerously under my skin.

"Get him out," she snarls. "He doesn't love you. He's a manipulative, abusive—"

The anger overflows, soaring through my veins as fists clench in my hands and it flies through the air like a meteorite falls to earth and her skin hits the knuckles and she collapses to the ground, crumpling like a rag doll and I can't help it, my vision is going red and my leg is flying out and I slam my foot into her stomach and she heaves and heaves—

Tears, blood, and vomit mix together on the metal floor. I spit on her like I would on a roach.

I stomp from her and onto the elevator. I ignore her cries. They echo against the walls. I ignore the blood spilling from her nose, the tears leaking from her eyes—everything. There is no friend of mine on that floor.

The elevator shoots upward. Calm wind flies through my hair, blowing the strands into a frenzy. Only seconds pass before the little bell goes *ding* and the door opens. Pulsating music drones out anything else as flashing lights illuminate the gray, metal hallway.

Micah leans against the wall beside the door. His black hair flutters softly in the wind. His eyes shine like emeralds. His arms open to me. I fall into Micah, my love, and let him smother me. He kisses the pain away. He kisses everything away.

"You okay, baby?" he murmurs, his lips at my throat. "That bitch give you any trouble?"

"I was the one giving her trouble," I smile wickedly. "You should've seen the mark I left on her face."

"You hit her?"

"I did more than that. She was puking by the time I left."

He's silent for a moment. Confusion sets a crease in his eyebrows.

I pull my fingers through his hair. "She said you didn't love me."

"You know how I feel about you," he grins.

I pull him close to me, smiling. "I know you do, and I love you too."

His lips press feverishly to mine. We lose ourselves in each other, our endorphins flying around us, encircling us in a tornado. Hands crawl across my body, finding the dress, the zipper, the clasp—

"Later, Micah," I mutter against his lips, tugging his hands away from my open dress. "I want to dance."

He grumbles nonsense and continues attacking my body, but I find his hand and twist my fingers through his. He wants more, I know he does, but I peel myself from him. His hand clenches my fingers until the skin turns white.

I lead him down the hallway. The music drones louder and louder until the sound is almost deafening. I smile whimsically, overjoyed to be back in the steady pulse of my everyday life.

We push the unlocked, metal door open and find Privies pressed against each other. I breathe in the rich smell of cologne and Clam, my two favorite potions. Micah leads the way, forcing us through the crowd of people.

Bodies surround me. I can't see anything. The music drowns out everything and the lights, flashing rainbow colors, clash against the gray hues of the apartment and blind me. I close my eyes, releasing my senses to this alien world.

Micah's hand is replaced with a cup. I drown the contents eagerly. The alcohol burns my throat and I melt in the fire willingly. It is spiked with Clam; I can taste the sweet heaven.

I'm in the heart of desire. Foreign bodies press against me. Hands, female and male, grab at me, but I don't mind. Micah grabs my waist as he places another cup in my hands. He pulls me close to him as I chug the spiked drink. Rum and Clam mix in my stomach and I couldn't think of a better dinner.

Neither of us speaks. No one does. The music eradicates all thoughts.

The lights blind us. There's no need to do anything but follow the drum of the music with the swing of our hips. We live. We're one.

Drinks fill my hand and then my stomach. Songs shake the walls. People leave the crowd to find bedrooms. Even so, we still dance.

His hands follow the contours of my body. A lump presses against my thigh as his hands become more ravenous. His heart thumps against my ear. He is a leech clinging to me, sucking all the life away. I try to remember the time or place, but I can't dive deep enough in the alcohol pool to find it.

I squeeze my fists, tightening my grip on the rope that is keeping me from falling into the deep end. The ocean sits below me, deep and black and full of mysteries. The water stings my toes. My grip loosens.

I close my eyes and let the beat carry me far away. The Clam takes effect, sending my senses away, sending my thoughts away—

"Open your eyes, Nova," a seductive whisper slips into my ear.

His caustic green eyes appear an inch before mine. He has pulled me away from the crowd. Rich cologne wafts to my nose. I catch my breath. Hormones ferment the air. It's so…wonderful. Eyes like the fires of hell watch me. He wants me. He will have me.

Time melts from reality. I pull myself from him and dive back into the crowd, pressing myself against a stranger until he wraps his arms around me. He can't have me. Not now. It's too perfect. I can't leave. My vision goes soft. My senses fall numb. I'm slipping away, I know it.

Micah disappears from the room and my mind. I'm lost. Hands grab at me, tearing the black dress from my body. It crumples in a helpless pile on the ground. Naked bodies surround me. It's beautiful.

A tiny bottle is pushed into my hands. Then it's gone. Someone hands me a smoke. I take a hit. The rich fumes ignite my lungs. A voice calls my name, but it's far away, very far away.

More shots. More Calamity. More smoke. It never ends. The world has spun into a haze of smoke and lights and music and I drift away, far away.

A voice calls to me again, wrenching at my arm, but I swing my fist out and it hits something and no one calls my name anymore. My knuckles are sticky with blood.

Hands pull at me, leading me away from the music, from the naked bodies and the music that pulses and the lights that blind and Micah's heart that thumps and into a room. Soft fabrics surround me. Cologne and Calamity mix together in the most wonderful of potions. Hands, multiple hands, flip me over, finding where I've longed to be found, and I'm gone into a haze of drugs and sex and pleasure and—

I'm gone.

There are three desires all of us secretly crave: happiness, pleasure, and ignorance. All of it can be solved with Calamity.

Anything can be solved with Calamity.

NOVA

I wake slowly. My Clam flight has soared away and left me here. I open my eyes, blinking four, five times before I can focus.

I am sprawled naked across a bed. I'm alone. Music shakes the walls as shouts erupt from down the hallway.

My mind is in a haze. Deep pain vibrates my forehead. I crawl over to the nightstand where a bowl of lemon drops sit. I stuff three into my mouth and suck on them eagerly.

As usual, my mind is an empty canvas. I remember nothing from the night. All I recollect is Ivy and Micah, swirling in a confused mirage in my mind. Anger lies underneath is like a hot brand ready to strike.

I better find Micah. He'll tell me what happened. Looking at the clock, I find it's eleven o'clock. The sun set only an hour ago.

I climb out of the bed as the lemon drops begin to take effect. I soon find myself in the midst of the party. Naked bodies are all around me. Smoke and the stench of booze twist through the air. Broken bottles litter the ground. I trace their shattered faces.

The rainbow lights dance across the room, casting random limbs into a spotlight and faces into shadow. The floor vibrates under my bare feet from the deep bass.

I find the first person in the crowd and pull him aside. "Have you seen Micah?"

"Who?" he shouts back.

I wave him off. He jumps back into the crowd, his genitals waving madly. I need to leave.

"Hey, sexy," a husky voice whispers in my ear, "you're looking awful broody. Have some Clam with me. Take your mind off things for a while."

"No, leave me alone," I growl. The predator backs away quickly, already searching for new prey. This cannibalistic nightmare sends shivers up my bare skin.

I push through the crowd, searching for Micah, for Ivy, but I find no familiar faces.

A hand clasps at my shoulder. "I can't believe you punched Ivy in the face earlier. That was wicked!"

I turn to the man, trying to find his face underneath the mass of dreadlocks. I give up and push forward, though questions push me back. What is he talking about?

A flighty memory flashes back. Ivy lies on the ground; vomit, blood, and tears mix in a pool beneath her. I walk away, my fists still clenched in white rage. Venom nearly foams at my mouth. I thought she was my friend.

I push my way to the corner where all the clothes have been cast. I dig through the pile and find my black dress and pumps. I dress quickly. Some men near me boo angrily. I ignore them. A hangover already fights a heavy storm in my forehead, though the booze still moves the floor beneath me.

I push my way toward the door as offers of a smoke, Clam, and a shot are insisted on me. I need to find Micah. How could he leave without me?

I walk down the hallway toward the elevator. I flip open my phone and dial his number, hoping, begging that he answers, but he doesn't. The line goes dead. I step on the elevator. I call my Oddity—the snitch—as well. No answer.

I leave the elevator and begin down the hallway. The metal hallway echoes eerily as my heels hit the cold ground. The lone yellow light flickers.

Click, click, click...

I exit the building as the alarms begin wailing. It's only then I realize I have no car to pick me up. I stand in the middle of the sidewalk, roaches staring at me from either side, as rain cascades from the sky. Micah's apartment is only two blocks down. I know where it is. It'll be quick, yes, it *has* to be.

I push through the Oddities on either side of me, plowing through their shocked faces. It's late out; not many roaches scurry about. Even so, the few that see me there, walking on the sidewalk amongst them, turn and flee the other way.

I keep my gaze down. I feel the eyes on me, noticing the absence of a green-striped jacket on my shoulders, noticing I exited the wailing building, noticing I'm on the sidewalk like them.

Bottles litter the street, collecting rain as it falls from the sky. I curl into my arms hopelessly; the wind bites at me, stinging me with its poison.

My heel catches on a crack in the sidewalk and suddenly I'm falling and tress swirl in a dizzy haze and roaches, there are roaches everywhere and my nose collides with the ground. Blood drips into the rain.

Click, click, click...

Groaning, I clutch my nose.

Click, click, click...

Peering through the strands of my auburn hair, I spot a Warden hurriedly approaching me, the blue on his jacket rippling beneath raindrops. I can't tell if the drops on his forehead are perspiration or rain.

The Warden stands before me as rickety as a drunken horse. He's nervous and clueless, I know. The corners of his mouth twitch uncontrollably. His hand nervously plucks at his belt buckle like a banjo, trying helplessly to keep his plump stomach off the ground.

I find my way off the ground, rejecting the extended hand of the Warden.

"Where is your jacket, miss?" The Warden towers over me. "You know the regulations."

"Do I look like a roach to you?" I spit at him.

The Warden shakes his head numbly, sweat beginning to bead on his forehead. "I apologize, ma'am. Privileges don't usually...they don't—"

He stops short and looks away from me, embarrassed. He holds his hat in his hands, despite the rain, and kneads it into dough. A cough sputters from his lips. I step back.

Muddy brown pits of hell stared back at me. He has roach eyes, that's for sure. I glare at the blue stripe on his uniform. He reeks of Oddity and the stench almost makes me vomit.

"I'm fine, roach," I spit. "Leave me alone."

I begin walking when his voice stops me. "Please, let me help you."

There is a silence from the oddly barren street and a slight whine from the street lights flickering out. Blood trickles down my face.

"No," I shout, deciphering the letters on his name tag, "not from you, *John.*"

"Miss, please, let me drive you home. It's dangerous at this time of night."

He glances around nervously, kneading and kneading that hat.

"Danger?" I laugh, my lips curling into an amused smile.

"Miss, please, if you'd only let me—"

My fingernails dig into his arm, staining the cheap fabric with my blood. "My name is Nova. I am no miss."

I stumble away, my feet catching on the many cracks in the unkempt sidewalk. The dreariness of the night drifts away like smoke tendrils. The skyscrapers become nothing more than a meadow full of black flowers as I walk and walk and walk...my nose finally stops bleeding. Time has melted away.

Two headlights and a rumble shake me from my dizzy dream. I spin around, expecting a horde of roaches rushing at me, but I find a red Mercedes. A white stripe borders the windshield. It's a Privilege car. The car spins onto the sidewalk in front of me, sending the bugs into flight.

Three men step from the car, one in the lead. The dim light casts them into shadows.

"There you are," a voice snarls.

The leading man steps in front of me, striking me across the cheek. I fall to the ground, holding the tender skin. It's Micah, my love, my only love.

He snatches my arm, his curses thick with booze. The men behind him laugh enthusiastically as he drags me into an alleyway. The asphalt scraps against my bare leg, sending sharp pebbles into my skin. I cry out, but it only makes Micah tug my hair. Tears fall in a river.

I wail, tell him I love him. but he doesn't hear me. My dress is torn apart. I'm pressed against the wall; familiar and unfamiliar hands grab and pinch and pull at my body. I try screaming put they only cover my mouth, muffling me and nothing works.

My senses die. I stop feeling. I stop thinking. I stop seeing and smelling and hearing because it's too painful and time stutters and I can't stop it. They're all around me, attacking, devouring, and hot breath melts my skin and the curses—Micah, my love—

Vines twist through my limbs and my eyes are bleeding remorse and my nose is bleeding pain and everything hurts and I can't see and they keep bleeding and bleeding and the pain—oh god, the pain splinters my bones and I can't see, and—

Arms never quit. Curses never quiet. Sympathy never saves me.

A heavy weight falls on me and I see it, the warm river of blood flowing on my cheek. The few lights fade. My weak breath catches fire in my throat. I deserve this. I deserve all of this.

The darkness suffocates me but whatever it does, it won't take me and I can't breathe and I keep gasping but all I suck in is that darkness pressing and pressing and pressing and help me, please—

My body is vandalized as they groan loudly one last time, finishing themselves on me as I lie broken on the rotten floor and footsteps and laughter and clap against the walls and then silence. My love is nothing. I am nothing.

I'm alone.

I want to fly away. I want Calamity to take me away and never, ever have to be here again. It's so painful and the blood and the tears and I can't see through it all—I'm blinded—where am I—Micah, my love—

Why couldn't you love me?

And I cry and cry and let the tears fall and mix with the blood and no one comes to help me because none of the roaches care and he betrayed me. He never loved me.

I lie here, in a pool of my own filth and the filth of the men and Micah and cry.

I'm nothing.

The darkness floods back, the pain gripping me in its iron fist and tightening and clutching and I can't fight it off and the skyscrapers are falling and I'm falling and I can't stay in this alleyway anymore and it's so cold, so cold and I can't breathe because the ice is gripping me and I can't take the pain anymore, it's too much, I can't—

Ivy was right. I'm a blind fool and now I'm loveless and broken and cast aside and friendless and I have nothing. I am nothing.

I punched and kicked and made her bleed and cry and vomit in the name of Micah's and my love for each other and here I am.

I've been punched and kicked and now I'm here, bleeding and crying and lying in a filth more repulsive than my own life.

I deserved it all.

I am nothing.

I will never be anything.

ROLLIN

It's late afternoon by the time I drift from sleep. The sun is on the opposite side of the sky, melting into a different horizon.

"You had a good nap?" Marco chuckles from beside me.

He's staring at the old television in front of him, sucking on a couple of lemon drops. It flips through different scenes. Most of them are within shops or buildings. Beside the TV sits a console, littered with different switches and buttons. In the corner of the observation platform, a telescope is set up. Its gold cylinder shines in the vibrant sunset.

"I didn't get much sleep last night," I grumble, rubbing the sleep from my eyes.

"Don't stress, my friend. I only woke up from my flight thirty minutes ago. I thought I'd let you sleep a little."

I stand from the lawn chair, my joints stiff. I roll my neck, pain stretching through the nerves. A mutilated, empty cigarette box lies on the floor. Marco is already working on the second box.

"Dinner is by your chair, if you're hungry," Marco says.

I tear the bags open and devour the food immediately. Hunger stabs at my stomach like a guilty conscience. My meal is a hamburger, not anything remarkable, but it is easily the most delicious meal I've had since I left the League.

It takes only minutes for the food to disappear. I nearly hurl after chugging an entire bottle of water on top of the burger, but I manage to keep it all down. I haven't had a decent meal since the pizza the other night.

Marco laughs. "I guess when you're a Privy you forget the importance of a good meal."

He turns back to the television screen, looking but not watching. His eyes glaze over as another yawn widens his mouth.

"What's on the TV?" I ask, holding my stomach.

"All the buildings in my little sector. I watch the insides of the buildings from this monitor and the streets through that telescope. The Binoc councilor had the cameras set up in all the buildings years ago. Most of them are dinosaurs, unused and otherwise unwanted relics from the past. The monitor switches between the cameras that are set up in each Binoc's sector."

"And that's all you do as a Binoc?"

He nods, his mouth drawn in a line. "If I need to call a Warden, for a Privilege's sake or a roach's misbehavior, I take out my phone and dial up my Warden."

I watch the monitor with him. Different scenes flip by, but Marco doesn't seem too interested.

"Some Privileges are having a party in a building down the street," Marco says. "I sent a Warden over there earlier. Two girlies were duking it out in a hallway. One of them punched the girl in the face, got her bleeding and puking everywhere. I think she was Asian, but it's so hard to tell with these cruddy monitors."

I shake my head in disbelief.

"The Warden came and patched the Asian girl up, but he couldn't get her to go to a clinic. Damn girl marched her way back up to the party only to get whacked in the face again!" Marco chuckles. "I wish you were awake to see *that*."

"Does that happen a lot?"

"Privies fighting? It'd be a strange day if it weren't happening. I switched off all the other internal building cameras in my sector besides this one. No other building is having a party so those don't need watching as much as this one does."

I take another sip of water, appeasing my rolling stomach. A muted cacophony of noise drifts up the skyscraper and to our ears. The sunset has faded into dusk.

"Isn't it kind of early to be having a party? It's barely dark out," I inquire.

"No, not here. Privies like to start early. Their parties could start at six and end at six, easily. There's lots of drifting into Calamity, waking up, and drifting into it again. It isn't considered a good party without at least one orgy."

"A little extreme, aren't they?"

He chuckles. "What else are they going to do? The Privies don't have anything to do all day beside party, take Clam, and wander around the city. Lather, rinse, and repeat."

We sit in silence, watching dusk fade into darkness. Rainbow lights flash from further down the street; they illuminate the black city in color, but still it seems darker than the pits of hell.

Marco offers me a cigarette and I take one happily. I haven't had a smoke since I left New York weeks ago. I cup my hands around the end while I light it, shielding it from the wind. I lean over the railing and let my head hang in the air. The wind licks up my scalp as I hold the first puff in, savoring the sweet taste.

"You ever worry about cancer, Marco?"

"No, no," he laughs, "I stopped caring about those things long ago. I'll probably be dead before I have to worry about that."

He goes back to his cigarette, tending the embers. I return to my own, taking more puffs of smoke. The nicotine calms me and helps me forget.

If only Marco knew.

Puff

He's not real. He's nothing more than a copy of someone else.

Puff

All his memories are fake.

Puff

My cigarette burns out. I ask Marco for another, and he kindly obliges. I immediately light it, puffing and puffing and puffing, but no amount of smoke can rid the knowledge festering in my head.

I keep telling myself that I'm not committing murder. These aren't people. They're clones. I'm merely correcting an experiment gone wrong. Each day, it gets harder to believe. Maybe the League is wrong after all…

Besides, that's a while away. I have to focus on finding her first, and then I can worry about that.

I roll my head over the edge again, letting fingers of wind comb my hair. Time begins to slip away. It will be a long night up here, on the Sears tower with Marco. He can't see time dripping away, but I can. Ever since I joined the League, I could see it.

Marco's bald head is suddenly illuminated by a single bulb hanging from the ceiling. An ugly glint appears on the shiny head. His coal black eyes stare ahead.

He jumps to his feet, heading toward the ladder. "I'm going to get some coffee and more cigs. You want some?"

"Yeah, sure," I say. "Thank you."

"No problem," he begins climbing down the ladder. "Make sure you keep watch of that monitor. I'll only be gone a minute."

As he disappears down the chute, it begins to rain. Droplets of water hit the ceiling with a dull *thud* as I watch the scenes of the monitor fly by.

There's a party going on, as Marco described. They're all naked, mindlessly having sex with each other in one massive orgy. Smoke casts the room in a haze. Lights flash across the room. Privileges pound back drink after drink of booze and bottle after bottle of Calamity. Broken bottles and people litter the scene.

The camera switches to a bedroom. A woman lies sprawled across the bed, naked as well. Her auburn hair flies in a wild frenzy about her. She stirs awake sluggishly.

The next scene goes to the hallway outside the party. Three men lounge against the wall. Empty bottles lie like a nest around them. They hold onto the wall for support.

Another hallway is presented. It is empty and bare. A lone yellow light flickers, casting dark shadows across the walls.

It flicks back to the party scene. More people have joined the orgy in the middle. Not a person in the room has a piece of clothing on. The auburn girl materializes from the bedroom, sauntering into the middle of the party.

One of the three men peeks into the party. He says something to the other men in a hushed whisper and the three flee down the hallway.

The next scene shows the three men charging down the dimly lit hallway to the front doors.

The auburn woman is now dressed and leaving the party, phone in hand. Men stop and harass her, pushing bottles and smokes into her hands. She takes some, but declines the others. There's a wobble in her step. She saunters down the hall, a phone in hand. She dials one number, then another. Neither pick up.

The three men sprint from the building. I jump from my chair and go to the telescope. I aim it at the building down the street, catching the men as they jump into a red Mercedes and disappear around the corner.

The auburn woman steps from the building. She doesn't catch a car. She plows into the group of Oddities surrounding her, huddling into her arms. A Warden—our Warden, I think—stops her. She pushes past him after moments of conversation. She walks a minute longer. The Warden goes the opposite direction.

The red Mercedes flies around the corner it disappeared behind earlier, peeling the asphalt as it spins onto the sidewalk in front of the auburn woman, sending roaches scurrying in all directions.

The same three men leap from the car and then—oh god—they're *beating* her—no Oddities stop them—they're dragging the woman by her hair into an alleyway and, and—they're tearing her clothes off and—

I rip myself from the telescope. Tears burn in my eyes. I can't watch anymore.

"Marco," a strangled cry escapes from my lips. "Marco!"

I scream his name, but his bald head doesn't materialize from the chute. Something's happening and I don't know how to call the Warden back and he should've taken her home, he should've *stayed*—

What do I do? I don't have a phone and Marco's not here and that woman is, she's—

I collapse in the lawn chair, screaming out for Marco but he's not coming and I can't help her. I go to the telescope again, shaking, and can only look for a second before my eyes blur with tears and I can't, it's too much, I—

What the hell is this place?

They say they're all clones, but they're people. They feel and breathe and see and smell everything. They may not be humans, but they are *people*, and people don't deserve getting beaten and raped.

What do I do? Marco's not here and he said it would only be a minute and then he'd be right back, right back up here, he said but he's not and not this Privilege is being raped and I can't do anything about it. I'm useless.

My fingers clutch the gold of the telescope. Pain strikes my knuckles but I ignore it.

"Marco!" I scream, hoping, praying, he will hear me.

I collapse beside the chute, sticking my head into the chute but it's pitch black and I can't see anything but still I scream his name because maybe, maybe he'll hear me.

"Rollin? Rollin, why're you screaming, for fuck's sake?" the faint voice returns.

"Call a Warden! Right now, Marco," I plead.

"Alright, just calm down. It'll be okay."

Seconds later I hear faint mutters drift to me. In the distance, a siren goes off. It echoes with deep melancholy.

I leap to my feet and go to the telescope. It's over. She's there, lying in a mess of filth. Blood runs a river from her temple. My heart clutches. The assailants escaped.

A minute passes. I'm frozen at the telescope. I hear footsteps behind me, but I can't tear myself away. A hand presses against my shoulder, but I resist. A voice shouts, but I can't hear it.

I couldn't save her.

"Rollin!" the voice screams, tearing me from the telescope.

I turn to him in a flash of rage. "She was being raped and I couldn't do anything about it."

"It's not your fault—"

"You said you would be gone for a minute," I growl. "You were gone fifteen. You left me alone up here without any way to contact a Warden and—"

He offers me a smoke and I snatch it from him. I light it quickly, inhaling the deep smoke into my lungs, holding it until it burns. However sweet the smoke, it cannot ease the anger.

"I'm sorry," he holds up his hands, remorse free from his eyes. "There was a roach girl down there waiting with my coffee and just *begged* me to have her. How could I refuse?"

Anger boils within me. My fists clench by my side. "You let a woman be raped because you couldn't refuse a prostitute?"

He laughs, collapsing in his lawn chair. "What can I say? Whores help keep the rustiness away."

I kick the lawn chair in blind rage. It slams into Marco, knocking the coffee out of his hands. It bleeds onto the ground and drips down the chute.

"What the hell?" he screams. "You wasted a whole damn coffee, you little shit!"

"Where's Buddy?"

"How should I know, you—"

"Call him right now," I snarl. "Tell him I'll meet him in the lobby downstairs."

He scoffs. "As long as it gets you to leave."

He dials the phone as I begin my descent into the darkness.

"Yes, Buddy. Your piece of shit wants to go home. Come clean him up."

I clench my teeth, but continue down. Rung by rung, I climb down from the height of hell and to sanity.

Tears blind my eyes.

I couldn't save her. Because of one ignorant man, I couldn't save her.

NOVA

I've been in the darkness for an eternity. Time has melted away, sending the minute and hour hands spinning and spinning into a black night.

I stop thinking. It's easier that way.

I drift through my mind, away from whatever tormented me before, away from the pain, the heartache, the tears…

I don't remember how long I go on like this, but soon, a hand is on my shoulder and I start to scream because it's the hands before that grabbed and touched and tormented and they're back again, THEY'RE BACK AGAIN—

But the hand doesn't touch or grab or torment. Its touch is soft, gentle. It shakes me as it shakes my nightmares away.

"Hello? Miss, can you hear me?"

I moan, the pain in my head throbbing a heartbeat that matches my own. Why does this man have to make me leave this darkness, so comforting and forgiving…? He shakes the nightmares away, but what else will he drive away?

"Miss, please, you've been hurt," the voice sings to me, but my mind focuses on only one thing…

"Calamity," I whisper.

It'll take me away, back to the darkness.

"Not yet," the voice says, "soon."

My eyes open weakly. Let me go back into darkness. I don't want to be here. I want to go away, far away…where is my Clam?

There's a large quilt draped over me, covering my naked body. A collage of clothing scraps composites the quilt, but all sorts of filth from my assault ruins the beautiful fabric. Mud, tears, blood, and unwanted filth.

"This is beautiful," I mutter, grazing my hand over the fabric.

"Thank you."

The quilt is an example of hard times, but it was ruined by the worst of times.

I turn my head to the voice and see the bright glint of a blue stripe shine down at me—a Warden. I expect myself to feel hatred and disgust for the roach, to tell it to leave me here to die and rot, but the softness in his voice makes me resist. I pull the blanket around me, even with the filth. It matters little.

"John?" I ask, my voice weak and so small, so terribly small.

"Yes, miss," he responds. "It's me. I'm here to help you."

"Thank you."

His head glimmers with sweat. A bead drops onto my head, but I don't move to wipe it off. I'm more disgusted with myself, with Privies in general, to do anything about it.

This man in front of me isn't a roach. I'm the roach. Privies are roaches. We are the evil vermin infesting this city.

"I deserved this," I whisper. "This was my fault. I'm sorry."

"There's no need to apologize, miss. This was not your fault."

"Yes, it was," I say, a tear falling from my cheek. "I'm weak. I'm a roach."

He doesn't say anything for a moment. "Where are you hurt?"

"I don't care."

"Miss, we need to help you. You're injured."

"I don't care!" I scream at him. "Give me some Clam and leave me to die."

I curl into a ball on the ground, hiding under the blanket, away from John, away from this terrible world that has nothing for me. I am nothing.

I sob and cry and it shakes me and it shakes the pain until I lie there, crying and John's rubbing my back, unsure of what to do, unsure of what to say, and I don't deserve anything. I am nothing.

"All I want is some Clam," I plead. "Please, John. That's all I want."

John ruffles through his jacket. I pull the blanket tighter around me, shielding me from this dark city and this dark world and the skyscrapers that stare at me with judgment in their eyes and the Binocs that sit upon them, watching and watching the Privileges go on and they couldn't stop them. The Binocs couldn't stop Micah or those men and now I'm here. Broken.

A slight *pop* sparks my ears. "I have some for you, miss."

I tear off the blanket, exposing myself to John but I don't care because there it is, that little bottle of happiness and love and joy and blissful ignorance and I grab it and cry more, tears leaking from me like a busted dam and I swallow the Clam, gulp it eagerly and throw the bottle down the alleyway. It shatters against the distant ground. I grab the second, the third from him and they all follow the same course. Glass shards rain on the alleyway like they did when Micah threw the glasses at me.

I feel it. Soon, I'll be gone. I won't have to remember this. I won't have to remember anything.

The familiar warmth floods my veins, taking away the pain in my temple and the soreness between my legs that I've been longing to forget and everything until I'm drifting away…and I fly. I'm free.

John encircles me in his arms and carries me down the alleyway, away from the pool of filth, away from the skyscrapers staring down at me, from the Binocs looming above, from the pain, the tears, the desperation, the depression…everything.

I'm free.

I fly away with John and into his Warden car. He lies me down on the seats in the back. Something soft is placed under my head. I snuggle into the cushion, my head floating on a cloud far away from everything that happened. What happened again?

What use is it? I remember it being awful, unpleasant, and I took the Clam and now I'm here, flying away and everything is wonderful and I feel wonderful with this quilt in the back of this nice man's car and it's okay. Soon everything will be perfect.

Something disrupts my thoughts. I turn, lifting my head from the pillow. Looking through the grimy window, I see a man talking with the Warden. He turns his head to look at me and his whole composure changes. Muffled yells echo through the window as he frantically waves his arms. Tears glisten in his eyes.

He throws himself at the window, banging on the glass and I scream. Things aren't so wonderful right now. *Why aren't they wonderful?*

This man…I recognize him. He's…he's…the man in the alleyway. Yes, he's that man who made things unpleasant *before*—

What was I thinking about? Oh, I can't remember. I ignore the man and sink back into my cushions, sink back into bliss, away from the world so I can fly…

The man doesn't stop pounding. I look up again as the man shouts at me, tears in his eyes. Maybe he should take some Clam. He might feel better about himself.

John takes the man, whom I see is an Oddity by the green stripe on his jacket, and throws him on the ground. There's a black man, too. He takes the man on the ground and holds him back in his arms. His eyes are watery. John crosses around the car and opens the door.

"—MIRA! MIRA, IT'S ME! MIRA, I—"

The door shuts. John starts the car and stares out at the two men outside.

"Don't worry about them, miss," he turns around in his seat. "We'll leave them soon."

"I trust you, John," I smile, staring at the men.

Something intrigues me about the two mysterious men. One is an Oddity with a green-striped jacket while the other is a Privy, clear as day. The Hispanic man with a deep brown tan—the frantic one—has black-brown hair, which is ruffled now, and the green eyes that sparkle like jewels. He is a handsome Oddity, that's for sure. Heat flutters in my chest. I wonder if I'll ever meet him. He seems like a wonderful man.

There is something familiar about him...the way his eyebrows crease when he screams or the way his fists tighten by his sides or maybe the way his teeth clench when he's cross. Yes, there's definitely something there. Oh, what does it matter?

I'm about to turn toward John, this wonderful man, when banging comes from the window. I throw myself down when I hear glass shatter. Shards sprinkle on me and I hold the blanket over my head. I giggle. This sure is a strange dream. Nothing like this could ever happen in real life. How...wonderful.

Screams erupt in my ear. "MIRA, LOOK AT ME. IT'S ROLLIN. PLEASE JUST LOOK—"

Suddenly, the screams cut off. I look over to see the black man with the Hispanic man in his hands. The black man looks like a Privy. He has a nice suit on, which is wrinkled now from wrestling with the Oddity. Have I seen him before at a party? No, not at a party. Maybe it was at the Clam shop...

I brush the glass off my blanket and to the opposite seat. I curl into a ball again, watching the strange pair. My auburn hair swirls in a frenzy about me. The Hispanic man stares daggers into my eyes. His eyes plead at me. I yawn. My eyes begin to close.

I hear the car engine rev. My body shifts back as the car peels from the curb. Wind flows in from the window. I hide under my blanket, but it is not thick or warm enough. It is wonderful though, one of the most wonderful things.

I hear John curse, looking into the little mirror above the radio. Hm, I wonder what that's for? He mutters more curses, pushing his foot further and further on the accelerator.

"Hold on, miss," he says to me.

Wow! This is like one of those action movies I used to watch from the olden days. There were car chases and bad guys who were chasing good guys but the good guys always won because they were good and that's what was supposed to happen.

I giggle happily, turning behind me to see a car following. It's black with a white stripe on the side. Oh, it's a Privy car! I wonder if I know them. John doesn't seem to like them though. He keeps glancing behind and swearing and sweating and I wonder why the car isn't a pool with all the sweat bleeding off him.

Bored by the car chase, my gaze finds my arm. Dried blood cracks against the skin. I start picking it absently.

The car jolts forward. I turn around quickly to see a car smashed into us. That Hispanic man I saw earlier is in the front seat, his eyes crazed and his hair crazed and his fingers clenched on the steering wheel like a crazed man and wow, I *swear* he looks familiar, but I can't put my finger on it.

I definitely saw him today, and I think I see him a lot. I know I would *want* to because he's a nice looking man. I think it had something to do with the alleyway, with why I'm all bloody and why my head is sticky and I don't seem to remember much of what happened. Hm…

"I'm sorry about this, miss," John grunts to me. "This man is crazed."

I laugh. "This is so wonderful, John!"

I should watch some of those movies again. I don't know why I ever stopped watching them. I remember one specifically. Ivy hated it, but it was my favorite. I can't remember the name, but there were wizards and short little men and potions—the bad kind that didn't make you feel so wonderful all the time—and things were adventurous and fun and even when things went wrong, they turned alright in the end.

"Where are we going?" I ask the nice Warden.

"To a hospital, miss."

I gasp. "They have hospitals? I thought we only had clinics!"

This place is amazing. I've been here for a while, but things have never stopped being wonderful.

I stop paying attention to the car chase. I'll watch it in the movies later. I lie down, cradling my head on that wonderful pillow and feel myself drift away. Yes, this is wonderful. Maybe if I go to sleep now then I'll wake up from this dream. Yes, maybe…

I'm gone. *Flying up in the air. I'm not bloody anymore and I'm beautiful and wearing my favorite little leather dress that has the studs running across my waist. Oh, I look wonderful! That Hispanic man will surely love me in this dress when I see him again. I must see him again. I'll use that makeup that Ivy gave me for my birthday a couple of weeks ago and he was so handsome and I'll be beautiful and I'll give him some Clam and then we'll fly away together and it'll be wonderful.*

Absolutely wonderful.

ROLLIN

Buddy holds me within his strong arms. The black muscles ripple as he struggles to keep me back. The Warden car disappears around the corner. Screeches erupt as the tires bend against the asphalt. Roaches on all sides have stopped and are staring at Buddy and me, the strange pair of roach and Privy walking through the streets, a wrecked car behind us and a Warden car vanished, leaving no trace but the curl of smoke through the air.

"Let me go!" I scream at him, struggling to tear from his arms. "It was her. It was her!"

My legs twitch with the urge to run, to sprint after her until my legs would crumple and my bones would break and my muscles would rip apart and I couldn't run anymore, even if I tried. I can't. Roaches are on all sides of us. Our car is destroyed. A scene has already been made and questions will be asked.

"Buddy, please."

He stays silent, holding me firm between his strong arms. The night falls quiet. The smell of burnt rubber twists through the air and…

She's gone.

I stop struggling in Buddy's arms. I collapse. The asphalt stings as loose rubble digs into my vulnerable skin. I watch the corner where she disappeared around. I watch where I let her go.

I need to believe that I will find her again, but my conscience tells me otherwise. It tells me I failed.

She didn't even recognize me.

I banged against the window, trying and *trying* to get her to see me, but she didn't. She saw right through me. She was bloody. It covered her porcelain body, making her look like a squished tomato. She was always proud of that porcelain skin.

Her auburn hair flew in a frenzy about her. Her face was ruined with streaking makeup, black and blue streaks running down her face against the blacks and blues of bruises covering her body…I almost didn't recognize her. She looked like a stranger to me, so painted and poised, as though Chicago graffiti had destroyed her vibrant canvas.

A rag of a blanket covered her body. She had no clothes underneath. Her chest was unveiled and she didn't seem to care. I barely noticed. All I could see was her. I had found her, but she hadn't found me.

I sit there, holding my bloodied fists in my hands. Glass shards stick into the raw flesh mercilessly. I don't feel the pain. I don't feel much at all.

Buddy's arms pull at my armpits, trying to bring me to my feet.

"C'mon, mah friend," he says. "We've gotta be a movin' 'fore people start lookin'."

"Let them look!" I scream, my voice scratching at my throat. "Let them listen to—"

Buddy's hand comes down hard across my face. My voice cuts short as I spit out blood. The roaches on the sides of the street are still watching, staring blankly with those bug eyes of theirs.

"I'll get you shipped to the suburbs for crashing my car, you roach," Buddy yells, his voice that of a stranger's.

Buddy's fingernails dig into my arm, yanking me to my feet. He drags me away from the street and the smoking wreck of a car. Cuts appear where his nails bite into my skin. The roaches have stopped watching. They continue about their errands, the event nearly eradicated from their minds.

"Keep walkin'," Buddy mutters to me.

He releases his grip, pushing me away from him. I know it's an act to divert the Oddities' attention away from us, but his words seem too harsh and his grip too firm. I grab a handful of Buddy's jacket and wrench him into an alleyway. I know what alleyway it is. I know where I've brought him.

I ignore Buddy as I stride down the alleyway. Fists clench at my waist. My knuckles turn white. My eyes stare wide ahead, concentrated at the pool of filth near the end of the alleyway.

I stop, scrutinizing the scene with every ounce of strength I have remaining. On the ground lies her dress in a pool of blood, vomit, and god knows what else. I look away in disgust. Blood lies in a short trail against the bricks. Bloody handprints stain the wall. I pick up the dress between two fingers. It drips with filth. I turn to Buddy.

"Do you get it?" I spit. "She was raped, beaten—"

"No, mah friend, ah understand—"

"Look at this!" I hurl the dress at him.

He dodges it and it hits the ground with a *splat*. Filth splatters onto Buddy's pant leg.

I begin toward him. "Did you love your mama, Buddy?"

"Yes, ah did, with all mah heart," he lifts his hands up in defense.

"What if your mom was gang-raped? What if she was left in an alleyway, bleeding to death and naked for all eyes to see?"

"Well, ah—"

"Would you be angry if someone told you to be quiet? If they told you to calm down and that everything was okay?" I spit, my eyes staring through this fake son of a bitch and I can't take him, I can't take this—

"Rollin, of course ah would," Buddy says, his voice cautious, his demeanor changed. He rubs his hands together, his eyes flicking from my fists to my face. He licks his lips and stares me in the eyes. "Ah'd find those suns 'a bitches and murder 'em. That's what ah'd do."

"Exactly," I whisper, my fists relaxing. "You'd find those bastards. You'd get revenge."

Buddy glances to the dress on the ground. "Ah never saw yuh as a vengeful man."

"I never had a reason before," I mutter, kicking the dress. It hits the wall, splattering more filth everywhere. It's everywhere. Her tears, her assault, her pain and remorse and violation everywhere.

"She didn't remember me, Buddy," I say, tears pricking at my eyes but I hide them, as best as I can. "She didn't even know who I was."

"But yuh found her. That's the important part."

I chuckle darkly. "I'm not so sure."

We stand in silence for a while longer. The wind whistles through the alleyway and sends shivers up my skin. I huddle into my thin jacket, but it's no use.

"I *saw* it happen, Buddy. I saw them take her, beat her, and push themselves on her. She couldn't do a thing. *I* couldn't do a thing. Marco was gone. I had no way of calling a Warden or anything. I could have stopped it, but I didn't."

"It's not yer fault, Rollin—"

"Then I ran down here to make sure the Warden got to her and everything was as okay as it could be. I didn't know it was her, I just wanted to make sure the poor girl was safe. Then I saw her. She was cradled in the back seat with that auburn hair and the Warden, he didn't understand. It was *her*. It was Mira. I tried so hard. I tried so hard for her to recognize me, but she didn't. She only stared and *stared* like I was the most wonderful thing on the earth."

He stands there and stares and just like her, he doesn't seem to recognize me. Dammit, I don't even recognize me anymore.

"What's worse, finding her dead or finding her so different than the woman she was?"

Buddy approaches me and raises his hand like he's going to pat me on the back, but pulls it down before he does anything. "Yuh really care fer her, don't yuh?"

I smile. "She was my friend."

"A rare thing, these days."

"And you wondered why I fought for it."

A glint of light catches my attention out of the corner of my eye. I turn toward the source and find broken pieces of glass littered on the ground like angel tears. A small gray bottle cap rolls aimlessly in the wind.

"What's this?" I murmur to myself.

Buddy follows my eyes. "That cap looks like those on 'em Clam bottles."

I kneel down at run my hand through the glass. It pricks at me, but I don't mind. There's glass in my hand already.

"She must have taken Calamity," I say. "That's why she was so incoherent when I saw her in the car. The Warden had to give her some so he could move her. That's why she must not remember me, right? The drug made her forget."

Buddy looks at me warily. "Ah don't know, Rollin. That Clam does a doozy, but ah don't think it can make a gal forget a friend…"

"But there's a chance, isn't there?" I plead with him. "She might still be there, under all the Clam. Mira might be there."

Buddy shakes his head. "There's a chance, but not a good one."

"I have to find her."

"Yuh'd be best with sittin' still. Yuh have to let her heal. It won't do yuh no good runnin' in there after she was *raped*."

I run my hand through my hair. I turn from Buddy, from the broken Calamity bottle and the pool of filth on the ground. I look out into the city as Oddities pass by. Only a few look in. The eyes that do find us don't linger long.

My hands hang by my sides. Pain stirs in them like an angered beast ready to charge. A heartbeat throbs against the red skin. Blood and glass stain the innocent flesh.

"Yuh best let me take yuh back to mah apartment and patch those hands up," Buddy eyes my bleeding knuckles. "Then yuh can tell me more 'bout yer gal and we can make a plan 'bout findin' her again."

I hear him, but I stopped listening a while ago. Things have changed.

The League didn't give me any way to communicate with them. They didn't trust me. My mission was simple enough, they said. I'll be there and back in a matter of months.

I wish I could tell them myself that I found her. They wouldn't believe me. They always thought I was a strange one. I was the Leaguer gone cripple.

"Why don't you leave with me, Buddy?" I turn to him.

His eyebrows crease with confusion. "What're yuh talkin' 'bout?"

"When I find Mira again and we're ready to leave again, why don't you come with us? There's nothing left here anymore."

Please, Buddy. Come with me.

"Ah don't know," he chuckles, waving me off. "Ah don't think ah could leave here. Ah couldn't bear without some Clam once and a while. Ah hate that fact, but it doesn't mean it ain't true."

"You don't have to decide now," I rationalize. "Think about it."

Maybe I don't have to murder him. Maybe I can save him. Maybe I can do one good thing while I'm here.

"Ah don't know…"

"Think about it," I plead. "You don't have any family here. You don't have anything waiting for you. You could leave all this behind and start new."

"Ah'll think 'bout it," he says quickly. "That's all ah'll promise."

I don't know what I'm thinking. Even if he did agree to go, even if he left Chicago before everyone died, what would the League say? I couldn't bring a clone back to New York.

Maybe he could escape. Maybe he could travel, escape all of this and never have to live any of it. Maybe he could do it.

I know he's a clone. I know there's another one of him back in the colonies, but dammit, he helped me out. He's a person, no matter what the League keeps telling me.

"C'mon," Buddy places his arm on my back, pushing me gently forward. "Let's go and patch yuh up 'fore yuh start talkin' again."

We make our way down the alleyway, past the ruined dress rotting in a mess of filth, away from the broken bottle and blood staining the wall and the source of Mira's pain and suffering and humiliation—

Breathe. Just breathe.

We walk away from it and enter the crowd of Oddities passing by outside. Buddy receives a few strange looks, but no one dares to question much. Buddy has a demeanor about him that demands respect. Oddities scurry at the sight of him.

"It's a beautiful night," Buddy smiles, looking into the sky.

"Yeah," I mutter. "Beautiful."

A city stained in blood, a world filthied with the acts of villains, the putrid smell of uncleanly roaches wafting through the air, the dark, soul-sucking skyscrapers consuming the sky, and the lone moon peeking though it all.

Beautiful.

NOVA

Being a Privilege doesn't mean you're privileged, as I once thought. You think you're flying, soaring through the sky with all the other Privies above the scurrying roaches and you don't look down. You never look down. You keep flying and flying and you never stop, because that's not the privileged way. That's not the Privilege way.

Privileges don't fly. We crawl. We rot in the sewers of the city. We sit and stew and ferment the air with our rotted flesh until the roaches scurry across the sidewalks, trying to find an escape from the smell. They never do.

I rot now. I fell long ago. The air doesn't carry the sweet scent of Clam any longer and the future doesn't hold the rosy hue of bliss.

Privileges take Clam to fly. Oddities take Clam to escape. I desire both.

I drift in darkness. I don't remember much. I fell into the Clam haze long ago and ever since then, I have been falling in and out of blissful ignorance. The darkness wavers, but it never ceases.

I dream of many things. I dream of Ivy and her bloody face. I hurt her in the name of love. Micah must love me. He must. I dream of Micah, too. Of course I do. He's the reason I'm here, in this darkness, is he not? Oh, Micah, my love…what happened? I know you love me, you must, but why did you have to drink so much? Why did you mix too much too soon? Something happened, but my mind is blank and weary…

I don't blame Micah for whatever he did. How could I? He is innocent. Society is to blame. It creates monsters in us all.

I don't know what I will do when I see him again. I don't know how I will act, what I will say. I don't even know if I will run toward him or away.

Our love for each other will never be broken. We are forever chained together. Nothing will tear us apart. Yet, fear lingers like a lost brother inside. I don't remember anything, but the emotion remains in the shadow.

I begin to drift from the darkness. Light peaks through. Clam leaks from my system. Groggy, my eyes blink open hazily. Bright lights blind me from above. I squeeze my eyes shut, pain stretching a familiar ache across the white plains.

"Nova? Can you hear me?" a voice calls from beside me.

I only groan. A deep pain spreads across my head. I pull my arm up to feel it, but gentle fingers hold it down. Wires and tubes extend from my arm. I'm a puppet on strings.

My eyes open slowly, squinting to adjust to the light. A masked face hovers above me. It's a woman with a white jacket. Brown hair flies from her head as blue eyes stare back at me. Her face is ordinary and her face spotted with freckles. Underneath her white coat she wears a navy shirt with a dancing cat. It almost makes me smile.

"What happened? Where am I?" I mutter, glancing around.

The room around me is all white and bare except for a couch in the corner and a dish of lemon drops on the table beside me. I lie in a hospital bed. Machines beep all around me. I must have been hurt pretty seriously if I'm in a hospital. Nobody goes to hospitals. Tears sting in my eyes. I let them fall.

"Micah..." I try to say something, anything, but nothing comes out. Nothing comes in. My brain jumbles the facts of the past. What did Micah do?

The Privilege doctor pets my hair, watching my vacant eyes. "It wasn't your fault, sweetie. He is a terrible, horrid man."

"It was my fault," I whisper, not knowing what happened but knowing that fact for certain.

"Shh, dear," the doctor puts her finger over my lips. "He won't be seeing you anytime soon."

"What happened to Micah?"

"We moved him to a different sector of the city. They have a Binoc watching him now. You can rest easy. There's no need to worry."

Tears pool in my eyes, blurring the doctor and the white room and the bright lights and everything until there's nothing. Not even Micah is here to hit me. At least then there was someone. At least then he could wipe away my tears and whisper sweet lies into my ear.

"I thought he loved me," I whisper, realizing the painful truth. He never said the words to me; I only thought he did.

"I know," she pats my hand. "I know, dear."

She checks on the machines as the tears make rivers down my face. I stare into the light, letting the pain settle until my eyes burn. I don't want to see this world anymore.

"There was a nasty cut on your head and you had a pretty severe concussion," the doctor calls to me, still analyzing the machine. "There're bruises and scrapes all over your body as well. You'll be okay, dear. You could leave today, if you wish."

I don't answer. I close my eyes, close myself, close the world. I wish Ivy were here. She always knew what to do. She always knew what to say. She was right, she always was, but she knew I'd hit her if she said Micah didn't love me. She should've known. She shouldn't have said it.

I don't sleep. They won't put any more Clam into my IV. They say that I've exceeded my dosage for any twenty-four hour period. Bullshit. I've taken more in a few hours than they've given me in a whole day.

I want to fly. I want to forget. I want to leave this city and fly higher and higher, away from these puppet strings, from these damn skyscrapers everywhere and even Micah.

I want to leave it all, forever.

Soon, I will.

ROLLIN

Buddy has a pair of tweezers in his hands and a pair of glasses on his nose. A pile of glass shards lies on the table next to us. Alcohol swabs and bandages are sprinkled about us. Buddy doesn't speak. His hands are steady and his mind unnerved. We took half a dose of Clam each to calm our nerves. I can't help but desire more.

"Yer gal," Buddy glances up at me, "yuh had a thing fer her, didn't yuh?"

"No," I quickly respond. "It wasn't like that. We were friends, that's all."

"Yuh sure 'bout that? Ah ain't seen a fella care so much 'bout a friend 'fore. Yuh sure did fight fer her back there."

"Yeah, well, things are a bit different where I come from, Buddy. When people form bonds, it's hard to break them."

His eyebrows raise at this. "Oh, really? St. Louis is so different than ol' Chicago?"

"Well… yes," I pause, "it's a lot different."

"How so?"

"Well, they don't like people getting romantic there. There are some rules. They don't even like people calling each other friends, but they prefer that over something like…girlfriend or wife."

Buddy smiles a bit. "So yuh do like her!"

"She's my friend, Buddy."

He only shakes his head and chuckles while I dismiss the image of Mira in the backseat of the car, her chest exposed. That was…well…I've never seen anything like *those* before. The image brings an unwelcome fire.

No, no, Mira and I aren't like that. We're in the League together. We can't have a romantic relationship. We're not supposed to have a relationship of any kind. When Leaguers were sent away and likely never to return, they didn't want other Leaguers to be distracted from their work. The mission is the number one priority. Everything else comes after, even our lives.

That's what we agreed to. Our lives for our colonies.

Of course we *wanted* to do things with each other. We got lonely. We got lustful. We resisted though, for the sake of the mission. It was what we gave up our lives for, so we couldn't throw it away for the sake of pleasure.

Mira told me that rumors were spreading of other Leaguers slipping out into the night to find the whores wandering the streets, though I doubt there were any whores to be found. Regardless, those Leaguers were the first to go and the first to die.

Mira was my friend, not my lover. She *is* my friend, and I will find her. I will bring her back from whatever void she has fallen through. I will save her.

"Alright, ah think ah got 'em all, mah friend," Buddy analyzes my hand closely before putting down the tweezers and his glasses. "Now, ah'm gonna swab it with some alcohol and wrap it up nice and tight fer yuh."

"Thank you," I say, flinching as the alcohol stings the open wounds. "Thank you for everything. You're a good friend."

Buddy smiles. "Don't thank me, mah friend. Thank the Lord. He shows me the path. Ah only follow in his footsteps. Ah beckon to his call and he called me to help yuh."

"I don't think the Lord had much to do with it, Buddy. You're the one who did it and I want to thank you."

Buddy frowns for a brief moment. "Yer not a believer?"

"No, I stopped believing a while ago. There wasn't much for me to believe in."

"Ah respect yer choice, but ah can't take yer thanks. Ah'll send them to the Lord if mah prayers allow it."

I shake my head. "If that's what you want."

Buddy ties the ends of the bandage together and pats the hand softly. I bring it to my side, flexing my fingers gently. Dull pain presses on them. Buddy pulls the cross around his neck to his lips. He kisses it softly, closing his eyes.

"Did you think about it at all?" I ask him, watching him carefully. "About leaving here with me? You've been so nice to me and I only wish to repay—"

"No, ah can't," Buddy pushes to his feet and turns away from me, a sudden spark of rage flaming his stride and igniting his face.

Anger trails behind him as the door slams closed. I hold my bandaged hand close to me. I hear the muffled sound of glass shattering. He'll be gone soon. It's almost midnight anyway. It's time to sleep.

Buddy said I could see her in the morning. He called Marco on the way back to the apartment and he told Buddy where the Warden had brought Mira. I wanted to go then and I tried to, but Buddy stopped me. It's better to wait until the morning, he said. Bullshit. I've waited long enough. A day ago, there was a chance I could find her dead. Now I *know* she's alive.

Maybe she'll recognize me when I see her. She must. She hopefully won't be on any Calamity and won't be sleeping and I'll come in and her porcelain skin will shine free of blood and there'll be bandages on her wounds and nothing will be wrong. That disgusting makeup will be gone from her face and she'll cry out my name in relief and tears will prick at her eyes and she'll be so damn happy. She won't be anything like she was before.

Then I'll find those bastards. I'll find them and make them wish they never raped and violated and humiliated my Mira. I'll make sure they'll never touch another woman like they touched her. Yesterday, Buddy said he didn't see me as the vengeful kind. Yesterday, I didn't think I was either.

Then three bastards came into my life. Now, blind rage flows through my body instead of blood. My fists clench without me thinking about it. I imagine their blood on the ground. I imagine their death on my hands.

Damn peace. Damn the League's mission.

I'm going to get my revenge, and I'm going to get Mira.

NOVA

It's morning. Bright light shines through the glass windows and hits my eyes. I squint but continue to stare. Trees flutter in the wind as the sunshine illuminates their pale leaves. It will be autumn soon. The trees will change colors, casting hues, a rainbow of colors, across this dark city.

I hate it.

The leaves fall, making every step of the roaches noisy. The weather gets colder. The air nips at my skin. The roaches get lazy. After autumn, winter comes, which is even worse. Roaches are found dead in the streets routinely throughout the day. Their frozen corpses stick to the ground. Sometimes, in the middle of the night, I can hear them chopping away, trying to dig the bodies from the ice.

They would leave them there to rot, but the Privileges would complain. They do it for our sake. Everything in this city is done for our sake.

The dead bodies don't bother me much. It'd be an unusual day if I didn't come across at least one. The ash bothers me. The Privileges have begun to call winter "Ash," though the ash begins to fall in autumn. Instead of snow, the ash of the burnt bodies floats through the air. People try to ignore it.

Tiny Oddity children beg in the street. They cup their hands in front of them, pleading for a drink or some Clam or some money or whatever they can get their goddamn hands on. They're pests, and disgusting ones at that.

Ash changes people.

I once saw a roach girl as young as seven offer a blowjob to a Privy man in exchange for some money. The worst part was the man accepted. Cries came from the alleyway minutes later. I tried to forget that, but a mind refuses to forget some things.

Once the first ash falls, Micah will be surely gone by then. He's part of

73

the southern visitors. Many of them come up in the spring and stay until Ash hits. They go back down after that. The summers in the south have become too brutal for most of them.

There is one perk of Ash. At least he'll be gone. At least he won't…he will never—

Oh, what use is it now. It's over. I'll never see him again.

Once the last of the Clam disappeared from my system, the memories came flooding back. Now, there's nothing I wish for more than to be back in that blissful state of ignorance.

I wish it was still the way it was before. I wish he had never raped me. I wish I had never punched Ivy in the face. I wish everything was how it was two days ago. Ivy was my friend and Micah was my best friend. Everything was perfect and I floated with Clam when I wished and sunk into reality when the former wasn't an option but at least I was *happy*—for the most part.

At least I wasn't alone.

I have no one.

A slight knock comes from the door. I turn to it lazily, tearing my view from the window and the trees and the ash already floating down from the sky. It's not autumn yet. Why is there ash?

"Ms. Aster?" the voice calls. "There's a visitor here to see you."

"Is it Ivy?" I ask, hope rising in my chest and oh, I hope it's Ivy because she'll be here and will forgive me and we can be friends again and I won't be so lonely and things will be okay. Things will all be okay.

"No, it's a man," she says, making my heart drop. "He says his name is Rollin and he's your friend."

My face crunches in confusion. "I don't know anybody with that name."

"Should I tell him to leave?"

I stare out the window some more, imagining that ash falling and falling on the trees and the skyscrapers and burying all the roaches until more die and more ash falls. It never stops falling.

"No, no," I mumble. "Send him in, I guess."

Footsteps echo softly away from the door. Maybe as a reward for my cooperation they'll give me some more Clam. I convinced the young nurse to pump some in my IV a couple of hours ago. He was quickly scolded by the doctor. They say I've had too much. I say I haven't had enough. My eyes have grown tired and my soul weary. I don't care to see this world anymore.

My gaze is fixated on those fluttering leaves when I hear the door swing open. Muffled voices come from further down the hallway as well as a machine beeping and the screams of patients and the groans of doctors and *beep…beep…beep…*

"Mira?" the voice asks.

I turn and freeze. My blood melts from my skin as I stare at him, my stomach on the floor shriveling in a ball and my muscles tense as I see *him*.

Black-brown hair. Green, emerald eyes. A Hispanic tan. That voice, like a lover's knife, cutting away at me with some foreign name and—

"Micah," I barely whisper.

His eyebrows crease in a way I've never seen them before. There's pain on that brow, weighing it down and his hands don't tighten and his voice doesn't come out like a saw ready to cut and stab and hurt me—

My hands clutch the rails of the hospital bed—I, I can't think—I close my eyes and clutch my hair and scream and yell until my voice comes out dry and scratchy—

He's rushing toward me, pulling my face in his hands and staring into my eyes. There's doctors and nurses and a black man all around my bed and I'm not so lonely anymore, not anymore and he's still there, staring and staring and *staring* dammit—

"Mira, it's me! It's Rollin—"

"Micah," I whisper and I can't breathe or think or— "You're Micah."

Those eyebrows crinkle again and it's not like him, not at all.

"Who's Micah?" he asks and his eyes, oh those eyes! Green emeralds stare back at me and I want to dive into them and climb about those foreign planets that float in space, storming and flying at millions of miles an hour but to us, it's so slow. We're not going anywhere.

"Your name is Mira Pevensky and—"

"Get out!" I scream and he's still holding my face and tears leak from his eyes, pooling down his face and Micah never cries and those green planets look so lonely, just like me, and I want to hug him, kiss him, let him give love to me and give me his pleasure because then, I'm not alone.

"Mira, please—"

"I'm not Mira," I cry, tears flowing and his hands fall from my face and who is he and who I am and I don't know, I don't know, I don't—

Then there are guards and he's being pulled away and the doctors sit there with their glum faces and the nurses sit there with their glum faces and the black man sits there staring and staring at me and Micah, me and Micah until I want to scream and I can't—

"Stop," I mumble but no one hears me, no one hears me. "Stop!"

The commotion stops. The guards stop pulling him. Micah stops struggling. The doctors and nurses avert their eyes. The black man stares at me.

His eyes, full of everything and nothing, despair and happiness, light and dark and I can't take it, it's too much, when will it stop—

I look out the window. I close my eyes and watch the ash fall, tumbling and billowing through the air. Some other people pretend it's rain or snow, but I don't. It's ash. It's death. It's my future and my past.

But I can't take it because I know they're watching me and I know they'll keep watching me and I want some Clam, just give me some Clam, please, PLEASE, HELP—

Fingers curl around my wrists, gently, and pull them from my hair but I pull out strands and they flutter in my fingers and they're wet with despair and his hands cradle my face, making me look into those gems and I can't, I won't—

"Mira," he whispers, so soft, so gentle. "Please, my Mira."

But I'm not Mira. I'm Nova, Nova Aster, like the stars. A nurse is at my IV, pulling an empty needle away. Thank you. Thank you, whoever the hell you are.

"Soon I'll be gone," I laugh, collapsing into the pillows, feeling their soft plush envelop my head and he's still there, Micah, my Micah, holding the air between his hands and staring and I don't know.

"Micah," I look at him, this changed, this strange Micah, "why did you do it?"

Confusion keeps attacking him, disfiguring his face and I wish it would stop. Why can't this all stop? I'm so tired.

"Do what?"

"Rape me, Micah," I whisper. "Cut me, punch me, kick me, brutalize me, make me lie and punch Ivy and—"

He takes my hands into his own. Micah never held my hands. Micah never touched me if it wasn't solely for his pleasure.

"I'm not Micah," he tries staring into my eyes, but I'm not looking at him.

He is Micah. He's exactly like Micah. The hair, the eyes, the little dimple on his left cheek, the birthmark next to his right eyebrow, the way his hair never folds over that cowlick he always hated. I laugh. He never could get rid of that cowlick.

"I loved you, Micah," I stare at him, giggling, laughing, the world spinning and flying and shooting into space.

I look away from Micah, this strange, strange Micah, and find an empty room. All the doctors and nurses have fled, leaving only the black man, my Micah, and a closed door.

"Please," his head collapses, his tears falling on our conjoined hands, our fingers interlocked, our minds on the wrong current, "Mira, remember me. If you're in there, if you're listening somehow—"

"Micah, you talk so strangely!"

More tears fall.

"But you're rather *wonderful*, I'd say."

Fists pound on the table.

"Even if you raped me."

A water cup is knocked to the ground, splashing all over the walls.

"And punched me."

A chair is thrown across the room.

"And cut me."

Glass shatters.

"And hurt me."

Curses are screamed.

"And never loved me. Not even once."

Micah, my love, what happened to you? I'm falling now, but I hope you come back. Maybe you will. I know I shouldn't hope for you, but I do. You seem different now but that's okay. I still love you. You're as wonderful as ever.

Hopefully you won't do that to me again, Micah. I loved you. I love you. You are my sun. You are my fire. You are my love.

You will always be my love, but I'm slipping, my Micah. I'm falling away from this twisted version of you, destroying things in my life just as you always have. Now, instead of you destroying me, you're destroying my life. Circumstances have changed but you have not.

I forgive you, Micah. I know you haven't apologized yet, but you will, and when you do, I forgive you. I always do.

I want to fly. I've wanted to fly. I can't smell or see or hear or feel anything anymore. The world is black behind my eyelids, all except for those flecks of ash floating through the sky.

Soon, Ash will be here. The dead will fly through the sky and the dead will walk through the street. I hope you stay for that, Micah. It's something as strange as you are acting now.

I hope you love me soon, my love. You've been hurting me in more ways than one. I want to know what it's like, inside there, inside the warm, rosy hue of love. I've only dreamt of it.

I forgive you, Micah. You didn't mean it. You love me, I know.

You're wonderful, the most wonderful man on the earth.

Of course you love me.

Soon, you'll always love me, and we'll always be together.

ROLLIN

Her eyes are closed now. A smile is still on her lips from when she drifted off, mumbling those words, those disgusting, vile words.

I'm curled on the ground, my fingers through my hair, pulling at it as I sit in more glass, shattered on the ground with the room strewn apart, and tears fall, watching that auburn hair flutter from the breeze coming through the open window.

I jump to my feet, the glass crunching as doctors and nurses and guards rush to me but I push them off, throw them on the ground because seeing her, my Mira, is making my head pound. She's gone. She doesn't see me.

I rush to her, cup her sweet porcelain face in my hand and brush away the tears that still lie on her face but it's no use. My tears replace the ones I wipe away.

"Where are you, Mira?" I whisper, pushing a strand of her auburn hair away from her face. "What happened to you?"

She doesn't hear me because she's drifting away in that damn Clam cloud, away from me and the city and pain and fear and remorse and every damn emotion that these people can't seem to handle.

"Rollin, maybe we should go," a soft voice calls from beside me. "Yuh can try to see her again tomorrow, if yuh'd like."

I turn to him, ashamed to look at her, this ghost of the woman I once knew. It's Mira, the woman who left months ago, the woman that went missing, the woman that was my friend, and she's not here. She's trapped in another world, leaving only this *thing* left for me.

"Who's Mira?" the voice spins through my head.

The room is completely destroyed. When she wouldn't see me, when she didn't know who I was, blind rage filled my body. I threw and demolished anything I could get my hands on, including the glass dish full of lemon drops and the chair beside her bed.

"They say her name is Nova," Buddy comes beside me. "She thinks yer the one who raped her in the alleyway."

"No, no," I mutter, "I don't understand. I saw it and called for the Warden. I *saved* her. I didn't do anything to her."

"Micah was her ol' boyfriend. She ain't seen him since it happened. They had an abusive relationship, they said."

I slam my fist on the table, my feet crunching on the glass underneath me. "I'm not Micah. She's not Nova."

"Yuh just need to calm down," Buddy puts his arm on my shoulder, holding my fists back, bringing them to my side. "Yuh need to settle. We'll figure it out soon enough."

"We need to figure it out now!" I scream.

"We need to go," Buddy pulls me toward the door. "They'll be gettin' suspicious of us if we stay here too long, especially after yer lil' episode. A roach and a Privy together is a strange enough pair. Don't want 'em callin' nobody."

The door swings open and a Warden appears. He stares at us methodically, his skin tanned and wrinkled like a discarded football, left to rot for years.

"I have to ask you guys to leave," the man says in a gruff voice. The blue stripe on his jacket glints an ugly sheen.

He gives us a queer look. We've been receiving looks like those whenever we've been together. Not often are a Privy and a roach together, but it has happened before. Buddy told me lots of Binocs have roaches to do most of their duties as they fly high on Clam. He also said Privies sometimes have roaches follow them to do their bidding whenever they want, like slaves from the old world.

Buddy takes me by the arm and pulls me along, following the Warden out the door. I look behind me once last time, seeing her peaceful face, free of blood and makeup, resting against the snow-white pillows, her auburn hair in a frenzy, her mind away from here, from this mess. The door closes.

We follow the Warden until he closes the front doors to the hospital behind us. The noisy city of Chicago awaits us. Roaches swarm around us. No sirens wail for Buddy to cross as they usually do when a Privilege exits a building.

"Yuh can try to see her again later, if yuh like," Buddy turns to me softly. "There's no guarantee she'll recognize yuh any different than before. Yuh'll figure it out, ah know yuh will. Yuh got the passion. Ain't no one—"

"YOU SON OF A BITCH!" a voice screams from beside me and I turn to see a tiny Asian woman staring daggers at me but something blurs in my vision and smacks into my cheek and I'm lying on the ground, holding my cheek and my nose. Blood is pouring out of both. I'm looking up at the

Asian woman, her fists still in the air, her anger still boiling in the air, and I feel it pouring out of me.

"What the hell?" I scream at her. "What was that for?"

Buddy reaches down to help me up. "Mah friend, ah think there's been a mix up—"

"You know damn well what that was for, Micah," she screams as tears run like rivers down her face. "I told her to stay away from you and she didn't listen to me! And now she's—she's—"

She cuts off as sobs steal her voice. She crumples into herself, sniffling into her shoulder as the tears fall. There's a group of Privileges behind her. Some give us their attention while others argue amongst themselves. They hold various signs that demand her release and Micah's banishment from the city. Mira must have found many friends when she came here if so many people are out here rallying for her.

"I'm not Micah," I struggle to get up with Buddy's assistance.

"For once in your life would you stop lying, Micah!" she screams. "You already caused Nova enough pain."

"I've already told you, my name isn't Micah," I tell her calmly. "I didn't rape her and I didn't abuse her. That woman in there, her name is Mira, not Nova. She's my friend and—"

Another punch flies. Bones crunch. More blood falls.

"Alright, mah friend. There's no need to get physical here."

"Shut up! Just shut up!"

Another punch. A kick.

"Please, he ain't the guy yer lookin'—"

A grunt sounds behind me. Pavement stares me in the eye. Red dances across my vision.

"Ivy, this scum giving you trouble?"

"That's the bastard who raped Nova!"

Kicks fly into my stomach. A sharp pain digs into my stomach, twisting and more people fall on top of me, limbs and knives and weapons of all sorts flashing across my vision. Pain comes from every corner, hitting and stabbing into every square inch of my body.

I can't breathe. I suck in air but none comes in. Fingers grasp my throat and squeeze and squeeze and pain rips my lungs out and the air is sucked my from body—

The fingers are pried off my throat and I hear Buddy screaming from beside me. Kicks and shouts echo off the hospital walls and blood is everywhere—on me, on them, it doesn't matter. That Asian woman is standing off to the side with her hand over her mouth like she didn't know it'd come to this, like she didn't instigate it.

"Alright, alright," a voice screams. "Enough of this!"

A man appears, the same one who escorted us out of the building and more Wardens come and pull the people off me and push the crowd back, putting some in handcuffs but the world is going dark and fuzzy and my eyes drift close. The pain pries every nerve from my body and I fall away from my place on the pavement.

Consciousness comes and goes, and with it accompanies the pain. I feel hands on me at some point, but they're gentle hands, soft hands, hands that care. Buddy's southern voice drifts to me but I can't make out the words so I drift away. I think of Mira and how she was before she left New York.

We were friends. Now what are we? Strangers.

Bright lights drift through the darkness and machines beep and hands probe at my skin and pain flashes where they touch but it's okay because there are no screams or kicks or punches and I'm okay. I'm okay.

Voices shouts at each other as the machines keep going *beep...beep...beep...*and Buddy's southern voice drifts through it all, shouting, "Help *him*, ah said! Ah don't need nothin'. Help him!"

Darkness drifts in and out but still I lie there, on this soft cushion that's different from the pavement with the blood splattered all over it. The pain comes and goes as reality does.

I feel the familiar chill of Clam rushing through my system and everything fades into white...the voices...the machines...the hands probing...the pain cutting into me like a hot knife...everything...

It feels *wonderful*.

NOVA

I'm drifting from the Clam world when I feel a hand wrap around my own. The fingers twist through mine, holding me there, to the hospital bed and my eyes drift open to see that little scrunched-up face, the long black hair and the large bruise covering her left eye and I cover my face, hiding the tears, hiding myself because I don't want her to look at me.

"It's okay, Nova," she whispers, pulling my hands away. "You don't need to hide anymore. I'm here for you. He's gone."

"Micah left?" I ask, searching the room for that black-brown hair, those emerald eyes, but he's gone. She was right.

"Yes, I, uh," she pauses, folding her hands over in her lap, "I saw him outside. Things got a little rough, Nova."

I stare out at the window, at the ash falling down. The leaves will change soon. Micah will leave soon. Ash will fall and nothing will be the same. I won't be the same. I can't let Micah leave. I can't let him leave me again. He's mine and we'll always be together. Always and forever.

"What happened?" I mutter, barely paying attention, watching the ash fall around the room, around Ivy, creating piles upon piles of ash. Ivy is getting buried in it. I can't see her. She's gone.

"I punched him," she says. "I punched and kicked and made him regret what he did to you. Our friends were there, Nova. They all know you from the parties and some of them knew Micah too."

"You beat him up?" I scream, my voice shrilling and I can't even see her, Ivy, who was my friend and best companion but now she's a pile of ash. Nothing more.

"Well, I had to," she returns, anger bending her brow. "He had to learn his lesson so he will never do it to someone else again."

"But Ivy—"

"But nothing!" she stands, fists clenched at her side. "He *raped* you, Nova. I don't think you realize the scope of what has happened. He abused you for months and last night he raped you. He left you naked in the alleyway, blood pouring from your body. You almost died, and that bastard is going to hell."

I laugh madly, holding my stomach as I watch Ivy, the pile of ash in front of me, lecture and scream and tell me I'm wrong and awful and that Micah is wrong and awful but the truth is—

"We're all going to hell," I laugh.

Micah pops in my head. He was here earlier, yes, I remember that. He was here. He cradled my face and called me strange names but it was okay, because he was here, he was mine. Only for a moment. Then he was gone.

But he was here.

His face is inches before me. The ash does not fall on his head. It moves around him, creating a mirage as the ash falls and falls and falls and Ivy is gone, buried in the ash. I hope she's dead.

"My love," I whisper, reaching for his face. "I love you, Micah. I do. Come back to me. I promise I'll be good. We can be together. We will never have to leave each other."

"Nova, who are you talking—"

"I can go with you to the south," I tell him. "We can leave together and never have to see any of these damn people ever again. We won't have to worry about them."

Something slaps my cheek but I can't feel it. I can only see him. I can only see Micah.

"Snap out of this, Nova! You're here, in the hospital, because that bastard sent you here!"

"RAPE!" I scream at the top of my lungs. "HELP!"

Guards rush in and drag Ivy, the pile of ash, out of the room while she screams and curses at me but I don't care because soon, I'm alone. It's only Micah, the ash, and me. A cool breeze flutters in from the window, sending the ash into a dizzy hurricane around me that no one can penetrate. No one can separate Micah from me again.

My hand flies to the call button beside my bed. The sound of glass shattering hits my ears but the slight *beep...beep...beep...*drifts to my ears and soon the nurse is there, staring at me with those eyes that see and judge and don't take time to *think*.

"Is Micah here?" I ask her. "Is he here, in this hospital?"

"Nova, I don't think it's best if—"

"Is he?" I scream, my fingers clutching the sides of the hospital bed, his face in front of me, his emerald eyes staring at me, his hair fluttering in the breeze. Oh, Micah, my Micah.

"Yes, he is," the nurse steps back, reaching for a needle in a drawer.

Soon I'll be gone. Far away from this. Far away from this all. I laugh, reaching up to brush Micah's face. He's so beautiful, and he's all mine.

"Miss, I don't think it's best if you—"

"What room is he?" I ask, petting his pretty face as ash falls on the nurse and I can't see her but oh well because there's Micah and me and the ash and nothing will take him from me.

I'll make sure of it.

"Nova, it's not a good idea—"

"What room is he?"

The nurse plugs the syringe into my IV and drains the contents. "I won't say."

I begin thrashing around and the IV yanks from my arm and blood and red consume my vision and I'm screaming and Micah, you better get them and the ash better cover them and I hope they die and suffocate and never wake up—

But I stop thrashing because I can't move anymore and belts are fastened around my ankles and arms and I resist against them and a prick stings my arms and I'm gone.

So wonderfully gone.

"Soon we'll be together, my Micah," I whisper.

ROLLIN

I haven't slept much. Slumber is not my friend tonight, as it rarely is any night. My eyes find the ceiling and I stare at it. Hours have passed.

I don't dare move my head. If I do, the pain will attack me again. I have so many injuries, they say I won't be leaving for a while longer. A broken nose, bruised face, stab wound in my abdomen, bruises on my throat, a broken arm, and a sprained ankle. Besides that, I couldn't begin to count how many bruises and minor cuts cover my body.

The Wardens arrested many of the Privileges as a show of authority, but Buddy tells me they let them go soon after the attack. Privileges are privileged any way you look at it. Ivy was let loose with no more than slap on the wrists, mostly due to how much she was crying, apparently.

I refrain from any movement. Any flinch or shiver causes pain to race through my veins like adrenaline's evil twin. I keep still. It's easier that way. The ceiling will be my companion a while longer.

Buddy sleeps in the couch on the other side of the room. They almost refused me treatment because I'm an Oddity, but Buddy demanded they take me in. They listen to Privies. They have to.

The only sounds that accompany me are the flutter of the drapes in the wind, the drip of the IV, and Buddy's soft snores. It's not much, but it's enough.

I close my eyes. I imagine myself at the League, all those months ago. I imagine her sneaking into my room late at night, closing the door behind her with a giggle. She would tiptoe around the room, trailing her fingers across the wall before pouncing on me like a hungry leopard. Her auburn hair would stick to my sheets and I'd have to pick them away after she left so no one would know she was there.

Those were the times before she left. The times before she disappeared without communication. The times before I had to go and find her, before I found a mockery of what she was. My Mira is gone and I don't have much faith she'll come back to me.

I hear a rush of sound as the door is pushed open carefully. No squeak sounds from the door as it usually does. The slight *beep...beep...beep...*sounds from the hallway before fading away as the door comes to a muted *thud* against the frame. A tiny giggle escapes the intruder as the lock sounds.

I don't care to turn my head and see. The pain wouldn't be worth it and I wouldn't see a thing anyway. The room is completely in darkness, beside for the limited moonlight peaking through the curtains.

"I don't need any more Clam, nurse," I say. "I don't want it."

More laughter escapes. I hear footsteps stampede against the tile flooring. Hands grab at my shoulders and a strangled cry escapes from my lips. A bloody hand is pressed over my mouth. I taste blood on my lips as it rolls down my chin. The same sticky wetness hits my arms as it drips off her.

"Micah! I'm here. It's me, Nova—"

"Mira," I gasp, my teeth clenched from the pain. "What are you doing here? You're bleeding, for god's sake—"

"It's okay, my love," a seductive whisper slips into my ear. "You don't have to pretend anymore. We can always be together."

She presses her lips against mine and I can taste the blood—*her* blood—and I gag but she continues to kiss me. This is *Mira*, even with her bare chest pressed against me.

I struggle against her but I'm so weak, so goddamn weak.

"There's someone here," I manage to get out before she attacks me again.

"He's so far into Clam he won't notice, love."

She's there, all over me and I don't notice the pain anymore because adrenaline rushes through me. She grabs a handful of me and I can't stop her, it feels so—

"Oh, Micah," she groans, giggling into my mouth. The blood is still there and all over my body. I see that auburn hair flowing in the gentle breeze and the moonlight hits her and I see, I see blood pulsing from her arm.

"Oh, god," I grab her arm. "You ripped your IV out, Mira."

"Shhh," she whispers, pulling her arm away and kisses me once more.

"No, no! You're losing too much blood. You'll die."

"We both can go together. Soon, we won't have to feel the pain anymore. We'll always be together, Micah. Always," she grabs at me more and she won't stop touching and bleeding and kissing and it's too much at once—

Cool metal touches my throat. Her other hand rips the bandages off my skin. Her weight presses on my broken arm. I cry out in pain, tears pricking in my eyes.

"It'll be over soon, my love, my Micah."

I wrench my unbroken arm away from her feeble body and shove her off me. The knife flies into the air and collapses on the ground with her. Cries erupt from below.

Banging erupts at the door. I push my anguished screams down to the bottom of my throat. The blood begins to dry on my body, creating a demonic scab across my body. My shirt sticks to me.

I try to sit up but I can't because she's there again kissing me and the knife against my bare skin and it cuts and I cry out more as my blood runs on the sheet but they can't get through that damn door and Buddy is gone, snoring away.

"Nova," I whisper between her kisses. I can't move. Pain splinters my bones. I can't fight back. She's too strong and I am too weak.

"Micah!" she sequels in delight, tearing the shirt from my chest.

"Nova, dear," I brush a strand away from her moonlit face. "You look so beautiful tonight."

I grit my teeth together because she's not Nova and I'm not Micah and this whole damn city is messed up.

"This is the only way we'll be together," she presses the knife at my throat. "We can be together forever. No one will ever tear us apart. No one will doubt our love."

"We can leave, love," I reach my hand for the knife. She only presses it closer.

"We can't, and you know that. Ash is coming soon and the whole world will be buried in the dead. We have to float with them, down on this city. We'll always be together!"

"We can be together here, right now," I say, my hand on the knife, pulling it ever so slightly from my throat. Her hand tenses and her eyes spin like a thousand hurricans.

"No we can't. They won't let us. They'll tear us apart again, my Micah, my love."

Sweat beads from my forehead, diluting the blood rolling from my face. My arm shakes at the effort of holding the knife from my skin. I can't tell if the blood covering us is more mine or hers.

"Let me have you right now, love," she whispers. "One last time. Then we can leave together and float with the ash."

Pain vibrates throughout my body. I can't see or hear and black dots float across my vision. The knife clatters on the ground and she's pressing against me more and my clothes are on the ground and so are hers and all we wear is blood. Red is everywhere, consuming everything and she's still there, forcing herself on me and blackness edges on my vision.

This isn't how it was supposed to happen. This wasn't how I was supposed to find Mira or how I was supposed to die. I failed the mission. I failed the League—

Everything stops. The blackness recedes as I see another dark figure in front of me with auburn hair in his hand and the weight has lifted off my body and her porcelain skin is bloody and bruised and stretched so think I can almost see the bones under her cheeks. I see the glint of metal in his dark black hand and the *shluk* of the knife and the cry, her anguished cry and tears fall and I can't stop them.

The knife clatters against the ground and a body crumples with a *thud* and I close my eyes, squeezing them as I hear her laughter drift to me.

"Hell is beautiful, Micah."

Then her last breath drifts to me and Buddy's hands are pulling a cover on me and red, red is everywhere and tears fall and I close my eyes to stop seeing and I beg and scream and nurses and doctors rush in and shouts and that *beep…beep…beep…*and nothing will stop.

None of it stops.

NOVA

I couldn't describe to you how it feels.
I'm twisting, turning, falling.
It's dark here.
The black presses on me from all sides.
But it's okay.
Don't worry about me.
I'm dying, but it'll be okay.
Micah will be here soon, I know.
Hell looks so beautiful through the eyes of a sinner.
I couldn't tell you what I was thinking when I found his room.
I couldn't tell you much of anything.
I'm crazy.
I'm a bitch.
I'm an odd Privilege and privileged Oddity.
This damn world full of people shitting on roaches and roaches shitting
on people and it doesn't make any sense, none of it does.
I couldn't tell you why it happened like that.
There was a time before all of this.
Calamity.
Ash.
Privileges.
Oddities.
Wardens.
Binocs.
There was a time before all of that.
It was a time before all this madness.
Things were simple.

People were people.
Drugs were drugs.
Life was life.
Ivy was my friend.
It was years ago.
I can't remember much of it.
It's slipping away, but only barely.
It's still there.
I can imagine it.
Vaguely, it's there.
I can't remember how many years ago I first came here to Chicago.
Seven?
Ten?
It's such a blur, a hazy fog in the depths of my mind.
I watched movies from the olden times.
I didn't drink.
I didn't party.
I didn't waste my life away.
I was strange back then, too.
I had a job and lived and thrived.
Ivy and I were friends, best friends.
I didn't have Micah.
I couldn't explain where things changed.
They just did.
I don't remember the past five years of my life.
Five years ago, Calamity was introduced to Chicago.
Five years ago, I was declared a Privy.
I was declared the asscrack of sainthood.
The Exterminator taught us to treat the other people—the Oddities—like roaches.
He taught us that Clam was the best thing this damn world ever gave us.
He taught us to never stop taking it.
The world was our fucking oyster.
My name is Nova Aster.
My name is nobody.
Finally, my mind is free.
There is no more Clam.
There is no more insanity.
There is only Nova, like I was before everything changed.
I am me.
Me am I.
Micah will be here soon.
It will be so wonderful when he's here.

I stopped breathing a while ago.
I don't know where I am.
It's still dark.
It's still vacant and lifeless and I drift.
Nothing much has changed.
Then there's a light.
It slits through the darkness like a knife and shines down at me.
It's hard to look at, but I do.
What else is there left to see?
My name is Nova Aster.
I drift toward the light, swimming through the darkness.
It's thick like ink.
My body is stained in it.
I pull through the edges of the crack.
Light spills on me.
The darkness fades.
I'm in Chicago again.
It's Ash.
It falls in a steady stream above me.
The heavy smoke streaming from the furnaces in the suburbs twirl into the air, sending ash with it.
So, so much ash.
Ivy is there.
She floats down.
I see the pieces of her, all burnt now.
They float around me.
I stick my tongue on and savor the taste as a fleck falls on it.
Micah will be here soon.
Maybe that black man will be here too.
I would like to fuck him.
Maybe Micah would join in too.
I giggle.
That would be fun.
The darkness folds around me once more, consuming the light.
I don't care.
My name is Nova Aster.
I am nobody.
I am dead.
I don't know what comes after this.
Maybe I will float in this darkness forever.
Maybe Micah will come soon.
No, he will be here soon.
I know.

If he loves me, he'll be here.
I know I cut him.
I had to.
The knife was sharp.
My wit was sharp.
My hands were steady.
What could have possibly gone wrong?
Oh, how I wanted him them.
How he bulged.
How his body yearned but his tongue receded.
How he stared.
Like he never had seen it before.
Those emerald eyes stared back at me.
Then the darkness fades away.
Those emerald eyes surround my vision.
I leap into them and dance across the plains.
I wish Micah was here.
There are trees on Micah's little green planets.
The colors have started to fade.
Bottles litter the ground.
Roaches crawl across them.
I close my eyes and push away the green.
Those eyes that judge.
Those eyes that burn.
Darkness returns.
I don't know why I'm telling you this.
I don't think I've left that room yet.
I don't think I'm that far gone yet.
I can still hear the screaming.
I can still smell the blood.
I can still taste it on my lips.
I'm trying not to think about it.
It is all so far away, but so near.
I feel hands on me.
I feel the blood stick to me.
I hear screaming, more screaming.
It won't stop.
Glass shatters.
A gust of wind brushes my hair, tickling my skin.
I giggle.
The familiar clatter of the knife hits the ground.
Micah's cursing.
I hear it all.

I smell it all.
I feel it all.
I taste it all.
But I don't see it all.
I'm blind.
The darkness doesn't leave.
It won't ever leave.
I'm dying.
I'm leaving this world.
My name is Nova Aster.
I used to have a friend.
Her name was Ivy.
I used to have a love.
His name was Micah.
I used to have a life.
I don't remember what happened in the past five years…
It was so long ago…
But I remember feeling…
…
and smelling…
…
and tasting…
…
…
and hearing…
…
…
and seeing.
The world is dark…
…
…
…
I'm not in that room anymore…
…
…
no, not anymore…
…
…
…
…
Micah isn't here…
…
…

neither is Ivy…
…
…
neither is Warden John…
…
he was nice.
There aren't much of those around anymore…
…
…
…
…
…
I'm leaving, aren't I?
…
…
…yes…
…
…
…my name is Nova Aster…
…
…
…
…it's coming…
…
…
…a tsunami…
…
…an avalanche…
…
…a midnight hurricane…
…
…
…
…I'm not scared…
…
…
…
…
…it smells like Clam cookies…
…
…
…
…

...tastes like Clam shakes...

...

...

...

...

...

...feels like ash floating on my skin...

...

...

...

...

...

...sounds like Micah telling me he loves me...

...

...

...

...

...

...

...and it feels *wonderful.*

...

...

...

...

...

...

...

...

...

...

...

So wonderful.

MIRA

"Come on, Mitch," I sigh, combing my fingers through my short auburn hair. "You sold it to me cheaper last week"

The minuscule man with dark eyes and midnight hair stares at me apathetically. "Supply and demand, my dear."

"Demand and supply are always high. Prices haven't gone up this much in months."

"Don't blame me. Blame this damn city and the damn roaches. They can't keep their claws off me. I've been running low on Clam all day."

"Mitch, you know we've been running low on money and the shop isn't giving us enough hours—"

"Honey, those aren't my problems. My problem is the amount of my time you're wasting."

I grumble as I fish out my money card in my pack. The green bars on it are running dangerously low. I don't know how much longer we will be able to go on.

I purchase two bottles, my rent for the next week. My landlord accepts Clam as rent, as many do in the city. I hope next week I don't have to resort to...not after last time...I almost...he almost...oh, I don't want to think about it. It's better that way. It always is.

This Clam shop is conveniently next to Sip and Sleep, where I work. I prefer going there because Mitch usually cuts me a deal, but I guess he wasn't feeling very kind today. Hopefully Clam prices go down, but this wouldn't be the first time that they've spiked so high.

I exit the Clam shop and immerse myself into the crowd outside. I keep my head down and my bag close. The crowds here are more forgiving than those in the roach sector, but some precautions don't hurt. It wouldn't be the first time if a roach got mugged, but it would be if someone cared.

Only thirty more minutes, at least, before I'm at home lying down to rest. I hope the straw mattress isn't still damp from the rain that came through last night. The roof held up more than I thought, but the leaking soaked through the straw by morning. It was a damp walk to work today.

Ah, work. The bane of my existence. I'm still wearing my uniform, an apron with a green stripe down the side. I've served so many Clam shakes today to so many damn Privies I think I might hurl.

The Privies that come in rarely treat me with respect. I don't blame them. I am a roach and they are Privies, but it's still hard to get used to. I've been here for months, but it stills seems like I walked in the city yesterday. Since then, it's been a constant struggle of surviving both physically and morally.

The bottles in my purse jingle absently. People press on me from all sides. It's hard to breathe. We're getting closer to the heart of the Privy district. Many, many blocks south is the wall to the roach district.

"Belle!" a somber voice sounds from beside me. "Did you hear?"

I turn toward it and see Yorry, my coworker, my friend, and my roommate. I smile as she squeezes toward me. Her apron flutters in the wind. Shake is still splattered on her face, as I'm sure it is on mine.

"What are you talking about?"

She slips her arm through my own as people press between us. "A Privy woman got raped."

"So?"

"No, no," she whispers, her brunette hair fluttering in my face. "She was *murdered*."

I look at her quizzically. "And…?"

She sighs. "It's been all over this city, Belle. You're so out of it sometimes! She went insane and cut this roach man up at the hospital she was at and another Privy killed her and the hospital is closed down and there's crowd of her friends out there and they're trying to get at the two men and—"

"Woah, slow down," I laugh. "Too much information, not enough ears."

She looks away bashfully. "Sorry…"

I laugh and shove her playfully. The roaches around us glare. Their ears aren't used to laughter.

"Go on," I say.

"Well, it's so strange. Apparently, she believed the man who raped her was the man in the hospital. The roach and Privy were together, too. Apparently, the roach man was an outsider. Mitch told me about it earlier. He came in with a black Privy a couple of days ago."

"From the *outside*?" I ask, my voice falling low, my heart beating quickly.

"Yes! Apparently, the two met beyond the gates and the Privy helped the roach man get into the city. Think of it: that man could be a secret spy or—"

"I doubt it, Yorry," I whisper. "There's been times when other cities have banished people or when roaches have escaped from the suburbs. They almost always used another traveler to get into the city. I'm sure the Privy man happened to come by a bad one."

"I don't know," she scoffs. "It seems a little *too* strange for my taste."

"You think finding dead roaches during Ash is strange," I joke. "I wouldn't worry too much about it. The story will blow over in the next week, as the other ones have."

"I don't know about that. There's a mob outside the hospital and another one at the rapist's house! They don't seem to be giving up any time soon."

Murmurs fly through the crowd as we pass by the hospital. As Yorry said, there is an enraged mob crowded outside. I haven't seen so many Privies on the sidewalks before. Some of the glass windows are smashed. The remains are littered on the ground.

Wardens surround the mob, pressing jacket-less roaches against the wall, cuffing them and throwing them to the ground. More than a dozen are lined up. They'll be going to the suburbs soon. They should've known better.

The Privies dance and wave in a frenzied chant. Some don't have clothes on. Some are pressed against each other. Some are throwing empty Clam bottles into the air, cackling madly when they clatter against the ground.

More Privies are passed out behind the crowd, drifting into the Clam world, far away from these trivial, human worries.

I wish I could be back there again.

No, no, I can't fall into that hole again. Any more Clam and I'll die like the other roaches. They'll throw me out in the streets, I'll freeze over, and they'll pick me up and burn me with the others. My ash will float through the skies and the roach children will play in it, thinking it's the snow they see in all the olden pictures.

Chanting from the crowd erupts in unison. A single voice drifts from the chattering, small and weak, but soon others begin to join

"Kill them, let her go! Kill them, let her go!"

I turn away and press through the roaches that have slowed to watch in front of us. Yorry yanks back at my arm, straining her neck to see over the other roaches. I tug her forward.

"Wait, Belle," she pulls back, making me trip over a crack in the sidewalk. "I want to see!"

"There's nothing to see, Yorry," I mutter, yanking her past the crowd.

She sighs and hangs her head, following me as we make a wide arc around the crowd. The building is very wide; it extends almost a quarter of a block. By the time we reach the end of the metal building, the crowd is far behind us.

An alleyway appears to the left of us. Glancing quickly, I see a door propped open. A person clad in denim appears pushing a dolly. A bloodied white sheet covers the body underneath.

"Shh," I nudge Yorry, pulling her behind a dumpster. "Look."

Two people are hurried out of the building by the man in all denim. One is dark in features and skin. An aura of blackness surrounds him like a plague. Blood covers his shirt.

The other man is a roach; I can tell by the green stripe running down his sleeve. It is barely recognizable from all the blood soaking the fabric. Bandages and blood almost cover him entirely. Two eyes peer out of the mummy's facade.

He limps severely on one leg. One of his arms hangs in a sling. He pulls his feet behind him and relies heavily on the wall for support as well as a crudely made cane.

The man in denim rushes them forward, looking nervously behind him. The crowd's chanting echoes distantly. The bandaged man trips on his feet and collapses on the ground. An anguished cry escapes him. The black man quickly throws him over his shoulder and races down the alleyway.

Yorry turns to me, squealing. "I can't believe we saw that!"

"Was that…?"

"The murdered Privy and the men who killed her. Belle, when everyone at Sip-and-Sleep hears about this, they'll go—"

"We can't tell them, Yorry," I shush her.

Whispers sound from behind us. People have crowded around us. I hurriedly get to my feet and bring Yorry with me.

"Can I help you?" I snap at the roaches. They dart away quickly.

I turn back to Yorry. "You see? People will be gawking at us if they hear we saw them. Keep it on a need-to-know basis, okay?"

She nods, biting her lip.

I glance down the alleyway. "I'll catch up with you later, okay?"

Without a response, I dart down the alleyway. My footsteps clap against the alleyway as I rush by. I slow down as I approach the corner that the group disappeared around earlier. Moaning comes from beside me and I stop, startled. He's sees me before him and lifts his head slowly. Deep cuts line his face, as though he was scratched, and blood runs from the wounds. A crude bandage wraps his head. His clothes are filthy and disheveled, but not enough so to see the blue stripe lining his sleeve. He's a Warden, or was.

"Please, miss," he croaks, reaching out for me. "Water?"

"I'm sorry," I tell him, glancing down the alleyway, quickly dashing past him.

It's not unusual to find roaches lying out in this alleyway. When roaches are so critically wounded that they need a hospital's care, they are sent out into the alleyway. This roach looks like he was pretty banged up, but not enough so that he had to go to the hospital.

Peaking around the corner, the group stands in a huddle around the blanketed corpse. The smell of rotting flesh drifts to me.

"That crowd is out there ready fer our blood," the black man says, holding his forehead in his hands. "Ah'm surprised we got out without 'em noticin'."

The other man, the one covered in bandages, lies in a crumpled mess on the ground. Blood almost completely covers his bandages. He groans loudly, causing the black man to look at him.

"Is he okay?" the man in denim asks. "You sure you can carry him? He doesn't look too good."

"Ah'll be fine," the black man sighs. "Yuh don't worry about me none."

"Buddy, of course I'm going to worry. I can't help feeling like this is my fault."

"Now, don't yuh start blamin' yerself, Marco."

"It is my fault!" he exclaims. "If I had only been up there when it happened, that bastard wouldn't have raped the Privy and—"

"Maybe he shouldn't of raped her," Buddy laughs darkly.

My eyebrows furrow as I stare at the black man. They say this man is the one who killed her. He sounds like he's one of the travelers from the south, but he acts like he's been here his whole life.

The chanting increases in volume. Glass shatters. Anguished cries drift to my ears.

Marco grabs the dolly. "C'mon, we better get going. They'll be looking for you guys soon."

"Ah know, ah know," Buddy drifts off as he crouches down to the bandaged man, shaking him slightly. "Hey, fella. Yuh feelin' any better?"

Buddy receives only a groan in response. He takes the bandaged man over his shoulder, wary of his injuries. The strange pair disappear down the stairs to the Pedway, a system of underground tunnels that lie beneath Chicago. The main tunnel goes straight from the northern Privy district to the southern roach district.

Marco grabs the dolly. He stares at the white sheet absently, tracing his fingers over the blood splotches. He raises the sheet and looks at the dead Privy. Tears well in his eyes. I strain my eyes, trying got see the body underneath.

He turns his back and begins walking away and I'm stepping forward, trying to follow him when strong arms wrap around me and pull me close and a hand covers my mouth and strong muscles ripple underneath me and

I try to scream but—

"Hello, dear," the deep voice sneaks into my ear. "Did you think I forgot about you?"

"Jax, you said we could leave—"

A cool knife blade presses against my throat and I wish I never left that damn street with Yorry yapping away—

"You know the rules," he whispers. "Maybe you shouldn't have left me. Maybe you should have done as I told you."

I open my mouth wide, trying to scream and shout even though no one would come, no one at all when—

Thump

The arms around me fall and I hear the satisfying *thud* of his body hitting the ground and I suck in breath, breathing and breathing and I turn to see—

"Hi," I gasp, staring at the roach man that I had walked by earlier. The roach man that the hospital had cast out of its doors. The roach man that had asked me for water.

He stares at me through bruised eyes. He holds a crowbar in white knuckles. He leans on one leg, and the other twists in an unnatural direction. Dim light shines through the crack between the buildings.

"My name is John, miss. Warden John."

MIRA

Nothing stirs inside me. No fear chokes my lungs. No adrenaline rushes through my veins. I stare at this man—he said his name was John—and all I feel is sympathy clutching my heart.

The alleyway is black and John is dark, staring at me with sweat beading down his brow and into those bruised and bloodied eyes and the sharp *klink-klink...klink* of the crowbar hitting the ground and Jax is at my feet breathing and oh god, I hope he's breathing—

"Are you okay, miss?" he asks, leaning against the wall, clutching his heart like the damn thing is about to burst out of his chest.

"Yes," I say. "I'm fine. Thank you."

Water drips from the pipes above. It hits the ground, the puddles, with a soft *plink...plink...plink*...and the whole world is dripping around me like *plink...plink...plink...*

"Will he be okay?" I look down at Jax, collapsed on the ground with that black hat soaking in the puddles around him and his mouth open and his eyes open and the memories flash back from before—

"Don't worry about him," John groans, collapsing into a heap on the ground.

I step over Jax and go to John's side. He clutches his ankle tenderly, pain squeezing his face together until it looks like it'll burst.

"What happened to you?" I whisper.

There is hardly any unharmed skin on this man. By the looks at him, he's so black and blue he could be a chameleon.

"I had a part in the, uh, incident you've been hearing about."

I step back warily. "You aren't the man who raped her, are you?"

This makes him smile weakly. "No, I'm the man who saved her from the rapist. No matter what a roach does, if he's involved in it, he's bound to be sorry."

"Who did this to you?"

"That mob outside," he winces as he shifts his position. "I came to visit Nova. I had some cookies for her, Clam cookies, but the mob wasn't so forgiving. They took their anger out on me, to say the least. The Wardens on guard stopped them and brought me into the hospital."

I stare at him in wide-eyed shock. "The hospital sent you out here, didn't they?"

"To live or to die," he agrees solemnly.

He groans as his face scrunches in pain. I dig into my apron and find a spare Clam cookie. I unwrap it and hand it to him. He eagerly accepts.

"Thank you," he smiles. "You work at Sip-and-Sleep?"

"Unfortunately," I strain my own smile.

He laughs, biting into the cookie again. I watch as the drug slowly eases the pain. His demeanor relaxes, his face unfolds, and his hands fall to his side.

The chanting that drifts from the street increases in volume. More glass shatters as the soft flickering of fire joins in. We share concerned glances.

"Do you feel well enough to walk?" I ask, glancing at his wounds nervously. He won't survive much longer if he stays here.

"I think I'll be okay after that cookie," he stands to his feet.

Wary of the crowd outside the alleyway, we opt to go through the Pedway like the group before us. We descend into darkness. No lights illuminate the dark space.

I reach into the bag on my back and pull out a flashlight. The sphere of light dances around the dark space. Water drips eerily. Rat droppings litter the floor, finding their way into the soles of my shoes. I sigh. It'll be a long night of cleaning them out. We press on, the noise of the crowd growing fainter as we do.

Neither of us is quite sure of the destination. I've never been one to use the Pedway system. Since the beginning of its deterioration years ago, it has only gotten worse. Horror stories have been leaked of roaches gone missing in its twisting tunnels. Privies have often wandered down here in drunken bliss only to be discovered dead the next day. Those are the stories that keep these tunnels bare.

My foot hits the top of a broken wine bottle. It goes spinning into the darkness, clattering against a nearby wall. I hear the familiar sound of glass crunching under my feet.

"Do you mind some conversation while we walk?" John says from beside me.

"Not at all."

I keep the beam steady in front of us, but it does little to penetrate the darkness.

"What did you do, before all of this happened?" I turn to him, but only find darkness.

"There isn't much to say," he laughs. "I've been a Warden since the Exterminator came. Life has been dull. I've managed to stay out of trouble until a few days ago. Needless to say, I doubt I'm still a Warden after what happened…"

"What happened?"

I feel his silence like an anvil about to fall.

"I was walking the streets as I do sometimes. I came across a Privilege woman stumbling across the sidewalks. Normal, right? I decided to help her, maybe bring her to a safe building where no roaches could get her. She refused and kept her way down the sidewalk.

"I got a call from the Binoc tower about ten minutes later. The man was frantic. Crazed, I would say. There was a Privilege being raped, he said. By the time I reached the scene, the assailants had vanished. I found the woman naked in the alleyway. Blood covered her body as well as other…filth. It broke my heart.

"Her name was Nova Aster. She wasn't in the best state of mind when I found her. All she did was ask for Calamity and she wouldn't move until I gave her some. I brought her to my car, and that's when things grew more crazed than they already were."

He takes a moment. I don't rush him. We continue on for a few minutes, silence disrupted by the scurrying of rats and the *plink…plink…plink…*of water.

"A man came up. I recognized his voice as the person on the phone. A black man was with him. He was crazed, I swear it. He began screaming at me, demanding that I open the door. He began banging on the glass, yelling her name.

"I was in the car, about to pull away, when the glass broke. His fists were covered in blood as he reached for her, the woman in my car. He kept yelling a name, but it wasn't even hers.

"I began driving away. I thought the crazy man was gone until he jumped into his own car and eventually rear-ended me. I was able to get away from him. He had wrecked his car so bad that he couldn't drive it anymore. I drove her to the hospital and they took her in. I left afterwards, and once I came back to pay her a visit, I was attacked."

"And now you're here," I say, glad I can't see John's expression in the darkness.

"And now I'm here."

"What did the crazed man think her name was?" I ask, curiosity lingering in my mind.

"He called her Mira."

I freeze. My feet stop moving. The flashlight slips out of my numb fingers and clatters on the ground. A whine drives through my ears. John says something and I can't listen. Vaguely, I feel his soft touch on my shoulder. The flashlight flutters across the dark tunnel as he picks it up.

"You said he called her Mira?" I whisper.

No one calls me Mira. No one in this city should know my name is Mira. They know me as Belle. Even back in the League, back in New York, they called me Mirabelle. Only one person called me Mira. He was the only one I let call me that.

Rollin.

"Yes," he says. "Now will you tell me what's the matter?"

"What did he look like?"

"What?"

"This man," I murmur. "What did he look like?"

"He was Hispanic, tall with black-brown hair and green eyes. He was a roach. There wasn't much else to him."

He's here. Rollin is here. He came for me.

"I don't think you should be looking for him," John says nervously, pulling me forward.

"Why is that?"

"Well, uh," he says, the flashlight bouncing with each step he takes. "He was the one who raped the woman."

"And the one in the hospital?"

"Yes, he's the one. He was there for her *murder*, too. This isn't the type of man you want to be looking for, miss."

"Call me Belle," I mutter absently and laugh. "I guess I forgot to tell you that in the rush of everything."

"Belle," he says to himself. "Belle, you need to listen to me. He's crazed and—"

"I need to find him, John," I turn to him and grab his arm desperately. "You may not understand it—"

"He raped her and—"

"—he's my friend—"

"—had a part in her murder—"

"—I don't think I can do it without your help," I cling to him like a leech, bleeding him for help. "Please, trust me. He's someone I need to find."

He sighs unwillingly, passing the flashlight back and forth between his hands. The beam of light flies across the dark tunnel like a drunken firefly.

"You're a Warden," I exclaim. "You know this city better than most. You know the people, the buildings, and you've seen him!"

Something flies across his face for a second. Something he's trying so hard to hide.

"You know where he lives, don't you?" I gasp as he turns from me.

"I can't help you, Belle," he grunts. "He's not a good man."

"Please, John. I'm begging you. He hasn't done the things you accuse him of. Something has happened and I don't—"

"Why does he mean so much to you?" he asks.

"He's my friend," I smile, "and he's come a long way here to find me."

John doesn't answer, only keeps walking and walking, his footsteps hollow against the cement walls around us.

The man in the alleyway, the one bundled in bandages and blood, that was Rollin.

It was *Rollin*.

"You're a part of this story, John. If...if I find this man and he's not...not who he used to be...you can take revenge on him for raping that girl or for eventually leading you to getting beat up and losing your job. Arrest him, beat him, have tea with him—I don't care. If he's not the man I knew, he's yours."

"Okay," he whispers after a moment. "I'll do it."

I squeeze him into a hug, making him fumble the flashlight between his thick fingers. Blood rushes to his face as I let go.

Rollin came for me. After all this time, he finally came for me. When I left the League, they told me another Leaguer would meet up with me in Chicago soon after. They said he would come months ago. They said he would be right behind me. They even went as far as saying he might catch up with me on the way. They lied.

Is he really here? I don't know, but I hope he is, and I hope he didn't do what John is claiming that he did.

"There's an exit coming up here soon," John says from beside me. "It'll come up on the outskirts of the roach district. We can find somewhere to hole up for the night."

The two bottles of Clam jingle mindlessly in my pack. I guess I won't be paying rent for awhile longer.

At least I won't be sleeping on the wet straw mattress tonight. At least I won't have more nightmares. At least the wind won't creep through the walls and slip through my jacket.

I pull the green-striped jacket closer around me. The apron flutters in a dull breeze coming through the tunnel.

"Someone must have opened a door," John mutters from beside me.

The flashlight hits something in front of us. It's only there for a second before John moves the beam to something else.

"Wait, over there," I whisper. "There's something there."

John does as I ask and returns the beam to the object. It's a dolly with a white, bloodied sheet. A body lies underneath.

"Let's keep moving," I whisper to John.

We try to maneuver around it quickly, but John trips on a rock and with

106

his weak leg, he knocks into the dolly. The wheels screech as it rolls away. I help John to his feet and rush past the screeching dolly, an arm of pure porcelain skin now hanging from the white fabric.

No water drips.

No rats scurry.

Only the wheels.

Eerrrt…eerrt…eerrt…

MIRA

I remember those days. They were the days of dull summer. They were days of brief happiness. Most of all, they were days of ignorance.

None of us believed what they told us. Killing the clones wasn't in our mind. It was never in our mind. We went about our training, our long days and short nights, with optimism.

The memory is resonant in my head. My family was stationed within some old bureaucrat's mansion in Germany. The halls were lined with marble and statues graced the walls. I remember my little sister Charlotte said the mansion was made just for her. Though she wasn't my biological sister, she was my only sister, and I treasured those special moments we had together.

Back then, I spent much of my days reading books upon books. There wasn't much else to do. They kept electricity extremely limited, even back there. I would wake at daybreak and sleep when the moon came up. Lights were considered trivial and unnecessary compared to electricity that powered the fridge or television. We burnt through many candles.

The knock echoed through the hall one day. It had the slight excitement of death attached to it, even then I could feel it. Charlotte and I were playing with some new dolls the officials had dropped by earlier that day. Our mom wasn't home. She was away, picking daisies for the dinner table. We were to have guests that night.

I never did find out who we were supposed to have over.

The men made the proposal to me. It was in extreme urgency, they said. If I agreed to go with them back to America and help exterminate the clones, they would assure the upmost safety of my family.

As I said, I read many books. I enjoyed the ones with adventure. I knew of knights and kingdoms; of dragons and monsters; and of selfish and unselfish people. I knew that being one of those unselfish people made you a hero and I knew everybody loved the hero.

My parents didn't return in time to say goodbye. It was only my little sister, her eyes like distant planets as they reached for me. Tears streamed down her face, but I had to turn my back and walk away. They told me I would never see them again.

It was a long journey to New York City. I had only seen the mythical place in pictures. I knew of the Empire State building that used to twinkle green and red during the holidays. It doesn't do that anymore, but I hoped it would. I knew there was a lady standing in the bay holding a torch. Lady Liberty, they called her, but what exactly did she liberate?

The best part of the entire trip was flying in an airplane. Again, I had only seen them in pictures, and even then, it seemed impossible that such a massive thing could soar through the air for so long. It was terrifying, to say the least, but I know I'm one of the few that can say they've done it.

Once we landed in New York City, they took me by car to a massive building—a skyscraper, they called it. They told me it was the Empire State building. I asked if it would twinkle green and red, but they only laughed.

The city was oddly barren. Later, I would discover the clones had already been cleared out of that city, but it seemed eerie to me when I first walked upon that pavement. No cars honked, like in the old videos. No massive crowds of people stormed the streets like they were going to battle. No other car was driving down the streets. No other person was walking around.

The League headquarters, they told me, was at the top of the building. The view up there was the most amazing thing I would ever see, they claimed. I waited in anticipation as we took the elevator—the actual elevator!—up to the top floor.

The doors opened to a group of people gathered on the floor. The room was bare except for the cushions people sat on. We were a very strange and diverse group. I later found out that it held people from all religions, ethnicities, colors, and sexual orientations. They were males, females, and transgendered people. Every type of person under the sun was there.

I sat beside an Indian woman. She spoke fluent Hindi and English. I asked her to tell me a story in Hindi. Though I didn't understand, it was beautiful listening to another tongue.

A woman came through the doors then. She was tall, with a hooked nose and a large mole under her eye. If I had been any younger, I would have thought her to be a witch. She wore a woman's suit and pointed heels. She placed her booklet on the table in front of her and began to talk.

"Hello, and welcome." She gave a pseudo-smile. "I'm one of the commanders in the League. As you all know, you've all been invited to become members of the League. We chose you all specifically based on gender, ethnicity, sex, race, and sexual orientation. It is important that we have a diverse group of opinions and values here, for our mission is that of human race, so it is important that every walk of life has a part of it.

"I'm sure you all know this story, but there is no harm in refreshing the details. Twenty years ago, a series of nuclear world wars destroyed the planet as we know it. After the survivors recouped, we decided to resettle in America, since the size allowed the rest of the human population to remain on one continent, and the infrastructure was not as damaged as in other major hubs of the world. The remaining population was situated in various buildings across the world that were left untouched by the war.

"We did not have the manpower to rebuild what had been destroyed, so the top scientists of the population were gathered to develop a method of cloning. Five years after the last bomb fell on the earth, they finally discovered the solution. Using the detailed health records left by previous generations, we were able to create massive numbers of clones. Some were people who already existed and some were of those long deceased.

"For ten years, the clones were sent to rebuilt the major cities in America. The rest of the country, mostly the suburbs of the major cities, was either left alone or repurposed into fields to harvest energy or food, or to manufacture products. This worked for a long time. The clones were programmed to be determined to finish rebuilding, but once they finished their task, something in their genetic makeup changed and they revolted. They began creating their own societies in the cities they rebuilt. The humans who governed the clones had been murdered. Some suburbs were transformed into massive incinerators to burn the dead while the rest remained to produce goods.

"For the past five years, we have been reconfiguring the societies to behave and believe they are actual humans. The scientists were able to remotely reconfigure the clones' brains to make them believe that they were humans. They implanted false memories into the minds to make them believe they had long and full lives. They remember nothing of their clone lives, but only of the lives they believe they had. Though the scientists could reconfigure their brains, they never created a 'destruct button' for the clones when they were first developed.

"Now, we are here. The League has assembled you all to help exterminate America of all clones. During the course of the next year, you each will be sent to different cities across the country with specific, classified instructions on how to exterminate the clones in the specified city. While you are waiting to be deployed, you will go through a rigorous schedule here. Each day, you will attend different enrichment sessions on history, literature, and survival, each being one hour in duration. Two hours of physical training, both in endurance and strength, will occur afterwards.

Your teachers may require you to spend additional time during the on various projects and assignments. A couple of days per week, our lab technicians will pull groups of three to train you on how to operate different equipment you will be given when you leave for your cities. Combat training will be held daily as well. Three meals will be served each day, promptly at eight in the morning, one o'clock, and six at night. Past six, there will be a few hours of free time. You may exit the League headquarters, but only during free time."

The woman continued to speak of the specifics of training and the enrichment sessions, but my mind drifted away. I met the eyes of a strange, Hispanic man. His eyes were the darkest of greens and held a deep mystery to them. His black-brown hair fluttered in the wind coming from the cracked window. He returned my gaze for a few moments and gave me a shy half smile.

I looked away quickly afterwards, hiding the blush flaming my cheeks. I didn't believe anyone noticed and hoped I was right.

"Most importantly," the woman's sharp tone catches my attention, "there is one rule that is critical. Amongst your fellow Leaguers, no relationships—whether they be platonic or romantic—may be formed. You are not to make friends. You are not to make relationships. Conversations are to be kept short and sparse. Soon, some of you will be sent away. Relationships of any kind will interfere with your work and the fate of mankind could be put in jeopardy."

She stretched a thin, pale smile across her lips, seemingly pleased with herself. "I'm beyond excited for our mission to begin. The sooner we complete our task, the sooner the colonists may return to America. This is their rebuilt homeland, and we mean to deliver it to them. The League commanders and the rest of the colonists thank you for your sacrifice. I know you all have been briefed on the consequences of becoming a Leaguer. Some of you will die returning our homeland to the colonists, but you will die as heroes. When the colonists return, your names will be repeated across thousands of lips. Above all else, your families are secured happy and healthy lives until the end of their days.

"Now, let us begin. We'll start by introducing ourselves to each other. Shake your fellow Leaguer's hand, state your name, and continue on. Do not linger. This is for ease of communication only."

Slowly, each of us stood up. We didn't move for a while. We awkwardly stared at each around, all of us too afraid to make the first move. We didn't want to seem like we were breaking the rule.

Finally, the Indian woman next to me broke the silence and turned to the man next to her, stating her name in a rich accent. Soon after, every followed suite.

The Hispanic man and I came together, pushed away from the other pairs introducing themselves around us. Our eyes met once again and we drifted toward each other.

"Mirabelle," I said as we came together.

"Rollin," he smiled, shaking my hand. "Nice to meet you, Mirabelle."

"You can call me Mira," I said quickly as he was about to turn away.

He paused for a moment, his eyes twinkling with confusion, but the stern-faced woman was staring at us so we separated. He walked away, greeting a young Chinese man. I shook my head, turning from him. The only person I let call me Mira was Charlotte.

Other people came to me and I told them all to call me Mirabelle. I had half a mind to go to Rollin and tell him to call me Mirabelle, but that would only raise the suspicion of the stern-faced woman.

After that initial meeting, we immediately dove into the schedule that the stern-faced woman explained earlier. The days were tiring, but I slept easy at night. We each were given our own apartment, stocked with a television, books, and other various means of entertainment.

Only two weeks had gone by when the first Leaguer was sent away. Her name was Lidiya, a young Russian woman who had exceled in all aspects of the League training. Her city was Los Angeles. It would be a long journey, but the League commanders was surely anxious to begin the process.

During this time, Rollin and I seemed to bump into each other more than usual. We would sit by each other during some of the meals. We stood near each other when we were training. We were even seated next to each other in some of our enrichment sessions. We never spoke during these occurrences, but a silent bond seemed to have begun to form between us.

As the Leaguers whittled down to half the original size, I started taking risks. I ripped pages out of a notepad in my room and etched notes out to him. Most of them were silly little things, saying hi or that I thought he was working hard lately. I slipped them into his hand every other day for two weeks, but every time I saw him throw it away. I knew this, but still I tried. It was against the rules, I knew, but I missed my family, especially Charlotte. I hadn't had a full conversation with someone in months. I missed being human.

One day, an unusually chilly spring day in April, Rollin came up to me during physical training. The exercise equipment was placed on the top level, and all the walls were glass windows that looked out onto the city. It was a breathtaking sight, and it made me look forward to my physical training. That day, we were working on our upper-body strength. I had just finished my fifth round of push-ups when he approached me. Sweat glistened on his skin and rolled down his face. The rich scent of his hard work drifted to my nose and I could not help but savor the smell. My mom never permitted me to spend time with any man except my father.

That made things here a lot harder than they were supposed to.

"Mira, would you mind, uh, spotting me as I lift?" he asks.

It was an innocent enough question, but I felt my nerves dance. There was a nervous twitch in his voice that suggested something more than platonic. Did he actually open one of my notes?

"Yes, Rollin," I said blankly. "Anything for the League."

It was the generic response. Many spoke it to avoid suspicion from the commanders.

"Anything for mankind," he affirmed.

I followed him to one of the many weight systems. He had asked for spotters before, but never from me.

I felt his musky scent drift to me once more. I closed my eyes and thought of my suite later. The League left various sexual aids for all of us. They supplied these to help with the natural sexual impulse. It didn't always work.

I watched him bend over to pull the bar up. His rear end stuck out and I felt an unnatural urge to grab the thing. I clenched my fists and looked somewhere else. My eyes only found his muscles, bulging as he gripped the bar. No, no, I couldn't look at that either.

A voice drifted to me as my eyes found the wall. What an interesting piece of brick!

"Mira, am I good?" the strained voice repeated.

"I'm sorry, what?" I snapped out of my trance.

"Am I good?" he exclaimed, his face turning the color of overripe tomatoes.

"Yes, yes!" I jumped, pulling my fists behind my back. "The League will prosper from your strength."

He dropped the bar with a deep *thud* and pulled a rag from the ground. He dragged it across his forehead. He thrust out his hand, thick with sweat.

"Thank you, Leaguer," he smiled.

I stared at his outstretched hand for a moment before impulse took over. I shook it numbly. A piece of paper was hidden inside his palm. I didn't react as he slipped it into my own.

"Anything for the League," I said.

"Anything for mankind," he confirmed.

I left him there and returned to the women's locker room. I smelt my hand unconsciously, savoring that rich, musky smell. Realizing my mistake, I shook my head in disgust and immediately went to wash my hands. I hope the other Leaguers did not see my mistake.

I entered one of the bathroom stalls and unfolded the note. His black handwriting was scrawled across paper from a yellow legal pad.

Meet me in the library at sundown. Come alone and inconspicuously.

ROLLIN

The dull lights of the alleyway fade away. Only Marco's dim flashlight leads the way, and even then, there isn't much to see. Darkness crawls on the edges of my vision. I lean against Buddy heavily, so much so that Buddy soon carries me in his arms. I don't resist; I feel my conscience slipping away and there's not much I can do to stop.

I listen to the soft patter of Marco and Buddy's footsteps against the rough ground, and the squeaking of the wheels echoing against the walls. I shut my eyes, though there's barely a difference between the open darkness and the darkness behind my eyelids. Pain stretches across my body, my abdomen especially. My face squeezes in pain when Buddy stumbles over a rock.

I find myself drifting away from the hurried walk in the Pedway, the squeaking of the dolly wheels, and the patter of the footsteps. I'm carried away from the pain, both physically and mentally, and leave the hell to happier times, though I didn't think so much then.

I think back to the League, during the first month I was there. It was a time when Mira and I weren't friends yet, but a silent bond formed between us. She would pass me notes, but I was always too afraid to open them, fearful of the consequences of being caught creating a friendship.

That was the only strong rule, besides following the daily schedule and swearing your life and hard work to the mission. The notes she slipped into my palm would go unopened, at first. Something changed after a few weeks. She kept trying, and I kept denying, but my strength began to wane. The loneliness I felt when I was young, traveling from home to home as an orphan, returned. I hadn't had a full conversation with another human since they first picked me up.

I saw her everywhere in the League tower. Wherever I was, she happened to be. I don't think either of us did it intentionally. It just happened. She was everywhere. Her shadow floated behind her like a long forgotten memory, only lingering long enough to feel déjà vu murmur through your ear.

I'd often find her by various windows, gazing out into the skyline. No one else did that. Many of the skyscrapers had been destroyed years ago, during the nuclear world wars. Though most of us had never seen one before, we did not find them particularly intriguing anyway. What we longed for was the familiar smell of home and the sound of our families' laughter. Other than watching the skyline, I often saw her going into the library during free time as I was coming out. We were the only two that used the dusty room.

She was a beautiful girl. She had porcelain skin, hair like molten lava, and eyes as crisp as a slice of the sky. Her beauty intimated me and made it easier for me to resist talking to her. I was nearly as afraid of speaking to her as I was breaking the League's rule.

I finally read the tenth note she handed to me. I expected a lot from it, but I think she had grown tired of writing so many notes only for them to be thrown out. She had scribbled out a crude picture of two stick figures holding hands and smiling. It was then I decided that I wanted the same as her: a friend.

When we went to our physical training time the next day, it took all my courage to ask her to spot me while I lifted. She was surprised, but obliged. I slipped the note into her hand soon after. She did her best to hide the surprise that sprung on her face, but I could see.

I arrived at the library an hour early. The time was mine to kill, but I still sat there alone for two long hours after I had entered those oak doors. Words had been etched into the wood, script from stories long forgotten. There I waited.

An encyclopedia sat before me. I was reading about the Dust Bowl from the 1930s. I thought it would be interesting enough considering the predicament we were facing. By that time, everyone had a bandanna around their neck in case we found ourselves outside.

Through the window, the melting, lemon drop sun dipped into the horizon, casting the sky into deep hues of red and orange. I watched it dip lower and lower, the book gathering dust before me. The doors did not creak open, but still I waited.

It grew dark and lonely inside the dusty room. Not even the books gave me companionship at that point. It was black ink outside by the time I stowed the encyclopedia away and began to make my way back. The corridors were dark. The elevator was dimmed. No footsteps walked about except mine.

When I reached the hundredth floor—one of the suite floors—I knew the commanders had gone to bed. All the candles were extinguished in the hall. Only the minimal moonlight peeking through the curtains lit the way.

The hallway was lined with doors. Mine was the first on the right. I turned to go inside, my hand resting on the doorknob, when I glanced to my left. Across the hall, the fourth door on the left was Mira's room. A sliver of light escaped from the underneath the door and the faint whisper of singing drifted to my ears.

I paused. She was awake. My feet shuffled toward her door and I stood outside, listening to her hushed singing. She wasn't the best singer, but she definitely was far from being the worst. It was pleasant enough listening to, especially since I hadn't heard anyone sing since I was young.

I stood outside her door for ten minutes, debating if I should knock or not, debating if I should go in, debating if even debating was too risky. I wasn't supposed to do this. I knew the rules, but loneliness stretched an all too familiar ache across my chest.

Finally, I raised my fist up and gave two shaky taps against the door. The singing stopped abruptly. Her hesitant footsteps came afterward, and the door slowly slid open.

Her face peeked out of the crack, her eyes wide pools of fear. Panic spread like butter across her face.

"Rollin!" she exclaimed. "How can I assist you, fellow Leaguer—"

"It's okay," I whispered, nervously glancing around the hallway myself. "The commanders are all sleeping, and no one saw me. Can I come in?"

"It's not safe."

"It'll be safer in your room than out here in the hallway, where someone could easily see us," I remind gently. "Please, Mira. You didn't meet me in the library like I asked."

She reluctantly opens to door for me and I slip into her room. We stare at each other for a few moments, tension like ice crystals in the air.

"Tell me you don't want a friend. Honestly tell me that, and I'll leave," I said, breaking the tension.

"What makes you so sure I want a friend?"

"Because you asked me to call you Mira the first time we met," I smiled, "but you made everyone else call you Mirabelle."

She stood there for a second, unsure of what to say or do.

I turned from her and started for the door. "I'll expect to see you tomorrow—same time, same place. Goodnight, Mira."

After I shut her door that night, things were different.

We met every day at the library thereafter. We perused the library shelves, finding different stories that we had read before. Her favorite was *Pride and Prejudice*, which I found just awful. Mine was *The Catcher in the Rye*, which she found awful as well.

Another favorite activity was leafing through the encyclopedias. She had never heard of an encyclopedia before, mostly due to the fact that she hadn't ventured into that section of the library. I showed her how there were different editions depending on what year they were published in and how they were categorized by letter. We had nearly gone through them all in a month's time.

During this time, we attempted to keep our friendship a secret but achieved little success. We received the contempt from other Leaguers, who believed—since we were not following a pivotal rule—that we did not take the mission seriously. They refused to associate with us. We tried our best to keep separate while in public. Once, during combat training, Mira accidentally sent a roundhouse kick into my head, knocking me out for a while. People questioned the legitimacy of our friendship for a few days after that.

As for the commanders, they knew of our friendship, but did nothing about it. Neither Mira nor I had anyone speak to us about it. We felt their eyes, though. They watched us more than anyone else. Mira joked that she'd draw a picture on her back so they would have something to look at.

Some nights, we snuck into each other's room. All we did was talk deep into the night, and sometimes we watched a movie, but nothing more than that. Those nights were seldom since we enjoyed the library so much more. Other nights, we would sneak out of the building altogether and explore the city. Those nights were special. We often would not return until daybreak. As everyone else was waking, we were returning.

Our friendship was platonic in almost all senses. We agreed that anything past a friendship was too dangerous. Having a friend, someone to talk to, was enough, we said. I tried to think of her as my sister.

Granted, there were instances were I felt something stir deep inside me, but I did my best to keep it away. Those were feelings of lust, more often, rather than romance. Everyone felt that urge there, but there were methods to keep it at bay.

The months drew on slowly. Soon, there were only a few of us Leaguers left. All the others had been assigned different infiltration missions and sent to their cities. More often than not, we were not informed of their assignments. We only noticed one fewer person at mealtimes.

I was shamefully happy that neither Mira nor I was assigned. I enjoyed my time with her, and that was the reason the League banned relationships. I had already promised my life to the mission if it came to that. Did they really have to take my happiness away too? Besides, the friendship didn't hurt, and thus far, it hadn't interfered with the mission.

I continued on with this mindset. I didn't feel too guilty. Mira did. She hated me at times. She hit me in an attempt to appease the anger, but all it resulted in was a few bruises. This only made her feel guiltier. I forgave her for those moments because I understood. She blamed me for her unfaithfulness to the mission. I blamed the League.

She liked to deny it, but she enjoyed being my friend. Time passed easier and it made the pain from missing her family not so…painful.

As the Leaguers diminished, Mira and I became less conservative in keeping our friendship a secret. The last Leaguer there other than ourselves—the Indian woman that Mira said she spoke to on the first day—knew very well of our friendship and despised us like the rest. Mira believed they hated us. I believed they were jealous.

Months passed, and there was only the two of us. Once we began wondering when they would tear us apart, a commander pulled me aside one day. His demeanor showed he wasn't afraid of what he was about to say.

"Rollin," he said in a gruff voice. "You're going to Chicago."

My heart sank. Everyone knew Chicago was far gone.

I told Mira the next day. She was heartbroken. We hadn't seen any other Leaguers come back, even though it had been more than six months since Lidiya had first left. They told us we probably wouldn't return, but we had been hopeful. It only made the future darker for me.

"Don't leave," she murmured.

"I have to go," I said. "I have no choice."

"Don't lie to me, Rollin. Not you."

I was set to leave in three days.

The first day passed quickly. I was excused from physical training and enrichment studies, but I went anyway. I wanted to spend time with Mira. When I entered the training room, the trainer screamed at me. I was to report to the laboratory for training and waste no time, he said. I followed the dim hallways sluggishly. I had all the time in the world to train, but only so much time to spend with a friend.

As usual, the scientists wanted to train me on new equipment. That day, it was a new device that started fires without kindling or matches. I lost myself in my thoughts, thinking of eventual loneliness, when my elbow knocked the fire starter onto the ground and it caught on my pant leg. The fire raced up my legs, tearing up the skin and destroying my nerves. Bubbling blisters covered my legs. The pain was so blinding I almost fainted. The nurses told me they were third-degree burns.

I was ashamed to feel it, but I was…happy. I wouldn't have to go. That feeling soon disappeared when the commander pulled me away after the accident. I sobbed after they told me the news. I waited until they had left me in the infirmary bed alone. The tears streamed down my face.

When they informed me of my mission two days prior, I was almost joyful. At least I would be the one to go to the most dangerous city in America, so it wouldn't have to be Mira.

Now all of that was ruined.

She found me in the infirmary soon after the commanders had left. No tears were on her face. She was wordless as she found me on the bed. I held her in my arms as invisible tears streamed down her face. For my sake, she didn't want to cry. I knew that about her.

She wasn't allowed to tell me anything about her mission, though she told me that they didn't tell her much. She said one last goodbye to me before she disappeared from the room forever. I sat in the hospital bed, wincing as my burns rubbed against the bandages, but the worst pain was looking at the door closing and hearing the *click* of the lock.

The next few months were nearly unbearable. An unnatural loneliness settled on my mind. The headquarters felt empty, the library desolate, and the halls vacant.

I spent a month in the hospital bed. The burns were severe and took long to heal. The scars proved it. Once I was able to walk, it all became worse.

They put me back in training. I walked the city. I ate food. But I did all of it alone.

I considered jumping a few times. Months passed.

The whole time I wondered. I waited. I heard nothing about Mira.

They wouldn't tell me anything, no matter how many times I asked. Time didn't seem to move.

Then, one day, a commander approached me.

"You're going to Chicago, Rollin."

My heart fluttered. "Another infiltration mission?"

The man before me was stoic, his features unnaturally still and his voice like gravel running down a slope. He revealed nothing, but I could tell there were words behind his scowl.

Something that he knew I wanted to hear.

"No," his voice wavered. "We've lost contact with Mirabelle. Your mission is not to infiltrate. Your mission is to find her."

MIRA

Journal #3: Mira Pevensky
Date: unknown
Season: early summer

Two weeks have passed since I left New York City and the League. I'm still traveling through the dirt and dust to Chicago. My faith wanes with the moon.

My thoughts are consumed with him. I hope he's recovering from his burns. I hope he's...oh, I don't know. I hope he's something. That's better than nothing.

We didn't leave on the best terms, no, but we left on some terms. He was supposed to go instead of me, but he was burned and I was the only one left to go.

I'm glad I came out here instead of him. It's awful. Slithers leap from the dirt and latch onto my ankle. If they hang on too long, they'll poison me, and I'll die without accomplishing the League's mission.

There are more dangers than that, though. Many clones wander out here, more travelers than I thought there would be. It's...unsettling. It's one thing to be knowledgeable of millions of deaths and another to look them in the face. Most of the clones keep their distance from me, but some, the strange ones, approach my fire late at night and ask to share it with me. Many times, they sleep cold.

They should be grateful. The League told me to kill any stranger that approached me, but there isn't enough darkness inside me to swing the fateful blow.

The dust out here is worse than it was in New York City. I wish I had two bandanas, hell, maybe even three. Dust blows at day and it blows at night. There's no rest.

Being out here, traveling, searching for weeks makes me realize why the League banned relationships. I only have the howling of the wind and the strange aura of travelers to keep me company. I doubt it's any better for Rollin in New York City. He has no one.

By my approximation, I have two weeks left of traveling to Chicago.

The worst thing is…I don't know what I'm supposed to do. I thought they would tell me how I was supposed to infiltrate the society or exterminate the clones or even get in the damn city. I only squeezed two tidbits of information out of them. One, I would be contacted once I reached Chicago. Two, another Leaguer would be coming shortly after I had arrived.

In short, they told me a little about a lot.

When they say that another Leaguer will be coming after me, it can only be Rollin. No one else is left. If I die before he finds me, which I might…that's okay. Maybe he'll have to go back to New York City and won't have to go to Chicago.

But that's just wishful thinking.

There's too much hell in this world for that to happen.

ROLLIN

Journal #1: Rollin Hale
Date: unknown
Season: early summer

I found this pad of paper in the library and the pen was rolling around under the table. I've come here frequently, but it never…well, it feels like a ghost roams the bookshelves. It haunts me.

I can't remember the last time I picked up a pen and sat down to write something. It's been a while. My handwriting is cruddy and my thoughts are scrambled.

In a couple of days, I set off and journey after Mira. The commanders say she has gone missing. They say that they haven't received any communication from her and her status is unknown. My mission is to figure out if she's alive, and if so, I have to bring her back to New York.

I don't mind too much. These months I've spent alone in the League tower have been some of the most torturous of my life. It's one thing to be lonely in a group of people and it's an entirely different thing to be utterly alone. I haven't had a conversation with anyone since Mira left. The most I've had is a couple of impersonal greetings from the commanders.

The mission is confusing in all senses. All the other Leaguers were sent off to infiltrate cities, their lives on the line. We never heard of Leaguers going after fellow members, but then again, they didn't divulge much information in any case.

The League tower has grown cold. I have to walk the halls with a blanket around my shoulders, like those kings Mira and I used to read about. If she were here, she'd sure get a kick out of that.

At least I'm not in the hospital any more. I'd rather be alone out here, where I can roam where I like, than alone in a room with the same four walls with the same color and same television with the same program running on it.

The commanders don't humor themselves on variety.

While I was recovering each day, the commanders only let me watch one hour of the same video about the discovery of cloning and how they were able to manipulate the clones' minds. Other than that, I filled many coloring books (don't laugh) and read many books (they weren't very good).

It was weeks before I could walk again after my accident. Patches of scars scrawled across my legs, almost like a map of the world, but a really ugly one that no one would want to live in anyway. I tried going to the library for a while, but there wasn't anything left for me anymore.

After that, I went on many walks throughout the city where I found lots of undiscovered treats. One day, I stumbled upon a massive park, or what used to be one. All the grass was long since dead and brown, but scrappy little trees still stood. I looked it up in one of the textbooks in the library. The bombs weren't kind here, but at least some of the foliage remains. It's a rare treat to see some. They called it Central Park in the olden days. She would've liked seeing that.

Sometimes, these walks would last for a day, maybe two. The commanders stopped worrying about me. They thought I was too weak to go on any infiltration missions.

This went on for a while. Days blended into the next. I stopped counting. Time went on and still she was gone and I was…alone. That's when they came for me and told me that I was going to go after her.

These past few days have been filled with vigorous physical training and extensive survival class lessons. In my free time, I exercise even more than before. The commanders follow me as close as a shadow. They mutter between themselves, always making sure that two are watching me at all times. I've lost count of how many commanders there are, but more often than not they look more bored since everyone left. They seem to change every day.

Tomorrow I set out to find her. I will take my pack, grab my light breakfast, and start the journey. I'll travel through New York City one last time. It's almost as though I'm going on another one of my walks.

It's almost dinnertime. We're having peanut butter and jelly sandwiches tonight. They know it's my favorite, so they made it special. The commanders say it will be the last good meal for a long time. Breakfast is going to be a few granola bars and a cup of water.

Hopefully they'll stick a few candy bars in my food stash. Nutritious or not, there isn't a damn thing in this world better than a chocolate bar.

I best wrap this entry up. I haven't talked about much. It's strange how people can do that: talk so much about so little. Hm.

MIRA

Journal #5: Mira Pevensky
Date: unknown
Season: summer

The sky is dark, the moon is out, and the world smells like shit. I'm inside a dumpster. No, I'm not kidding. I'm lounging on trash bags of rotting garbage. The scent is about thirty minutes from becoming unbearable. Before I explain how I got in here, I have a lot to tell.

I was correct in my travel estimation. It took me two weeks after the third journal entry before I reached Chicago. The terrain was decorated with rubble, big and small. More and more travelers began to stop by my fire as I got closer to the city.

The clones were there, roaming toward their eventual deaths, as well as a few massive trucks rolling by. I hid from those. I felt it in my gut. A traveler told me later that the trucks were headed for the suburbs, where all unruly roaches were kept. I didn't quite understand what she meant, but I knew enough from her tone to know I should hide from them.

One of the travelers who stopped by my fire was a mighty proud man. His hair was gold as the sun and it fell past his shoulders—even longer than mine was, before I cut it all off a week ago.

Anyway, this man wore no clothes at all. He was completely naked. It didn't seem like it mattered much to this man, but it mattered a lot to me. His eyes were wide with insanity and his smile wide as the galaxy. How he had survived without clothes or equipment, I couldn't say. As I have said before, my mom didn't even let me see my father work outside with his shirt off. Even that was too much for my young eyes to see, even though he was my father.

124

It shocked me to say the least, but this strange, insane man was shocked at my shock. He was very proud of his body and wanted to show it off. Wonderful.

Obviously, I did not allow him to sit by my fire that night.

The night after that, a black man came to my fire. His voice was thick with the south and his manners holy in nature. He clutched a Bible in his hands and wanted to read it to me, but I declined.

"No, I'm no lady of God," I said.

He frowned a little, "I ain't so sure about that. You as holy as they come. I can see it on your skin. Pure as snow!"

"No, no," I smiled. "I don't believe in any god."

After saying that, this man didn't want much to do with me anyway. I had a talent of driving people away by their own preferences before mine came to surface. He was a peculiar man. Not as strange as the nudist, but strange in a different way.

After talking to this man, a conversation between Rollin and me drifted to my mind. It was one we shared on a walk through an old church. We threw rocks and broke the stained glass. A piece of Jesus' head fell by his feet. He picked it up then and glared at the fragment.

"I wonder why so many people believed in this man," he said. "He isn't all that good-looking."

I laughed. I remember that. Rollin threw the glass at the wall and it shattered into a thousand pieces. That was the day we discussed religion. We went back after our walk to the library and pulled book after book about religion. It was then we decided that no god could exist. Not here.

Those are the moments I miss the most. I hadn't had many of those kinds of memories before the League. Most of my days were spent in my family's mansion. My mom didn't like me venturing out of it much. She said it would ruin me. I said staying inside would ruin me. Both of us were right.

Most of my memories were spent between the same four walls, with the same three people (most of the time with my little sister Charlotte), and in the same damn place.

When nudists and followers of God come to my fire, it's a strange experience for us all.

These instances were my first indicators that Chicago was what the commanders had told me. The clones' society had grown far more complex than I had expected, but it was hard to see why the League considered Chicago the worst off.

The next night, I saw my first glimpse of the skyline. The past few nights it had been both misty and cloudy. I couldn't see a damn thing. It made traveling quite the adventure. The skyline was beautiful, sure, but I'd seen enough of New York City. It didn't hold my interest for very long.

Soon after, I found the entrance. There were guards there and they weren't very keen on niceties. Their eyes followed me as I walked up to the gate. They looked me up and down. Though not as strange as the two before them, these men were dangerous. I could tell in a single glance.

They asked me a simple question: "Oddity or Privilege?"

At the time, I didn't know what the hell they were talking about. It wasn't until later that I realized my mistake at this. I don't understand why the commanders were so reluctant to hand out information like this to us. I almost died at those gates.

"What?" I said. "I need to get inside the city."

Don't think me a fool. There was a massive wall surrounding the entire city, and I wasn't about to waste days of walking to find another entrance, if there was one at all. I knew my options were limited, and I couldn't scale the twenty-foot wall unnoticed.

"You from around here, little lady?" they sauntered up to me, lust rolling a storm in their sickly eyes.

"No, no," I muttered, standing my ground. "I'm a traveler and I wish to enter the city."

"Do me a favor," the man licked his lips. "Turn around and let me see that little behind of yours. Maybe then I'll let you in."

The other men laughed and joined in, all of them prowling toward me like I was some meat on a hook ready for them to snatch. It was disgusting.

I didn't know what to do. I know lust when I see it. I saw enough of it in Rollin's eyes to know. Unlike these men, he was able to control it.

I guessed their motives and damn me if I was wrong. I...I didn't know what to do. They were coming closer and closer and...and...their hands reached out for me and...I knew what was coming...or at least, I think I knew.

"Men, please" a voice spoke up, a deep gruff voice from far off. "Leave her be. Let her go in as an Oddity. It won't do you any harm."

The men stopped in their tracks, turning away from me and toward the man, whose voice came from the right. He was short in stature but made up for it in his booming voice. He was cloaked in shadows, so I couldn't make out his features.

"Oh yeah?" One spat on the ground. "Why?"

"For god's sake! Leave her alone. You had another not too long ago. I think you can hold off a little longer," the man screamed.

The men backed away. I hiked the pack on my back close to me, adrenaline shaking my legs. I didn't want to defend myself, even with my training at the League. I could tell I'd leave the scene with a body more broken than before.

They let me through, but not without many scans up and down. I felt hands brush against my side. I tried to ignore it. They wanted a rise out of

---

me.

I entered the city, the long dreaded, cursed place. People bustled about. Some people stopped and stared at me, wonderment in their eyes. Curses from the people behind them soon sent them on their way.

I didn't know where to go. I can't say I was afraid, necessarily. I have long accepted the fact that I would die in my efforts for the League. I'm not afraid of my own death. I'm afraid of failing the League.

So this brings me to the story of me ending up in a dumpster. It's dark out now. I can barely see the paper in front of me. I doubt if any of this is legible.

Anyway, I didn't have a single clue what to do. The guards at the gate said I was an Oddity. I didn't know what that was. I understand now, of course. Chicago has a caste system. The Privileges are the higher tier and the Oddities are the lower tier. There's not much else to it.

I asked a man on the street. He seemed very bothered and confused when I stopped him, but he gave me the answer with some persuasion.

"If you want to get started here," he said with a smile, "you can give me a little show and I'll pay you in return, baby."

After that, I immediately left him, ignoring his catcalls. I had more sense than to stick around the pervert. My days in the League and in my mansion back home did not prepare me well for the lust of men. I could see it in every one of them. They stared at women like meat ready to be cooked. The women weren't at fault either; I saw some of them grab at the pants of passing men, or pulling out their breasts and waving them for all to see.

It was quite a culture shock. I wandered the streets until dusk began to fall. Danger crept onto the city with the darkness like a dense fog; I could barely see through it all.

Stranger people began to appear. Many of them, the ones who were walking on the sidewalk at least, were all wearing the same jacket with a green stripe. I received many stares while walking along the sidewalk.

Some man with a blue-striped jacket—he called himself a Warden—approached me and asked me where my jacket was. He demanded to see my payment card as proof of my status. A line of other jacket-less people stood glumly behind him. He could clearly see I had no idea what he was talking about. I told him I had arrived that day. He almost didn't believe me, but he left me alone on the condition that I would find a jacket soon.

That's how I ended up in this dumpster. Between the solicitation of sex acts and seeing strange people lurking about, I knew I had to find shelter away from all these people. There was only one place I could find that would shield me from this damn city.

I found one of those jackets with the green stripe in here. I assume it marks the people as Oddities because all those who are driving in cars, not wearing jackets, are the Privileges, as the man explained to me earlier. I don't mind wearing it. It gives me some warmth.

I don't know what else to do. When I agreed to leave the colonies and come here, I never imagined it would lead me to lying here in a dumpster. I thought I would be helping clean up the cities so the humans could come home.

I was wrong.

The League hasn't told me what to do. They only gave me one command: wait to be contacted. How long am I supposed to wait?

I see now why the League didn't want us to have friends or lovers within the League. Once you leave, the loneliness is only worse. They were trying to wean us away from having companions so the loneliness wouldn't be as bad once we left.

This type of loneliness is awful. I'm the only human in this damn city. I'm surrounded by pseudo-people who think they are humans. Their lives are a lie, and only I know the truth.

I couldn't say what I'm going to do when I wake up tomorrow. I have no plan. I have no ideas. I don't feel like the hero they told me I would be.

ROLLIN

The streets are dark and bare when we ascend the stairs, leaving the Pedway and Mira's body behind us. Marco disappears around the corner and slips away into the night. His bald head glimmers for a moment in the moonlight. His denim is crusty, ruined by the filth below.

I pull my roach jacket tightly around me, stifling a groan as pain rips across the muscles of my arms. Every step sends knives dicing up my nerves. Buddy flashes a warning glance toward me as he crosses the street.

A fog had settled on Chicago while we were underground. No headlights pierce the eerie blanket. The streets in this part of the city haven't been kept up; pebbles and cracks riddle the asphalt. Buddy's careful footsteps are soft as they fall on it.

Few people are out. They flit about, jittery as shadows. Their dark clothes melt into the black buildings. Not a whisper races through the street.

There are still skyscrapers here. I don't know why I thought there wouldn't be, but I was hopeful. I can't stand any more black giants staring down at me.

I clench my teeth as my muscles strain. One foot in front of another. One at a time. Left, then right. Left, then right. It's so simple, but the fibers of my muscles seem to peel away from the bone each time I force a foot forward. Left, then right. Left, then right.

I will make it.

Blood seeps through my bandages. I feel it pooling under the white cotton like a blister ready to pop. My clothes suffocate my limbs. I had to find spare clothes tossed in the dumpster to cover the bandages. Everyone in the city knows my face now, but a bandaged fool is far easier to spot. Not many roaches leave a hospital at all, bandages or not.

I'm the rapist. I'm the murderer. I'm a damn fool, that's what I am. Maybe I'm just unlucky. Maybe none of this is real at all. Maybe I'm dead and I'm revisiting my past. Maybe I'm still unconscious from when Mira gave me a roundhouse kick to the head all those months ago. Maybe I'm still at the League, and maybe she is too.

I'll wake up in a few moments. Mira will be there, shaking me awake with a smile on her lips but a crease in her brow. She could never help laughing when someone got injured. A nervous habit, she said.

Something slams into my arm—the broken one—and pain shatters the bone into a thousand pieces and they rain onto the cement and stars appear and I scream out—

"What the hell, man?" a voice growls. "Get yourself together, you piece of shit."

The man walks on, spitting on me as he goes. The glob hits my cheek, or what would've been my cheek if the scarf that's covering my bandages weren't there. I pull it closer around me, conscious of my bandages, conscious of my familiar face and the murders' guilt on my skin.

I feel Buddy's glare burning into my back. *Don't make a scene*, he said. *No matter how much yer in pain, don't bring no attention to us.*

I'm trying my best, Buddy. I am. My abdomen had barely stopped bleeding before they booted us out the back door of the hospital, the stitches are crude and minimal, bruises cover my body, my arm and nose are broken, and a sprained ankle tops it all off. I can barely walk normally. I'm proud of myself for even attempting it.

Beside the physical pain, there's more, a demonic fury stirring inside me, but I push it down, away from me, away from now. I can't think of these things now. I can only focus on what's ahead.

Buddy still walks across the street, his feet dragging against the gravel. *If ah look drunk*, he said, *no one will ask no questions.*

I'm following him. Where our destination is, I don't know. They said it was safe. That's enough for me. Marco went ahead to scout it out and make sure.

Neither of them has been here much, here in the roach sector, since they used to be Privies before Nova's death. They can't say they've never come here. All Privies find their way into the roach sector at some point in their lives. There's no whorehouses in downtown Chicago, the Privy sector. Filth rots with filth, they say. We're all here to rot together now.

Buddy stumbles to the left, turning down a dark alleyway. I follow on the other side of the street. Shadows flicker in dark crevices.

I think of Buddy, of what I've put him through. He says he's okay, but I see the demons lurking inside him as they have been with me. Murder stains everyone a deep, blood red.

I press forward, ignoring the pain as best as I can but I can't. It's too much. It's flooding through my system. I wish Buddy would carry me again like he did while we were underground. No, no he can't do that. I have to act normal. People know my face.

People think I'm a rapist. A murderer.

But I'm not.

I swear I'm not.

I didn't do it, Mira.

I didn't do it.

The skyscrapers swirl in front of me but I see Buddy marching ahead, stumbling and tripping and yelling out.

The words swirl in my brain.

"Hell is beautiful, Micah."

I'm not Micah, Mira! I'm not him—

"We can always be together."

We could have been, Mira. What happened to you? Where did you go?

"They'll tear us apart again…"

They already have.

You're gone.

My feet drag against the rubble on the ground but I ignore that and the pain, a pulsating heartbeat, in my head, and the agony stretching across my skin and piercing it to the bone and my bones aching and my muscles crying out—

Buddy's gone. Darkness surrounds me. Shadows flicker, but I see no people scurrying about. Black clouds my vision, stretching across the edges and creeping into my conscience…I am weak…tired…can't stand…or think…

Arms surround me, pulling me away from the street where I have to walk normal and talk normal and act normal because there shouldn't be anything wrong with me but there is. I'm beaten and bruised and dying but I can't go to a damn hospital because the mob outside will kill me before I get there.

"Rollin?" a voice calls but I ignore it because it's bright where I am. It's finally bright. Darkness fades away until faces appear above me and their eyes blink slowly. Sweat beads on their foreheads and worry destroys their smiles and dirt has muddied their clothing and blood has splattered on their collars and rips tear at the cloth and—

"Hey, pal?" the voice calls again but— "You okay?"

Of course I'm okay. I'm only bleeding and broken and bruised and nothing in my body seems to work but that's okay, of course it's okay or else why would they be asking me if I was okay?

"What the hell am I doing here?" I mumble, staring up at the faces as they stare at me and we're all staring at each other because everything's okay.

Of course it's okay.

"Rollin," the black man says, yes, his name is Buddy, that's right, "ah think yuh need some rest."

"Yes, what a test it was!" I laugh, throwing my hands in the air, but then pain spikes in my arms and I hear screams echo and hit my ears and there's a hand covering my mouth and I can't breathe, dammit—

"Stop screaming, you damn fool!" the bald white man says with his moon head and infuriated eyes and oh, how red his face is.

So I stop thrashing and the pain settles to that of a hacking knife but at least it's better than an incinerator so that's a perk if anything could be called one and I pant and sit there and pant some more because they're still looking at me, staring at me and asking—

"Are you okay, Rollin?"

—and I'm not okay. I never was okay because the devil was released a while ago and it's stirring inside me and biting and pinching and tears prick in my eyes because the agony is worse than the broken arm or nose or knife wound or ankle sprain or bruises or anything.

It's hell on earth inside.

I see her bloody and broken and in my vision, twisting away and white and pale and she never was that pale before, *never*, and she's falling away and I reach out to catch her and I scream her name but Mira disappears. She's gone.

That's when they get it. They finally understand.

They are silent for a long time. My tears fall and they stand still. I couldn't say how long time passed, but the well ran dry and the tears stopped coming. I shut my eyes to them. Maybe they don't understand. I don't understand. She was my friend. She was my *friend*.

Hands tickle my skin as bandages upon bandages are peeled away. The blood crusts over. I drift into sleep as water trickles onto my skin.

I dream of before. Here, she's not dead. She's Mira, not Nova. She's real.

We visit Times Square. We take pieces of the road and chuck them at the massive plasma screens that still stand from the olden times. She laughs and laughs and *laughs* as each rock embeds into the screens.

"Rollin! We shouldn't be doing this," she says, lobbing another rock into the sky regardless. "The commanders won't be happy."

"I've had enough of the commanders," I smile. "They don't need these damn things anyway."

"It's a museum," she argues.

"It's a graveyard."

The memory blurs away as another resurfaces. We're inside her room at the League headquarters. We're working on our latest assignment, a paper on the destruction of the old world based on the lectures we received the day before. Mira's auburn hair is thrown into a messy bun, the strands flying out like they're trying to escape.

I reach over and pluck a hair from her. She yelps in surprise, her notebook flying as she leaps at me.

"Rollin! What was that for?"

I laugh, holding the hair above her. "I need it for cloning, Human 271."

She purses her lips. "Stop messing around, stupid. We've got a paper to work on."

"Oh, quiet," I wave her off, holding the ginger strand in the light and scrutinize it. "I'm working here."

She leaps onto my back and reaches for the strand. I stumble, almost collapsing to the ground, but I regain my balance quickly. Her fingers snake around the thin strand and she yanks it from my fingers.

"You're not cloning me," she whispers in my ear as she slips from my back.

"Oh? You like being special, don't you?"

She smiles. "Why would I *want* a clone? Don't you think it would be weird to have someone walking around who looks exactly like you?"

"Well, it won't happen. You know that."

"But what if we *had* been cloned?"

I sneak around her and snatch the strand back again. "Be ready to have a clone, Ms. Pevensky."

"No!" she laughs, pouncing on me once more.

We fall into a mess on the floor. She's straddling me, her hair no longer in a bun but flying in a frenzy about her. Her hands hold mine against the floor and a low-cut shirt reveals more of her than I anticipated.

Silence wraps a seductive blanket around us. Her chest rises and falls with heavy breathing.

"So here we are," I snigger, trying to ignore the heat and urge rising inside. "You can have your hair back. There are plenty in my mouth to chose from."

Her eyes don't leave me. Her mouth parts as though she's going to say something, but nothing escapes her thin lips.

"This is like one of the *special* movies they give you, right?" she whispers.

I resist the urge, but only barely. "Yes, it is."

"They give the girls those too, you know."

My fingers clench under her hands. "They do?"

"I've watched a few of them."

"Mira, why are you telling me this?"

She stares me in the eyes. "Because I want you to kiss me."

I sigh, fighting myself, kicking myself. "Mira, you know we can't—"

"Kiss me," she says, her face stone cold. "Just this once."

"No," I struggle against her, but she doesn't release me. "You're my *friend—"*

"But you want to," a smile turns her lips. "You don't think I can feel that lump under me? I may be inexperienced, but I'm not an idiot."

I wrench myself from under her, making her topple to the ground. I leap to my feet and rush to the door, pausing with my hand on the knob. Fear beat in my heart instead of blood. Being friends was one thing...but this was different.

She told me to kiss her. I'm outside her door, leaning on it with my head in my hands because she asked me, she *wanted* me to...to *kiss*—

"I know you're out there, Rollin," a soft voice comes from the other side of the door. "I could hear you cussing from the next room over."

"The rooms are soundproof," I mutter. "You can't hear anything."

She laughs. "Tell that to the guy in the room over. He blasts those movies *so* loud, groaning all the while and *man*, he takes forever to—"

I grimace. "Men have their urges."

"Yeah, I just wish he could be a little more quiet about his!"

"Mira, we're off the subject here."

I hear a suppressed sigh. "Come back in. I'm sorry for...coming on to you, though I know you wanted—"

"Mira," I groan. "We're friends."

She's quiet for a moment. "How much longer are we going to be friends for?"

"We've already broken enough rules," I whisper.

"Maybe not enough."

ROLLIN

Darkness surrounds me, but I accept it. A memory comes to surface. I hear it before I see it. There are moans, the pleas, the anguished cries, oh god, it's all here again—

Then she's there. Blood covers her body along with ruined makeup trickling down her face. Not an inch of clean skin can be seen. There is only blood coating her entire body, she's red, even her auburn hair is dripping in red and I can't, I—

"Oh, Micah," she groans, kissing my neck and pain holds my body in a tight grip and it won't let me—I can't—Mira!—MIRA?—

I'm not Micah. "I'm not Micah," I tell her. She's not Nova. "You're not Nova," I say, but she doesn't hear me, only tearing off my clothes, exposing me with bruises coating every single inch of my body, the broken bones, the—

She grabs me, takes a grip of me and squeezes and I cry out in more pain and she only smiles and squeezes harder, darkness edging on the side of my vision, falling—help—HELP—

"Don't lie to me, Micah," she growls in my ear. "I know you want it."

"I don't," I cry. "Not like this, Mira. Not—"

"Stop calling me Mira!" she screams, releasing her grip on me and sitting up. "You'll never leave me again."

"Mira…" I whisper.

She latches onto me again none the less, screaming out Micah as she pushes herself on top of me, rocking back and forth, back and forth, crying out as blood rolls down her body—

I don't want this. I don't want any of this. I push it away, back into the darkness and watch it drift away, thankfully, oh thank you, sweet darkness—

135

She's gone. The twisted version of Mira, the nightmare, is gone. I'm free.

Images of her float across the darkness. Not Nova, or whatever the hell she called herself, but Mira, *my* Mira. She laughs and those freckles that the American sun created dance joyfully. Her porcelain skin shines in the sunlight. Her orange hair lights on fire under the sun, blazing her into a breath of beauty.

From the moment I saw her, she caught my eye. She was the sun, and I couldn't resist the warmth. She was a proud lion underneath her skin, never letting anything get in her way. All those close encounters, the accidental brush of my hand, her tendency to jump on my back, her laugh, the smell of her perfume, her crystal eyes that saw everything—

I wanted her so badly, but not like that. Not like she did. She wasn't the same. For god's sake, she didn't even know who I was! Her freckles didn't dance. Her hair wasn't a fire. She stared at me with those crystal eyes, broken, broken…

She was a shaved lion, stripped of her pride. The Mira I knew wouldn't let a razor close to her.

Another image resurfaces. It's the first day of the League. People huddle in the small room at the top of the Empire State Building. Mira catches my eyes instantly, but another face holds my attention more.

It's…Marco.

He has a full head of hair, but his face is unmistakable. Denim covers him head to toe. He sits quietly in the corner, his attention held to his twiddling thumbs. He bites his lip nervously, glancing around at the others with a perplexed look upon his face. His attention quickly returns to his thumbs.

Marco? He was in the League? He must have been one of the first sent off if I don't remember him…and he shaved his head! What's he doing in Chicago? I thought Mira was the first to come here?

Mira.

And I can't help but feel the heat rising inside me and she's back with blood dripping down her chest, the bare chest that was unveiled to me when I saw for the first time in Chicago and she rocks back and forth, back and forth—

She's not Mira. She's a shaved lion. My Mira is gone.

The image disappears. Her naked body, her bloodied skin and conscience, are all gone. She's dead. She's gone. She's never, ever coming back and I have to accept that. I can't.

Buddy thinks I'm in love with her. He thinks I'm dying of a broken heart. He carried me through the Pedway, my body so broken and bruised I could hardly walk. He said it wasn't my bones that made my legs jelly. It was my heart.

I told him his mama told him too many love stories. He said she did, but he was always one to catch the spark in-between two people, regardless of the stories.

"Yuh look at her different," he said, "like she's the only damn star in the galaxy."

"She's my friend."

He smiled warmly. "She's more than that to yuh."

"My sister, then, fine."

"If that's true, ah wouldn't want to be yer sibling!"

I punched him for that. "Leave it, will you?"

"What happened 'fore yuh came here?"

"Huh?"

"Tell me?"

"Why do you want to know?"

"'Cuz ah do."

I thought about it. Before I came to America, before I left the colonies, my life was simple. I was alone. I never met my parents and I couldn't tell you why. There was a woman who cared for me up until the age of five. Her image is a blur, but I remember it vaguely.

She was an elderly Hispanic woman. She would go into the trees near us and bring back juniper berries to dye her hair. Everyday, she'd escape in the forest for hours. It kept her sane. There were days when she couldn't find them, and those days...a bolt unscrewed in her mind. She'd walked for hours, as long as it took, to find her juniper berries. One day, she never came back.

After that, I wandered. I would travel from city to city, stealing and foraging for my food. People offered their homes to me or to find another home for me to live in, but I always declined. There was a black hole on the left side of my chest.

I stayed in that state for years. I didn't have anybody. One day, I was sneaking a roll from the market when a hand caught me. It wouldn't have been the first, but I hadn't been caught in years. I was angrier at breaking my streak than getting caught.

There was a large man, but he was hidden behind a black scarf around his head. A suit held his body together.

"You shouldn't be stealing," the man said, his voice deep, almost mechanical.

I smiled at him. "A hungry stomach ignores morals."

"Come with me."

I did. I was tired of asking questions, so I listened.

That was the day the League came to find me and that was the day I followed. It wasn't long until I was in a crowded room and I saw a pretty auburn girl with a smile that held the wonders of the world.

"I was alone," I said to Buddy after telling him my story. "Nothing more than that."

Buddy's quiet for a moment. "And yer gal, Mira?"

"She was my juniper berry."

"And nothin' more?"

"Loneliness has no preconceptions; it only knows itself. When you hide underneath the floorboards of a home, staring into darkness and shaking at every footstep above, you don't want love. You want a friend."

I forget sometimes. In fact, I forget all the time. Buddy doesn't understand life in the colonies. He only understands the fabricated life he was given.

Life was what his mama told him by the fire as she knit, or the smell of cookies baking in the oven as dad came home from work. Life was going to school and sleeping in the same bed overnight. Life was a perfect calamity.

The colonies were a nightmare compared to that. He doesn't understand. He will never understand.

He's fake.

He's not real.

He's somebody else, far away.

He's a manifestation of science, not of love.

Juniper berries float across my mind. Their rich scent tickles my nose, as does the scene of my nana scrubbing them into her swollen scalp.

"You'll see, niño," she'd mutter in her thick accent, rubbing and scrubbing. "I'll be beautiful."

I never told Mira where I was from. She told me her story the second night we met up in the library. She prodded for my story, dancing around it as she finished hers.

"What was your colony like?"

"Didn't have one."

"What about your family?"

"Didn't have one of those either."

She didn't ask much after that, but I always felt her gaze, watching, wondering…*who is Rollin?*

I couldn't answer her question myself.

Another vision emerges from the pool of darkness. It's Mira.

She had entered Chicago recently. No green-striped jacket adorns her back. Her crystal eyes hide fear underneath the proud irises, but I can see it nonetheless. She pushes through the crowd gathered on the sidewalk. I notice their stares. I see the judgment, the wonderment, the embarrassment. They think she's a Privy, with the way she's walking, the absence of a jacket, the healthy glow to her skin. No, she hasn't felt it yet, they thought. She doesn't know what it means to be desperate.

Claws grab at her. She freezes, squeezing her backpack around her.

"What are you doing in these parts, little Privy?" a gravely voice matches an equally disgusting man.

"Excuse me," she growls. "Did I look like I wanted a conversation?"

He snarls. "Go back to your nanny, Privy."

She pushes forward, but there's a jitter in her step, a flutter in her heartbeat. It thumps within the darkness, pulsing, pulsing, pulsing—

Then the memory floods back. Hands pull her into an alleyway, tearing her clothes off, biting at her skin and a flash of metal against her head and blood, blood EVERYWHERE—

Oh no, oh no, oh please no, it's happening again, help—HELP—

Dammit she's there, bleeding and the men and I can't help her, I can't—

I told her I would always be there to help, to talk to, whatever she needed and now she's, oh god please someone HELP HER—

My fists clench and screams are tearing through my throat and I can't breathe, I CAN'T BREATHE—

—SOMEONE HELP HER—

I thrash and kick because I have to help her, I have to, somehow, someway, but someone is holding me down and I can't get up HELP—DAMN YOU ALL—

"Rollin!" a voice shakes me away to a big dark face and those brown eyes and that southern drawl. "Welcome back."

MIRA

John and I are safe from harm, hidden in an abandoned building located in the deep south of the roach sector. He let me take the bedroom upstairs, but even still, I can hear him snoring peacefully on the couch in the other room. I stare at the wall beside my bed, and my mind drifting away to dark memories of the past…a time when I lost myself…

No rooster wakes me, not the glorious sunshine of a new day nor a dog nudging my foot nor the smell of a hot breakfast nor a kiss from a loved one nor a radio alarm nor anything slightly reminiscent of my past life.

The smell of rotting garbage wakes me.

The stench is unbearable. So much, in fact, it makes me vomit up an empty stomach. I never understood why that happens, but Rollin told me once that people are more likely to throw up on an empty stomach than a full one. I never believed him, but I'm starting to get the gist of the idea.

I push the lid away from the dumpster and clamber out, bits of my vomit still clinging to the strange jacket I put on last night. The green stripe glistens horridly in the early dawn.

My food stores ran out the day before I entered Chicago. I can't remember the last time I was hungry like this. The League fed us three times a day and every Leaguer had a personal snack stash in their room. They thought the extra calories were good so we could build up fat for the long journey. I stare down at my flat, hollow stomach. I wish I had indulged on a few more chocolate bars back then.

Even when I was traveling to Chicago, I never was this hungry. I rationed my food enough so I *didn't* get hungry. This is hunger. It's a crippling, gnawing carnivore in the pit of my stomach, tearing away the lining of my stomach to reach that precious fat my diet had previously allowed. It's not there, but it keeps digging anyway.

140

I stumble to the sidewalk, dragging a sleeping foot behind me. My eyes squint as the bright yellow hits my unaccustomed eyes. They were so used to tearing up at the smell of rotting food and seeing nothing. A dumpster does not allow plentiful lighting or a pleasant atmosphere. Go figure.

An elderly Hispanic woman wobbles past me. Rags cover her body, but she huddles into them nonetheless. A green-striped jacket adorns her feeble body and few hairs grace her tanned head. Dark slits of eyes stare accusingly from stooped brows. I touch her arm gently, but she yanks it away nonetheless, as though my touch was poison.

"What're you doing that for?" she growls.

"I'm sorry, ma'am," I look to my feet. All the books I had read with Rollin talked about servants looking to their feet whenever they'd been scolded.

"Ma'am?" her eyebrows furrow as she tries to see under the thin wisps of hair covering my face. "You think I'm some kind of Privy, do you?"

I shake my head, the social tiers confusing my weak mind. "Is there a shelter somewhere around here? Somewhere that gives food and a bed to sleep on?"

The woman blinks at me absently, her eyes wide in a mixture of shock and horror. "You talking about a whorehouse, are you?"

"No, no! A shelter for people who can't pay for food or a place to sleep."

The woman cackles madly, holding her sides painfully. "Oh, you're a mental one, you are! Just go in that alleyway there, dearie, if you're looking for somewhere to sleep eternally. They'll come to pick you up soon enough. Every day at midday, as always."

She hobbles away, still holding her sides, still laughing madly. Few others pass by, but none look at me. They keep their heads down, pushing their feet faster as they cross in front of me.

Do people here not have shelters? All the books Rollin and I had…well, there were always compassionate people. They would help the poor and they would hate to see any soul go hungry. There were always good Samaritans helping the poor so they could be happy in the afterlife. I thought…I'd hoped…

Oh, I don't know anything.

Did that woman…did she think I was…or was going to be a prostitute? What use is it now?

A young girl, no older than eight, stumbles on the sidewalk in front of the alleyway and collapses to the ground. People around her either step on her or walk around her. She clutches her nose, blood cascading from it. Tears stream from her eyes but no sobs shake her body.

I push through the people and help her to her feet. "Are you okay?"

She stays silent. I lead her to the alleyway I was before, escaping from the accusing eyes around. They stare at me as I help the limping girl sit on the ground.

"What are you doing?" She stares at me, holding her nose with her green-striped jacket. Red bleeds into the green.

"You fell down…I was only helping."

"If you're one of the whores," she curls into herself, fear bleeding her like a leech, "I don't do nothing…nothing to…I don't care if you helped me! I'm not going to—"

"Oh, no!" I gasp, rushing to the girl who shrinks away from me, hiding her tears in the jacket. "I would never ask you to do anything."

She peers from the jacket, sniffling softly. "You promise?"

"Pinky promise," I smile, holding my finger out.

She glances at it strangely, her eyes narrowing. "You're a strange lady."

Her jacket crinkles. Crusted dirt sprinkles from it. We sit in silence for a while longer, neither of us quite sure what to say.

"My name's Mira," I tell her. "I can help you find your mom, if you'd like."

"My mom? I don't have one of those."

I open my mouth to say something to her, but nothing comes out. I close my mouth and fold my knees to my chest. I know that the clones don't age, that this little girl has been little for more than ten years, but I thought they at least had families…where am I?

"Why do you talk so funny, lady?" she turns to me, pulling the jacket away from her nose for a moment. "I haven't heard no ladies talk like you before."

"I talk like you do."

"No, no…" she mutters. "You talk weird."

"Why do you say that?"

"You talk with no fear."

"You don't seem too afraid," I say.

"You learn to hide it. The crazy ones like the fear."

I sit with her for a while longer, watching the people pass by the alleyway. They don't peer in much, but when they do, I don't see fear on their faces, only confusion and lust.

"Is there a church around here?" I turn toward her, aware only now that I don't know her name. Even if I asked, I doubt she'd tell me.

"A what?" she asks, pulling the jacket away thick with blood.

"A church. You know, where the worshipers go and pray."

"I don't think we have one of those, lady," she stares at me, clambering to her feet, "but I have to go. The Privy market throws away the burnt bread about now. Bye, strange lady."

She disappears into the crowd on the sidewalk, which has grown larger during the time I spent with the girl. I sit in that alleyway for a while longer, thinking about the girl and the old woman and all things wrong with this damned city.

I would have sat there the entire day, if it had been up to me. I had no desire to discover more things wrong with the city, but my stomach had different plans. I eventually pull myself from my asphalt seat and merge myself into the crowd. My stomach growls at them, partially impartial and partially upset at those with round stomachs and fat-flushed faces.

People around me shove as I slow to a pace they are not accustomed to. Curses under the breath are frequent as well. I walk with the crowd for hours, looking for scraps of food in garbage cans or on the ground, but I find nothing. I have no clue where I am or where I am going, but that matters little as long as I find food by the end.

A large truck passes by on the street, the first I've seen. I force my eyes to the ground and don't look at the cars for a while longer. In the bed of the truck were bodies upon bodies, all wearing the same green-striped jacket.

The crowd I march with moves in a steady rhythm. Few people break away from it and even fewer join in. We left the center of the city long ago. We're in a distant part of Chicago now. Occasionally, a person hidden amongst the buildings will cry out or scream or a gun will sound, but no one seems to flinch except me.

Every now and then, a person shouts out "Calamity for sale!" and those are the times when the most people leave the crowd. They flock to the person who cried and jut their hands out with cards in them, all with a few green bars across.

We pass these people quickly. Not many stores grace the buildings here as they had in the larger section of the city. Cars are few and far between.

I've been walking for a long while, so long in fact that my legs have gone numb and the movement of putting one foot in front of another has become mechanical, almost automatic. I've stopped feeling or thinking much at all, but only walking, my stomach gnawing away and my sanity with it as well. Only the strange cars passing by with their stranger passengers keep my mind alert.

I push ahead, following the people in front of me until they leave and then I follow their replacements. I see this obscure city and the destruction many leave behind.

People lie dying in the alleyways. Trucks stop, workers fly into these alleyways and carry the deceased into the bed of the truck, some still groaning. Most don't put up a fight. They're thrown on top of bodies upon bodies, no longer people. If they don't die from their wounds or disease, they will soon die from suffocation as bodies are stacked on top of them. A truck passed by and an arm was sticking from the mess of bodies, reaching for the sky as though there was a god. There aren't churches here anyway.

At some point, the cars return in more frequent numbers, fewer trucks pass by with bodies piled within, fewer people scream from the alleyways and fewer gunshots sound. There are these strangely dressed Oddities walking about with an air of dignity about them. I hear people mutter "piece of shit Wardens" under their breath. Regardless, they still walk straight, hide their wounds and avert their glances.

One of these Wardens snatches an Oddity walking beside me earlier, curses "damn roach" and throws him to the ground, kicking him repeatedly, all while the man cries, "I didn't know she was a Privy, I swear I didn't! She was asking for it. She was walking on the sidewalks, she was—"

The Warden kicks the man in the head one last time, and he stops his begging. He's pulled into a car and driven away. Others beside me whisper, "He's going to the suburbs, damn fool."

Life continued like this for two days.

Two days without food, without shelter, and without sanity. The only water I found was various puddles on the ground after it rained. I knelt to the ground, pressed my lips against the murky water, and slurped eagerly. Keeping the water down was difficult.

I tried begging for food, water, anything—but people only spit on me and told me to die. Walking became too strenuous without the food to fuel it. I tried eating some of the garbage even—banana peels, the leftover gunk at the end of a bottle, or some toothpaste thrown away with a little left— but all of it only made me vomit in the end.

Two days my life went like this.

I survived as an exoskeleton and nothing else.

Every night, I curled up in the dumpster again, afraid to sleep in the alleyways where predators could easily grab hold of me. I saw it happen on the second day. The woman was napping when a man strolled into the alleyway and began ripping her clothes off. Her screams echoed through the city, but no one stopped to help her.

Dawn ripples against the bleak gray sky. My head swarms with the effort of climbing out of the dumpster, but I do so anyway. I have to try. Maybe today I can find some of the burnt bread that little girl was talking about.

My arms fail under me and I collapse to the ground, crying out as I do so. I hold my stomach, the pain like digesting a thousand knives. At least that would be something. My stomach feels the equivalent to a shriveled peanut, but my hunger is a thousand times that size.

The world goes dark as my eyes drift closed. This is where I will die, lying on the cold asphalt, the early sun gracing my skin, with the League's mission incomplete, and my duty failed.

That's when gentle fingers shake my shoulders and my eyes flutter open to a man hovering above me.

My eyes go wide as this man with a tight, black cap with beady eyes peering from under the brim smiles at me. He wears all black besides the standard Oddity jacket.

"Please, leave me alone," I stammer out. "I don't have anything."

"Let me help you up," he holds his hands out to me. "You look hungry."

My stomach growls as an answer and my hands reach out to him without thinking first. The prospect of food is all it takes for my wits to leave me.

"Do you have to bed to sleep in at night? Food to eat?" he asks gently, holding me up.

"No, I don't."

"I can provide that for you. I have a shop down the street a little. I sell Clam there and—"

"Clam?" I look at him a moment.

"Calamity, you know," he says. "The drug?"

"Oh, yes," I lie, "I remember. The hunger's going to my head."

"I sell Clam there," he continues without acknowledgement, "and sometimes the men like to have some fun before they pass out. Your job would be to…please them, and in exchange you'd receive food—three meals a day—a warm bed to sleep in at night, a—"

I freeze, the blood running cold in my veins. "I'm no prostitute."

He shrugs his shoulders. "Think of it more as a mistress."

I shake my head, leaving his grasp and stepping away from him. "I—I can't."

But when I step away the world spins from the hunger and I throw my arms out and he catches me.

"You're starving. You need some food."

"I—I don't know," I stammer out, ashamed of myself, of everything, but I'm hungry, so goddamn hungry I can't feel my morals shaming me.

"C'mon," he holds out a hand. "Let's get you something to eat."

My mouth waters at the thought, and dammit, I can't resist. I'm sorry. I'm sorry, but I can't resist. I take his hand and he leads me through the streets. His hands are soft and warm, like hot cookies from the oven.

People pass by us on either side, parting their way as we move back the way I had originally come from. Some of them actually smile at us while others laugh and throw empty little bottles at us. The man leading me doesn't think much of it; he only smiles back at them and continues on.

He stops at a door and leads me into a store. A single counter stands in the tiny shop. A man stands behind it with a thousand tiny bottles stacked behind him in various boxes. They all contain the same milky liquid inside, quivering slightly as our footsteps rock the floorboards beneath them. Alone on the counter sits a dish of lemon drops.

"This is my shop," he announces and then turns to the man behind a counter. "We've got a new one."

The man behind the counter smiles. "Who's going to be the first to try her out?"

The man leading me ignores him and continues on through the shop to a set of stairs hidden behind a wall. He leads me up them, partially carrying me because I'm so weak. Smoke hangs in a cloud on the upper floor.

"This is where you would be staying," he tells me.

At the top of the stairs, the length of the whorehouse is unveiled. Two scantily clad women lie lazily on couches, their eyes searching the length of me.

"A new one already?" one shouts. "We just lost her this morning."

I turn toward him. "What is she talking about?"

The man dismisses us with a wave of his hand and goes to another staircase. I follow him, or rather my nose follows him. I smell food. My stomach ignores my wits once more.

"The floor we were just on is where the business takes place," he explains. "Up here is where you would live."

A small room with three beds crammed together unveils itself to me. A table in the corner sits with three mismatching chairs beside it. The smells of sweat and smoke mix, spun around by a fan rotating at the top.

"Come, sit down," the man beckons to a chair. "I'll find you some food."

I listen to him and rest myself in an old lawn chair. It creaks as I sit, but holds my weight. The man disappears back down the stairs.

I stare at the room around me further. Wallpaper covers the walls in patches; tiny Hawaiian women with hula skirts cover a yellow background. Each bed has a different raggedy quilt on its mattress, which I see is no more than straw stuffed into a sheet.

At least it's something.

None of the beds have a pillow. Only one is made; the other two are a disheveled mess. Footsteps echo as the man comes up the stairs. He appears, a hot plate of food in his hands.

I devour the plate of food without a word, nearly choking on it in the process. Once the plate is cleared, I pick it up and lick the last remains of it. I ignore the questionable look from the man; I'd do anything to keep that carnivorous beast away from my stomach.

"You eat like you won't see another meal," he comments.

"Well, I don't know if I will," I push the plate toward him. "You eat fast or not at all."

He sighs. "If you stayed here, you wouldn't have to worry about that. You'd always have a meal and a bed to sleep in. All you'd have to do for me is please my customers any time they desire. The more you please, the more *you* are pleased."

"I—I don't know…" I sigh, staring at the empty plate. If I deny, I won't be seeing any empty plates, or any plate at all. I'll be hungry. "I don't even know your name."

"Jax," he smiles. "I forget the formalities sometimes."

"My name is Belle," I smile, thinking of it on the spot. The fewer people who know my real name, the better.

I stare at that empty plate, unable to pull my eyes away. Is this what the League wanted from me? To be a prostitute, unable to afford a meal any other way? Is this what justice is: sleeping around and barely scraping by?

"You'll be comfortable here, I promise," he says gently. "At first, you'll only have to serve a customer once a day. As you grow more accustomed, we'll adjust the schedule to you. If it gets to be too much, you can leave at any time."

"Any time?" I look at him.

It's the best thing I've got. I don't know the first damn thing about this cursed city. I don't know how to go about getting a job. I don't know where to get food. I don't know where to start getting money. You need a house to get a job and you need a job to get a house.

I think of Rollin. The League told me someone would come after me to give me further instructions, and who else would it be besides Rollin? He's the only Leaguer left. Is he close behind me, or still in the headquarters at the League? What would he say if he came here to find me a prostitute?

Well, if I don't accept, he'll more likely find me in the alleyway outside, dead from starvation. Which would he prefer?

"Jax," I mutter out, barely a whisper. He leans forward in anticipation, his chest bumping into the empty plate and I know it, I know I have to. "I'll do it. I will."

He nearly jumps from his seat, a smile on his face so wide it'd cross a chasm. He folds his hands together and takes the empty plate in his hands. It'll be the first, the first plate of many.

"As a thank-you, I'll give you a bottle of Clam for free," he fishes in his pocket and procures a tiny bottle like the thousand on the first floor. "Come meet the other girls."

He hands me the bottle and I follow him downstairs. I slip the bottle into my pocket, saving whatever is inside for later. We reach the last step and I find the two women, still scantily clad, still sitting where we left them minutes ago.

"This is Yorry," he gestures to the first woman. She is thin as wire with hair blacker than night. Her skin is as porcelain as mine. She wears white lace lingerie and sucks on a cherry stem. "This is Estelle." Estelle is a larger woman wearing a costume reminiscent of a sailor's. Dark brown curls adorn her head. She may be larger than Yorry or me, but she is as beautiful as either of us.

Both Yorry and Estelle greet me casually with a wave of their hand before going back to primping themselves.

"Some customers will be arriving shortly," Jax explains. "Otherwise the girls wouldn't be dressed so provocatively. Oh, that reminds me."

Jax disappears behind a curtain and reveals a black and pink lingerie set. "You better get dressed. The rush will be coming soon."

I take the scraps of clothing and go behind the same curtain Jax retrieved them from. The jeans that stayed on me for weeks fall off, as does the roach jacket. I slip into the underwear. Shivers attack my skin.

While I change, I hear Yorry begin to talk. "She has virgin skin, Jax. I know it. No man has touched her before. You sure you want one of those?"

"I know," Jax says, "that's *why* I want her."

I finish dressing and pull the curtain away. My old bundle of clothes is in my arms. The tiny bottle of what Jax called Clam is in my hand.

"You have a beautiful body," the larger woman, Estelle says. "Do you take only men, or women too?"

"Well…uh…" I stammer, holding my clothes close, my feet burning to sprint down the stairs.

"Leave her alone, Estelle," Jax snaps at her. "Don't scare her off."

I swirl the milky contents in the bottle around, staring at it as the others stare at me.

"You're supposed to drink it," Yorry laughs.

I stay silent as I snap the cap off the bottle. My fingers shake as I do, the cap tumbling from my hand and to the floor. I put the bottle to my lips and swallow the contents and…warm ice fills my veins…taking away everything…the bad memories of hunger…of my travels…

The bottle drops from my hands and clatters onto the floor. "What…what is in that?"

Yorry smiles and picks up the bottle. "It's Calamity, the best damn thing this city has to offer, and we can have as much as we want."

I collapse on the couches, the cushions enveloping me in their soft, plushness and I feel absolutely *wonderful*. Everything slips from my head and I'm empty, complete empty, staring up at the ceiling and the fan going around and around—

"Belle, are you ready for your first one?" Jax calls from downstairs.

"Oh, I'm ready," I smile and giggle, pulling the lingerie to expose myself. Warmth spreads across my veins, enveloping me in a luscious glow and everything, everything is more *wonderful* than I could ever ask.

The girls laugh as the man comes upstairs. He lies across me and I lose myself.

Everything is *wonderful*.

My life continues like this for a long, long time.

Months go by, and still no word from the League, no Rollin, and no way to contact them.

Nothing changes.

Nothing moves.

Everything stops.

For a while, I'm okay with this.

I breathe.

I eat.

I sleep.

I survive.

That's all I need for a while.

Then I need more.

I stayed at Jax's shop for two months. What happened during those days, I couldn't say. My life has been a constant juggle of paying my dues to the shop and drifting out of my Clam sleep enough to complete those dues. It has been a cycle that has never ended and an ending that has never cycled.

I became addicted to Clam. It wasn't hard. The shop held a seemingly infinite supply of the drug. Every time I tried to quit, I fell into a deep depression that hinted at suicide. Every time I felt the urge to fly away, which was quite often, I went downstairs to Tommy, the store clerk, and he gave me one. He didn't care, as long as I showed him my chest. The more I let Tommy do to me, the more perks I gained while he was the clerk.

I...I don't know what happened during those two months. I remember lots of men tearing my lingerie off, sleeping, eating, laughing with Yorry and Estelle, turning away Estelle's midnight touches and then accepting them when she offered me some of her meals in exchange.

That continued for a while, and it was beneficial for us both. Estelle got the pleasure she didn't receive from the men and I got the food my stomach always craved. Three meals a deal was sufficient, but after wandering hungry for three days, my body always desired more. As my body gave a healthy glow, Estelle shrunk into herself and lost all the weight that had made her special. Our business deal didn't last long. We found Estelle in the alleyway outside two weeks later, flayed alive.

Jax suspected it was only a vengeful Privy looking for some midnight fun. Yorry and I thought differently. We knew that man Estelle had refused wasn't too happy about it. His pants were bulging and like many others who came in, he had a preference for larger women—though by that time she wasn't much larger than us—and Estelle was picky. She didn't take everyone.

After her, Janice came. She was quiet at first, as I was, but she soon opened up. More men fancied her, but Yorry and I fancied her less. We missed Estelle, but more so, we missed the extra meals.

Time didn't seem to move. Nights rolled into midnights into mornings into afternoons into evenings over and over again. Nothing changed. Nothing stayed the same. My senses turned off, but now I've awoken. My memories are returning. My morals, my conscience, has returned, and damn, it is relentless.

Rollin, my Rollin, my friend, my always faithful friend. If only…if you saw me now, you'd be ashamed. I'm ashamed, Rollin, but I was scared and confused and hungry and alone and I didn't know what to do. I didn't know, Rollin.

I did what was easiest, and what is easy isn't always right. My choice wasn't right. It was wrong. I wish I'd worked hard, found a real job, found some food, found something.

I don't know where you are or what you think has happened to me, but I'm sure death would have been a more noble cause than this. You probably think I'm dead. For the last two months, I *was* dead. Nothing stirred inside me for a long time.

My body was robotic. It learned the routine. It washed and repeated until I'd washed it so much there wasn't anything left to wash. Judge me all you want. I can't turn back time. The hands will keep ticking. Rollin, I've only now awoken from this dizzy dream. I've tried to ease off the addiction, to stop taking so much Clam but then I think of you and how I'll never get to see you again and how goddamn awful everything is and—

When these thoughts become too much, I take the Clam and everything, everything is okay then. The thoughts go away. My feelings disappear, leaving me alone, floating through the world on a cloud made of cotton candy.

I was supposed to come here to save the colonies, to do my duty that I agreed to when those men came to my door and took me away. I came here to exterminate the clones, but I only exterminated myself.

Men come and go in the night. I've stopped keeping track. They undress me, penetrate me, finish themselves, and then they're on their pretty little way. I make the noises. I move with them. I do what's necessary or they'll complain. I stop feeling. I only do.

It's awful, I know, but you don't understand, Rollin. If you were here, you'd understand. This world is so goddamn awful, it's so…twisted. I understand why they said Chicago was the worst off. People consider the worst atrocities everyday business here. Murder is casual. Suicide is common. A person who isn't addicted is an outsider.

This city is so fucked up I can't tell where it began.

I didn't realize it when I came here. I didn't realize it at all. I didn't understand why the commanders told us to be afraid. I didn't understand why this city was the worst.

Now I do.

Rollin, I hope you forgive me, wherever you are. I know you aren't hearing this or know what has happened to me or what I've done, but someday you might, and I hope you'll understand and forgive me then.

I'm letting myself think about all of this for the first time in a while. Usually, when these thoughts come to my head, about how fucked up my life is and how much I fucked up the League's mission, I take Clam and everything's okay.

I can't do that anymore.

I've committed myself to stopping. I'm going cold turkey, and today marks the first day. I will beat the depression. I won't fall into the addiction once more.

It's dawn now. Two months have come and gone and here I sit in bed, snores echoing softly as dawn breaks through the windows. I haven't woken up at dawn in months.

I leave Yorry and Janice to their slumbers and climb from my covers. I'm naked. The other woman sleep the same way. At first it made me uncomfortable, but after being naked so much of the time, wearing clothes became the uncomfortable thing.

It's strange how those things happen, isn't it?

I don't bother to dress as I climb down the stairs to the lower floor. Pastries and fruit are out on the table for us. I bite into them, savoring the chill that's usually gone by the time we reach them at noon.

In the corner of the room sits a tin box piled high with today's supply of Clam. I avert my eyes, focusing on the rich cream flowing from the flaky Danish pastry, but my eyes find the bottles once more. Footsteps coming upstairs shake the floor, making the bottles sing a familiar jingle.

Jax's familiar black cap appears first, followed by those beady little eyes. His face lights in surprise, but not at my naked body. No, he's seen it enough to have grown tired of it. The excitement of surprise has long since faded from him. Yorry says he's been in this business longer than anyone.

"Up so early?" he asks, moving about the room and tidying up from last night's rush.

"The birds woke me," I mutter sleepily.

He gives me a queer look. "Birds? I think you've forgotten we're in a city, dear."

It was the first excuse that came to mind, an excuse reminiscent of the olden days, when there really were birds that woke me up in the colonies, and even sometimes at the League headquarters. Those mornings were rare, but they were beautiful all the same.

I used to run to Rollin's room and shake him awake. He'd swat at me like a fly, grumbling about some dream he was having. He claimed he never was a morning person and didn't care for birds anyway.

"I don't remember you having too many people last night," Jax says, straightening the pillows on the couches. "Not any more than usual."

My sleeplessness didn't arise from birds. My withdrawal spurred it. I lay awake all last night, my mouth watering at the thought of the sweet taste of Clam running down my throat. It took every ounce of courage and strength to not run down a flight of stairs and fly away.

"I can leave any time I want, right?" I ask quietly, my voice taken away by the pain, the desperation, the longing.

He stops fluffing the pillows and turns to me, concern creasing his brow. "Are you thinking about going, Belle? I saw you were acting strange, but I didn't know—"

"No, no," I stammer out, "just a fleeting thought, that's all."

I shake my head, returning to my Danish and devouring it heartily. Cream flows down my chin as warm hues of red and orange break through the glass window, disrupting the cold chill of the morning. Goosebumps cover my skin, but I refrain from finding a blanket. The chill will take my mind off of…it.

"Do you expect lots of customers today?" I ask, watching him sweep up the floor.

"As busy as any other day," he laughs.

I never knew that Jax woke up every morning to clean up like this. I always thought Tommy did or another one of the clerks. I always thought Jax was too busy or sleeping instead. He's up as late as us girls.

I finish the last of my breakfast, stuffing the cream-filled bread into my mouth. The sweet cream runs down my throat and I smile satisfactorily. It takes the edge away, the longing deep in my chest for Clam, to feel happy, to not feel like this.

"You should get some sleep, Belle," Jax comes and takes my hands. "You'll be tired later and you need to…"

"I know," I whisper. "I was hungry, that's all."

The reds and oranges have faded away to a bright sunlight that streams through the glass, the color of melting lemon drops. It breaks across the floor and casts Jax in a halo. It's too bright. I can't look at him.

He wraps his arms around my waist and holds me tight. His touch isn't one of lust but one of concern.

"Get some sleep," he holds me tightly, and for the first time since I stopped taking Clam, I feel…not terrible. He…cares. The feeling is so foreign it took me a second to recognize it.

"Okay, I'm going upstairs," I say. "Thank you, Jax."

Jax kisses me on the forehead gently and sends me on my way. I make my way up the stairs and hide under my covers, melting the goosebumps away.

Yorry stirs beside me, turning over in her sleep as her eyes flutter open.

"Hey, Belle," she smiles. "I thought I heard you up."

"I can't sleep. The birds woke me."

"There's no birds here," she giggles. "It's the Clam, Mira. I saw you refuse Janice when she offered you some last night. You're trying to get off it?"

"Yeah, I'm trying," I mutter, "the best I can. You should get some sleep."

She turns over without another word, laughing about birds under her breath.

There were birds one time. In the colonies, at the mansion with Charlotte sleeping in the room next to me, the birds would chirp and stir me awake. I'd smile and drift back to sleep.

"The birds woke me."

When Yorry finally wakes, it's near midday. We were all up late last night so I don't blame her. There was quite the rush last night. She throws her arms out above her, stretching as she yawns loudly. Janice grumbles and turns over. I smile at Yorry as her eyes meet mine.

"Didn't you sleep at all?"

"No, not really," I mutter. "I couldn't, and I wasn't very tired anyway."

She shakes her head. "If you say so."

Pulling the covers away, her naked body is revealed. It doesn't bother either of us. We're so used to seeing naked bodies around us that whenever Jax comes upstairs to check on us, his clothed body almost makes us uncomfortable. He joins in the fun sometimes, but only rarely.

"I have other things that pleasure me," he said once.

Yorry jogs down the stairs and returns with a plate of breakfast. She sits at the small table across the room and invites me to join her. I crawl from my covers and sit beside her.

"I had the strangest dream last night," she says, covering her mouth with her hand. A half eaten cream-filled Danish sits in her hand.

"What was it about?"

"You were there, Belle. We went on a walk and passed by this store...oh, I forget what it's called now, but we went inside and asked to work there. They agreed and we left this place. We left it for good."

She goes back to her pastry for a while as Janice stirs and calls out in her sleep. She does that frequently. She has nightmares about what happens here and thrashes around. I used to have nightmares, but then the Clam took over and it stopped.

"Why don't we?" I ask, watching her reaction.

She pauses mid-bite and stares at me. Her eyes blink absently as she chews methodically. She doesn't say anything for a few moments, only chews and swallows, chews and swallows.

"What?" she whispers, glancing behind her as though Jax had heard every word we had said.

"We wouldn't have to do this anymore," I say. "We could have lives, Yorry. We could find a place to work at and another place to live at. We wouldn't have to live like this anymore. We could—"

"We have everything we need here, Belle."

"I'm tired of spreading my legs to earn my meals."

She grimaces, half of her wanting to bend to the truth. "We have food and a bed to sleep in…all we have to do is have sex with men who don't have half their wits with them anyway."

"Don't you get tired of it? I get sore, Yorry, and half the time it hurts more than anything. The men that come through those doors are, more often than not, twice our age. If I see one more tiny, wrinkled—"

"You're right!" she exclaims, squeezing her eyes as though she doesn't want to believe it herself. "You're right, Belle. I'm tired of it, and I've been here twice as long as you."

I smile warmly and steal a grape from her plate. "When I went on a walk the other day, I saw a store was looking for more roaches to work. It's right down the street. We could go right now if we wanted to."

"Which store?"

"Sip-and-Sleep."

She groans and throws her head back. "Out of all the stores, you had to find that one? God, you know how much I hate that store. It's a hellhole of Privies there."

"It's not so bad. We could make shakes and cookies all day. We would have to serve the occasional asshole, but how's that any different than what we do here?"

She eats the last of the fruit on her plate with a frown. We don't get fruit too often here, and when we do, we know it's Jax's way of saying thanks. Men were coming in right after another, nonstop until hours past midnight. Fruit is a luxury we don't often get.

I reach across the table and take her hand in my own. She smiles and squeezes it gently.

"Let's get dressed and go check it out," she says.

Inside the tiny table between the beds, I find my old clothes. I haven't worn them since I first came here, two months ago. Yorry finds clothes similar to mine, ones she first wore here half a year ago.

When Jax found Yorry, she was hours away from dying. He offered her the same business proposition as he did to me, and it's hard for a desperate soul not to agree with the worst. More often than not, it's better off than what was before.

Estelle was there even before Yorry was, months even. Yorry says Estelle used to be skinny, but when she saw that some of the men preferred larger girls, well, she had quite the time indulging on all the sweets Jax would give her.

The third girl, the one I replaced, was named Heidi. She had been there for years. No other girl had lasted as long as she did. Even Jax couldn't remember when she first began. The years were growing on her and the other girls were wondering when her time would run up.

A few weeks later, she was found hanging from the ceiling pipes from a noose made of the bed sheets. That answered their questions.

Nobody lasts long in this business. We'll be lucky if we make it out alive.

I glance over to Janice still dozing away under her covers, thrashing away and screaming out occasionally. She won't make it long. A man will come along, take her to the alleyway, and finish her like Estelle.

I remember going to the alleyway with Yorry. There was Estelle. Flayed alive, guts pulled from the stomach and the blood used to write a message, the simplest message:

THE END IS COMING

I hope it is. I can't stand much more of this life.

Once Yorry and I are dressed, we leave the screaming Janice to her problems and descend down the first flight of stairs. We're almost there. We've almost reached freedom.

Our footsteps are meticulous, but they still seem to clap against the walls, proclaiming our decision to Jax. The clothes on our back are awkward and uncomfortable, shuffling in our march. Yorry files behind me, peeking above my head like we're two children sneaking out after dark.

I inch around the corner to see Jax lounging on the couches, a fat cigar smoking in his hand. He twirls it between his fingers, letting loose a long drag of smoke. He leans his head back on the couch, our arrival unnoticed.

"Jax," the word squeaks from my mouth, "how's the cigar?"

The words seem foreign coming from me, and Jax notices it. He looks us both up and down, giving us a quizzical look.

"What are you ladies all dressed up for? Why don't you grab a bottle of Clam from over there and fly away with me?"

"We're just going for a walk," Yorry stammers, folding her hands in front of her like it's the only thing keeping her from springing out the room. "It's such a beautiful day."

"Yes, beautiful…" Jax mutters, taking a drag on his cigar. "What's going on, ladies?"

We inch a few steps forward, sensing the tension in the room, realizing our narrowing window of escape.

I couldn't say why we're afraid of Jax; he's been nothing but nice to both of us. Not one incident has led us to fear him, but a level of intimidation comes with a man like Jax. He looks at you like his property and less of a person. His eyes narrow when something isn't right.

Yorry and I remember what he did to the man who murdered Estelle. There wasn't anything left of the man for them to collect the next day. He's a man you want to like you.

"We're—"

"We're quitting, Jax," Yorry blurts out, stepping in front of me. "We're going to look for a job."

Jax doesn't say anything for a long while, almost so long that I don't think he'll answer at all. He pulls his cigar to his lips three, four times, each time taking a slow drag, savoring the smoke until it pours from his lungs. His eyes flick between us and nowhere else.

"You have a job," he growls.

"I'm sorry, Jax, but—" I start, stepping forward.

"Shut up!" he screams, pulling his cigar to his mouth and dammit, I can see his face growing red and that vein on his forehead bulging and—

"No," I say. "We're leaving, and there's nothing more to it. You're just going to have to find more girls. You said we could leave any time."

He stands to his feet, growing more and more red. "You're not leaving."

I step toward him, silent, but knowledgeable that I have the strength to keep walking past him and through the door. For the first time in months, I remember.

Anything for the mission. Anything for the League.

His face flips from stoic to furious in a millisecond—his arms twitch from their customary spot by his side and snatch my arm in an iron grip—his fingernails dig into my skin in—blood teardrops appear—he takes his cigar from his mouth, carefully, like he's savoring it—he presses it into my arm—I cry out, tears spring my eyes—Yorry's scream echoes my own.

I yank my arm away—fingers curling and my fist clenches—pulling it back—*oomph*—the crunch of my fist on his cheek—he cries out in pain and collapses against the coffee table, groaning in pain and clutching his cheek.

"I'm done being your sex toy, you vile bastard," I push through clenched teeth, anger igniting me as I hold my burning arm. "I'm not yours to sell anymore."

I land a kick into his side, forcing him to turn over and retch his stomach. I feel Yorry's hand find my own and we sprint from the store, our feet clapping against the floorboards for the first time since we came here, announcing our escape, announcing our freedom. Tommy gives us a longing look as we run, his attention more focused on our bodies than our intentions.

Sip-and-Sleep happily gives us positions at its store. For the first few nights, we sleep inside dumpsters, as I had months ago.

Time changes, but the world doesn't.

Yorry almost gives up hope. She is moments away from walking away and returning to Jax after only a few nights on the streets.

"Nothing is worse than living in a dumpster," she screams. "I can't live on the streets again! I can't."

I ask her for one more day, and she gives it to me. We find an apartment about a thirty-minute walk away from Sip-and-Sleep, but we can afford it with our small paychecks. The ceiling drips water onto our straw beds, but it is enough. We can live without Jax and with dignity. I can live one step closer to the mission, whatever that is. No one has come for me yet, and I have long given up hope that they would.

This is our life, and we enjoy it far more than before. We are away from Jax, from Tommy and Janice and the ghosts of those who never escaped like we did. We make our own money, buy our own food, and do what we want to with what is between our legs. No one owns us. We are free.

Neither of us mind the work. It is better than having unwanted sex twenty times a day. It is better than sleeping during the day and working during the night. It is better than being a lady of the night.

It is only two weeks into this new life when we first hear of the newest scandal. Yorry is insistent on checking out the hospital where the pair of men, a Privy and a roach, murdered a Privy woman. I promise to go with her, but only because I don't feel like walking home alone in the dark.

The crowd is thick, but the night is thicker and dark as blood.

ROLLIN

My eyes drift open slowly, ignoring the voice, ignoring everything. A bright light blinds me and I quickly close them, shielding myself from reality. Before, it was so…oh, I can't remember it, but I remember the feeling. She was there. Mira.

The street has vanished; a disgusting room surrounds me and Buddy's face looms above.

"Yer awake," he says. His once vibrant voice has seemingly lost its luster.

Buddy's weak smile stretches taunt across his dark face. I close my eyes again. Pain stretches a dull hum across my muscles. I try to ignore it. It doesn't work very well.

"Mah friend, yer gettin' better," Buddy struggles to keep his smile up, his voice weak, his eyes lackluster. "Every day, yer gettin' better."

"How long have I been asleep?"

Buddy looks away. "Rollin, ah don't think—"

"How long?" I growl, my fists clenching, my knuckles turning whiter than his eyeballs.

"Two weeks."

"Two weeks!" I exclaim, trying to pull myself to a sitting position, but I can't, I'm too weak, I'm still hurt. "We've got to go—"

"Woah, woah," Buddy pushes me down gently. "Yer barely fit to be traipsin' 'round the city. Yuh just get better, mah friend."

"I don't care," I resist against his arm but it's no use, he's too strong and I, I'm too weak and—

"What yuh in a rush for?" he pulls back his arm softly, his eyes tired and weak and he collapses back in the chair. "Do yuh 'member what happened 'fore?"

I close my eyes. Get me away from it all. "I remember."

"Then where yuh goin'? Yuh ain't got no place to go, not no more."

"I know," I whisper. "I forgot for a second there."

Silence leaves us mute for a moment.

"Marco's cookin' us up somethin'. We thought yuh'd be hungry after only gettin' yer nutrition through Clam—"

"You put me on Clam for that entire time?"

Buddy looks down, the words like daggers to his soft skin. "Yessir. There wasn't no other way."

"You drugged me for two weeks?"

Buddy holds his hands, trying to keep me from sitting up again but it doesn't work, it doesn't work. "We had to! Ain't no other drug as cheap and plentiful as Clam, ah tell yuh. We gave yuh small doses, just enough to keep yuh knocked out."

"But *why*—?"

"Yuh was dyin'," Buddy says softly, his eyes melting like lemon drops in the sun. "Yuh was losin' too much blood and we didn't know what to do so we had to trick yuh body to forget it was dyin' and it worked, but—"

"I was dying?" I ask, collapsing into the bed and the pain burns at my muscle but I ignore it, like always. Buddy's frantic, clutching a pillow between his hands and staring at me with tears pricking in his eyes, as if me almost dying was worse for him than...well, than murdering her.

"Yuh was! Ah can't believe yuh made it as far as yuh did comin' out. Yuh was bleedin' from yer stomach and yer bones weren't set right and—"

"Thank you," I interrupt. "I don't know how I can thank you, Buddy."

Buddy relaxes a bit at this. "Ah'm a man of God. If ah can do right in the world, ah'm only doin' mah duty for Him."

"Well, thank him for me, will you?"

Buddy gives me a half smile, his hand twitching to the Bible on the coffee table like a reflex. "Ah prayed fer yuh every day, ah did. Ah put mah cross 'round yuh and prayed yuh'd make it through, ah swear it. Marco called me crazy but it worked. Yessir, it did."

The scent of food cooking drifts from the kitchen. I inhale deeply, savoring the rich aroma.

"What's that smell?" Buddy cocks his head, his eyes watering.

"It's juniper," I smile. "Marco's using juniper berries."

"Juniper?"

"An old scent...that's all, like the cinnamon your mama used to bake with."

"Juniper...ah don't think it. It don't even grow in Chicago, not nowhere near here."

Buddy's eyes hold my gaze for a few moments longer, the dark brown of his skin dull and worn, like old leather shoes. Bags hang from his eyes and I notice he's still wearing the same clothes he was when we left the hospital.

He peels himself away from me and drags himself to the kitchen, lured by the scent of juniper. It *is* juniper. It has to be. Muffled argument finds my ears and I stare ahead, aware of my surroundings for the first time

I lie on a couch, the cushion ripped apart as though a rabid dog had run rampant through the small room. Tattered wallpaper dangles from the plastered walls in shreds. The sunflowers that used to be cheerful are now dying, hanging from the walls and reaching toward me. Their death ferments the air. Dirt covers the floor. It creates hills and valleys, unveiling the destroyed floorboards underneath. Insects squirm in the filth.

I turn my head away, trying to ignore the disgusting turn of events. If only I was on Calamity now...I wish I was. I wish more than anything that I was.

I sink back into the couch, letting the cushions take my head away. I close my eyes and try to drift away, but I can't. Dreams won't rescue me this time. My body has had too much sleep in the past two weeks, and the chatter coming from the kitchen is noise drilling in my ear.

Buddy and Marco emerge from the kitchen, three steaming bowls of potatoes and chicken between the two of them. He hands one to me and I begin to devour it eagerly. Sweet juices run from my mouth and drip down my chin, but I could care less. I can't remember the last time I had a hot meal.

"Uh, Rollin..." Buddy trails off, staring into his untouched meal, "ah was wonderin' if yuh could tell us a bit more 'bout yerself."

I put my fork down, staring at them curiously. "Why's that?"

"Well, ah was just thinkin' earlier. Ah've spent so much time with yuh and ah still ain't gotta clue where yuh came from or where...*she* came from."

"I told you, Buddy. I came from St. Louis to find Mira."

Buddy shakes his head. "All the way fer her? She ain't family, Rollin."

I groan. "Are you going to go on about that again?"

His eyebrows furrow, his eyes dismal and watering at the corners. "What're yuh talkin' 'bout? Ah've never brought this up 'fore now."

I stare at them a second, my brain whirling, trying and trying and *dammit* I'm trying but I did tell him. We had a conversation about juniper berries and how Mira was my juniper—

But he didn't remember what juniper berries were. He asked about them earlier and—

"It must have been a dream..." I mutter, "I'm sorry."

"Ah shouldn't have brought it up," he whispers, placing his uneaten meal on the ground beside him. "Ah'm sorry."

"It's nothing too exciting," I explain quickly, watching his hung head.

"Mira left for Chicago and I didn't hear from her for months. One day, I decided to go after her. She was my only family and I couldn't, I wouldn't let that slip away…"

"Ah understand," Buddy nods, still not looking. "Ah had a fella like that down in Texas. He was an elderly man and his body knew it. One day, he was climbin' a hill and tumbled right down, that he did. Ah found him at the bottom of the hill, bruised and mangled, vultures hoverin' above like they was waitin' for him to die. Those birds can sense it, ah know.

"After that, ah traveled up here fer the first time. Ah stopped in a few cities, St. Louis bein' one of 'em. Right fine city, ah'll be damned. Ah made mah way to Chicago through the dirt and dust. That's where ah first became a Privy, damn me if ah'm lyin'.'"

"How'd you become a Privilege if you were new to the city?" I ask, digging into my half-eaten meal. I know the clones know nothing of the League and don't remember the nuclear world wars years ago, or even that they once were clones. It's interesting to see what Buddy believes to be true.

"They ran mah records. Ah didn't know shit 'bout the city 'fore ah came in, but ah told 'em at the gates to look me up. As yuh know, every city runs their government differently, so ain't two cities alike in how they treat travelers. The other cities had me down, all right. Ah was a pretty uppity citizen, if yuh ask me. Ah had money, mostly from mah friend, the old man," Buddy looked down forlornly, moving his meat around with a fork.

"Did you leave once you got here?" I stare him down.

"Oh yes," he mutters, "ah couldn't sit still. Ah was here fer barely two weeks 'fore ah took off 'gain. The other Privies didn't like me. They didn't like mah travelin' blood. Said it was too flighty, they did. Ah didn't care much fer 'em anyway, so ah left.

"Ah did a lot of roamin', let me tell yuh. Ah can proudly say ah've been to all the damn states in this godfersaken country. Ah've seen lots of destruction and not a lot of prosperity. This city ain't the worst. Ah've seen chaos so crazy, people was slittin' their own throats to escape from it all.

"Ah did a lot of things ah wasn't too proud of. The last straw was…killin' someone. Ain't no one deserve a killin'. Ah made mahself go home after that. There wasn't no place left in Texas fer me, so ah went to Chicago. It was the only city that didn't drive me crazy while ah was there. Ah had this plan of settin' up some sorta shelter fer the Oddities since lots of 'em don't have much. 'Fore ah could get to it, yuh found me, Rollin.

"Ah was determined to repent myself. Ah was sure ah would never fall into the devil's traps again. Damn me if ah was wrong, ah said. But ah was wrong. Look at me now. Ah've gone and killed some more. Ain't nothin' ah can promise to the Lord that ah won't break, I guess…"

Silence holds the air for a few moments longer. Not even our forks move. Marco stares ahead frozen, his eyes glazed over. I can only assume he took some Clam while he was in there. He hasn't said a word.

"Ah killed her," Buddy mutters, tears pricking at his eyes. "Ah killed a woman. Ah killed her with mah own hands, fer God's sake."

He takes the bowl in his hands and smashes it into the wall. It shatters and flies across the room, bits of food and glass going everywhere. Sobs choke the air from him.

"Buddy, you're—"

"Don't yuh tell me it was the right thing to do!" he says, tears pouring and pouring— "Killin' someone ain't never the right thing to do. Ah killed someone, Rollin. Ah took a life from this world and if ah was ever a man of God, ah sure as hell ain't one now!"

His knuckles clench, turning white and then almost blue and that dark face of his goes darker and darker until I don't think it can go darker any more but it still keeps going and—

"Ah ain't desrvin' of this world," he murmurs, staring directly into my eyes the entire time. "Devils can't repent nothin'."

ROLLIN

Days have passed, and I have been making progress in my recovery. During the two weeks while I was in a comatose state, my body healed significantly, but not enough so that I could walk around or sit up even. Now, I can sit up without aid and take a few agonizing steps with the help of Marco or Buddy.

Neither has been the best companion the past few days. Marco sulks around, missing the comforts of his apartment up north, missing being a Privy, and hating every second of running. As for Buddy...her murder haunts him day and night.

"Ah considered suicide," he whispered yesterday, the pupils of his eyes going wide. "Ah considered a lot of things, but the Lord has taken me under his wing. He ain't lettin' me go so easy. Ah want to repent, and ah don't want to go to hell 'cause of sin takin' me there."

I was about to tell him that two murders makes him sinner aplenty, but decided against it. Buddy doesn't need more reasons to commit suicide.

I sit up on the coach and reach for the book that's hidden within the folds of the couch. It's an old, battered copy of *1984*. Buddy found it outside in a dumpster when he went to find food and had the good sense to bring it inside. I open the book and begin reading about Big Brother and this world of George Orwell's.

The couch sinks as Buddy sits at the opposite end. I continue my reading as I hear the flutter of his Bible being leafed through.

"'Pray for us, for we are sure that we have a clear conscience, desiring to act honorably in all things,' Hebrews 13:18. Ah always loved that quote, Rollin. Ah thought ah'd share it with yuh. Ah look to it in times like now, when the past is black as sin and the future a hazy fog."

I look up from *1984*. "It's a good quote to live by."

He smiles at me, biting his lip in a nervous jitter. "That's why ah have to confess somethin'. Ah met Mira 'fore ah met yuh."

My eyes fly open as I stare at him, this man, this lying man.

"What the hell are you talking about?" I yell.

Buddy scoots away a moment when he sees my reaction. "Ah met her when ah was travelin'. It wasn't near Chicago, but somewhere in Indiana, which don't make sense if she was comin' from St. Louis."

A nervous sweat breaks across my forehead. "I don't know why."

"Well anyway, ah went up to her fire and asked if ah could share it. Ah was talkin' with her 'bout our Lord, yuh see, but she didn't like that none. Ah didn't think much of it until yuh brought her up a couple months later and ah didn't know what to do…"

I squeeze shut my eyes, a pounding heartbeat vibrating through my temples. "Why didn't you tell me this, Buddy?"

"Yuh wasn't doin' so hot and ah had just met yuh, mind yuh."

"But you should've, you…" I mutter.

I ignore Buddy as he blabbers on about all his excuses. It becomes white noise in my ear and I close my eyes, away from him, away from all of it.

He killed Mira.

I shake my head. No, he didn't. He killed Nova. How did she become…Nova? What happened to her? Will it happen to me?

Does something…happen to people in this city? Marco has barely said a word to me since the incident on top of the Binoc tower, Buddy is losing his mind with grief and regret, and Mira lost her memory and who she was.

She didn't recognize me. She kept calling me Micah, the one who raped her.

I pull my hands to my head, shielding myself from the destruction, the chaos, the misery. I can't do it. I need to leave. I can't be here anymore, and there's nothing left for me.

"I need to go," I whisper.

"What?"

"Once I'm healed, I need to leave the city."

Buddy is silent as he stares at me. "But yer…but ah'm…"

"There's nothing left here for me anymore," I stammer. "She's gone. I failed. All that's left for me to do here is kill the man who raped her."

"Yer not thinkin' 'bout no revenge, are yuh?"

I turn to him and direct my confused look at him. "I don't even know where he is, Buddy. There's not much of a lead to go on."

He's silent for a moment, staring ahead and folding his hands in his lap. His eyes twitch back and forth, unsure.

"Ah can't have no part in it," he says. "Ah've gotta stay holy. Ah've gotta please the Lord. Ah gotta do what's right, and goin' after this man ain't what's right, ah'm sorry."

I sigh, but I understand. It's the advice I gave him, anyway.

"Ah'm sure Marco will help yuh out, though," he glances over at the sleeping corpse on the couch beside us.

I think on that, glancing at Marco. "What…what should I do? I don't want to kill the man but…he ruined everything. He led Mira to madness and if I go there—I don't know if—"

"Whatever happens, yuh ain't gonna be anymore damned than ah am."

I laugh morbidly. "I guess not."

Time continues in its ever-changing way. A day passes as slowly as my strength returns to me even more so. Soon, I can take a few steps on my own. We play cards to pass the time. Buddy can hardly play Go Fish, but Marco has had his fair share of playing time from nights on the Binoc tower. Marco sweeps every game we play.

I'm the first to fall asleep and the last to wake up. By the end of that day, I can stand without assistance and take a few steps. By the next night, I can walk. I may be in gut-wrenching pain, but I can walk.

Buddy and I prepare breakfast the next day. Until now, we had been using the fresh food Marco had stolen when we first fled the city. Now, every meal comes from the abandoned house next door. Our meals will be coming from cans for a while. It's not a glamorous life, but it's living.

I sit beside him on the couch, flinching slightly as the pain twists through, but it passes quickly. I hold my stomach gingerly as I ease back into the couch cushions. We discuss what the future holds for us. Buddy stands firm on his decision to not intervene with me, and Marco agrees to help. Marco pulls a cigar out and lights it with ease. He puffs on it thoughtfully.

"You want to kill him?" he asks.

"If I have the chance, if we find him quickly…" He doesn't say anything for a while, only puffs and puffs his cigar, pulling away the stress of his life.

"He'll be leaving the city soon, but I don't think he'll be able to flee the city before the mob gets control of him. He'll go up into flames and spread across Chicago if he likes it or not and damn me if he does."

"If we can't find him tomorrow, then I'm going to leave Chicago for good," I turn toward Buddy. "There's nothing left for me anymore, and there's nothing left for you anymore, Buddy. I hope you thought about coming with me."

"Ah have, but ah can't. Ah've decided to open up a home fer the roaches in the city that ain't got a bed or some food in their stomach, just like ah told yuh ah was gonna do way back when. Ah'm sorry."

Marco laughs, taking the final puff of his cigar and smashing the end into the ashtray. "You're as damned as I am, Buddy. There's no use trying to reverse it."

"It's the Lord ah trust," Buddy stares at him, "not yer opinion."

MIRA

I couldn't describe this feeling: my heartbeat is a drum inside me, my body an eggshell ready to crack, my fist a fish stranded on shore, my whole body shaking so bad I'm surprised it's even here at all. I need some Clam. I need to calm down.

John's hand appears on my shoulder, soft and comforting, the only thing that's not shaking right now. I hold it close to me, smelling the rich aloe lotion he put on earlier.

"It's okay," he whispers to me. "Don't be afraid."

But how can I not be afraid?

Outside the red brick building, messages are burned and scratched into the sidewalk:

Rapist

Murderer

He's not.

The red brick building is deteriorating; many bricks have fallen from the mortar or are close to falling. All of them are eroded. The red color has long since faded, leaving a dull pink behind. The cement steps leading up to the door are cracked and crooked. No longer the fresh white when they were first laid, the cement is dark gray, almost black.

Thorny bushes lie underneath the windows, their bare branches clawing toward the glass panes, reaching for the life inside. Flowers haven't grown on them and it's nearly fall. Soon, all the other flowers in Chicago will be dying.

I stare at the door. It's black as night and covered with spiderwebs, dust, and fly carcasses. It glares at me menacingly, tempting me, daring me to go inside. My fingers twitch, wanting to turn the knob, but they don't move. My mind has stopped my body and nothing works, nothing works anymore.

They say this is where a man named Micah is supposed to be staying. It's located in the roach district, only a block away from the wall. The Privy councilor put him here to protect him against the mobs, apparently. Has Rollin changed his name to disguise himself, like me? John claims Rollin is the one who raped the girl, and when pictures began to surface of this Micah, it was him. It was my Rollin.

John tells me that people burned the names into the sidewalk because they were too afraid to go inside. Once a murderer, always a murderer, they said. On the inside, they had Wardens placed to protect this Micah. That's what the Wardens told John.

"I can't go in," I whisper, turning to John. "What if he really has changed? What if…all these rumors—"

"They're not rumors," he takes his hand away. "They're facts. He raped her and then murdered her. This isn't much else to it."

"Maybe he was mistaken for someone else! Maybe he's not the same person," I try to figure out a way where this isn't true, where he won't be the bad guy. "It can't be true. I…"

I lose track of my thoughts. The world tilts a little, spinning out of proportion and I can't take it anymore. It's too much.

"Sit down with me, Mira," John gestures to the cement step in front of the door.

I sit with him and we are silent for a moment. We watch the street, people coming and going but no one ever stays the same. Crowds of roaches, not as many as in the Privy sector, move across the sidewalk, rarely stopping.

Some of them stare at us. I ignore them. Their gazes flick from our faces to the words burned into the cement in front of us, and it doesn't take long for them to turn away. Most roaches avoid anything that could harm them, and that means other odd roaches as well.

Even though we're Oddities, we can still become stranger.

A car passes by. It's a Warden car, distinguishable by the blue stripe on the windshield. The man inside spots John's face and gives a hard look, pressing his accelerator. The Wardens know John is innocent, but also know he isn't supposed to be alive. They want to take his side, but in doing so, they would bring their own death.

"That was Warden Thompson," John mutters. "I knew his wife and twins, baby girls, before they were kidnapped and never seen alive again. Their bodies were found in a dumpster around the central part of the city. I was the only one there with him when they found the bodies, and I was the only one to keep him sane. He would've hunted down whoever did that to his family, but I knew better. I held him back. If he did anything to a Privy, it would mean death or to the suburbs. I couldn't tell you which would be worse."

"What's it like in the suburbs?" I ask, curious.

He doesn't talk for a long while, as though if he would speak about it, the horrors would come to life right before us. He only takes his hands and rubs them in front of him. His eyes look off into the far distance, seeing everything and nothing at all.

"It's hell on earth," he whispers. "It's as if Ash was alive and real all the time. It's...I don't know what to tell you, Belle. I've only seen it once and...if I ever had to go back, I'd ask for death instead. Most people there don't last more than two weeks, anyway. That's why Wardens are so eager to send roaches to the suburbs; they always need more. The lucky ones are sent to the farms, fields, or production lines to produce goods for the city. The damned get sent to the incinerators."

The atrocities leave me speechless. I only stare at my fingernails, which are filled with dirt. I scrub them into my jacket and try to get the dirt out. Filth has been following me ever since I was in that alleyway.

I turn around and look at the monstrous beast behind us. We've spent the past two weeks searching for this building, asking the Wardens who would talk to John, asking the gossiping roaches, asking anyone who would talk to us. Now that I'm finally here, I sit outside it on the steps, talking to John as I have been for the past two weeks.

It's funny how things work out, huh?

I look at John, a sweet, humble bumblebee, as I like to think of him. He'd hate me if I ever called him that. He is a bumblebee, though; so many people are afraid of him, but he's only as harmless as their fear makes him. If he had a choice in it, he'd never hurt people or send them to the suburbs at all.

"When I was a child, I wanted to be a doctor," John had told me when we were searching for new leads a few days ago. "That was before everything happened...before the world crashed and burned and before I ended up here. I wanted to help people. I wanted to save people when no one else would. I wanted to be the last resort."

It was at that moment I first wished I would find John in the real world. He's out there, in the colonies somewhere. If I ever make it back there, to the colonies, I'm going to find John, the real one. I'm going to say hello and ask how he's doing, long after the John beside me is gone. Maybe he's happy. Maybe he's a doctor. I'd like to think that.

It's strange how well I know the man beside me after the two weeks we've been together. I've told him so much, more than anyone else I've met in this damned city. He seemed...honest, and that was something new and strange to me.

I told him about Rollin. I told him why I wanted to find him. I told him he was like family, a brother almost...but not quite. No, not after those lonesome nights, not after the lustful days...though I didn't tell him about that.

It took me a few days to ask John why he was helping me. John couldn't answer that question for a while, until one day he told me about his aspirations as a child.

When he found himself in Chicago, he became a Warden because it was the closest thing to being a doctor. He wanted to help people, even if they were snobby Privies rolling around high off their asses in the middle of the night.

"You needed help," he explained, "so I helped you. You offered revenge, but I don't want that. I want to be a Warden again, and this is the closest thing to it."

It wasn't anymore than that, he insisted. I didn't believe him at first, but I've grown to trust the man. He reminds me of a middle-aged Rollin, like the one who always tried to gain my trust and be the best he could be, despite the circumstances.

Now...Rollin is behind me, just some bricks and a couple of wall away. He's right there. I haven't seen him in months, and he's *so* close, but somehow, I don't feel like it's him. The Rollin I knew would never have been called a rapist or a murderer because he would never do that. It makes my stomach turn and my head pound and my feet refuse to move.

I turn my attention back to the street and the herd of roaches marching along its barren path. *RAPIST* and *MURDERER* catch my eye but I turn away from them, trying not to think of that. I can't.

A bright yellow hat catches my attention on the ground, so sunny in a field of darkness. It reminds me of one Yorry had, long ago. She bought it from a clerk in the market one day. She spent her whole week's earnings on it, but she loved it. She nearly cried when it was stolen by a Privy two days later.

Oh, Yorry...she's probably worried sick. She either thinks I'm dead or was sent to the suburbs for one reason or another. When a roommate doesn't show up for two weeks, it's an easy assumption to make.

She was the one to help me get away from Jax's shop. If she hadn't...if we hadn't...I might have never found Rollin. I might have stayed there forever until I ended up like Estelle, flayed in the street.

I stand to my feet, my hands no longer shaking. I bound up the stairs without a word to John and ram through the door. I can't stop now. I have to keep going. If I stop, I don't know if I'll ever gain the courage to get up again, to go up these stairs and knock on that door and he'll open and god forbid he be a rapist and murderer. Please, if there is a god, don't let Rollin be either of those.

John's soft footsteps echo from behind me as I climb the first staircase, then the next. The roach that told us this is where he lived, said he was on the top floor. He'd better be there. Please, let him be there.

I reach the top faster than John climbs the first set. I go down the hallway, like the roach said, the third door with the black oak frame and the writing all around. Slanderous and demeaning words are scratched and burned onto the black oak and tears prick in my eyes because it can't be true.

My fingers grasp the doorknob as John's steady footsteps approach closer and closer. The door swings open. I freeze, my hand on the handle as the door drifts open and I could go in, he could be in there, I could see him and finally know the truth—but he could be dead—no, he's not, he's not dead!—he might be though, he might—

"Belle?" the voice drifts from below me and I push the door open because if I see that chubby, honest, Rollin-like face staring back at me again, I know I won't gain the courage to push through this door and see the real Rollin again.

The first thing that catches my eyes is three words:
BURN IN HELL

I freeze, entranced by the words and nothing moves, I can't move, I won't move and I hear John's footsteps coming closer and closer and there's no turning back now, I'm here and I can't go back. I'm here. He'll be here. John will be here.

John's panting alerts me that he's behind me before his voice does.
"Belle?"

I listen but don't hear. I see but don't watch. I touch but don't feel. Nothing registers. Nothing clicks in my head, nothing. Only darkness.

It's empty. The room is empty, all except those words.

He's gone.
BURN IN HELL

ROLLIN

The day begins in a haze. Colder days have come. Soon, as Buddy informed me, Ash will arrive and we'll all go to hell.

Buddy hasn't been here for a season of Ash since he spent so much time traveling, but Marco has, and even he doesn't want to talk about it. When we brought it up, he kept his head down and stared at his bowl of oatmeal. It was the only thing we could find for dinner.

"Pray to whichever god you pray to and ask to be gone from this city before it comes," he muttered, staring at the oatmeal but never at our eyes, never.

That's when Buddy chipped in. "Ah heard all the bodies they've kept holed up fer so long have been rottin' in the back of a truck fer as long as the last Ash ended. Once the fall hits, they'll take 'em to the suburbs and the workers will be slavin' away, puttin' 'em in giant incinerators and lettin' 'em burn and burn…"

"If I have anything to do with it, he'll be out of this city before it happens," Marco mutters. "There hasn't been ash falling from the sky, and let's hope there isn't any for a while."

"But what if we're not?" I turn toward them. "It's fall now, isn't it? It should start up any day."

Marco shook his head. "For your sake, I hope it doesn't."

The sky has gone gray. I haven't been in this damned city long, but I can tell when something bad is coming. The clouds roll across the sky dark as night, light pillows burdened by ash that's ready to fall. Any day now, he said. It will come.

That was last night. It's morning now, but the sky is still gray. The world hangs in a foggy mist that doesn't let up in the hours after dawn. The world is dark and damp. No birds fly. No trees sway. No animals quiver in the dark morning light.

Nothing moves.

We don't talk about it. Buddy pretends it's not happening. He jokes with a nervous smile on his face, pretending he's not a murderer, pretending he can repent his sins.

Last night, he kept screaming out into the night, pleading to the Lord to forgive him. His cries kept Marco and I up all night, but neither of us said a word to him when we met for breakfast this morning. We know demons lurk inside him. The angels have left the poor soul to suffer with the damned.

The memory of Mira's death haunts him even more than it does me. I've tried to forget it, but memories that you try to forget seem to linger even more so. It's the important ones that slip away.

She was on top of me, covered in blood, screaming out my name as she held a knife to my throat. She wanted us to be together. She didn't know what she wanted. Right when I thought she'd do it, when the blade would pierce my skin and our blood would mix together in the most deadly concoction, she went limp in my arms, a knife through her chest.

Buddy was there, the knife in his hands and a dark stitch in his heart. Things ended, for her and for me. I've had nightmares about it, the most recent one being last night.

A hand shakes my arm, making the memories go away, but only for now. They'll be back. They always come back. The good memories, from the League and my home in the colonies, those are fading.

"Rollin?" the soft southern voice asks, shaking me some more but dammit, the memories won't fly away. I can't fly away.

It's then I realize I've been sobbing. Chokes have shaken my body and two concerned pairs of eyes look back at me. Buddy has stopped shaking me, but silence continues except for my cries.

She thought I was this man…Micah. The crowd outside the building thought I was Micah. Mira died because of him, and she thought I was him.

My fists clench as I stare at the two men around me, buried in the dirt covered floor and the drying flower wallpaper and the disgusting apartment that I can't be in any longer.

This…Micah made Buddy contemplate suicide. It ruined both Marco and Buddy.

"I'm going to kill that bastard," I say through clenched teeth.

No more questions are asked. We gather our things in silence and start out the door. The day mourns like a widow.

There are no newspapers in Chicago. The only computers are used to swipe the Chicagoans' payment cards. There are telephones, but only the Privies have those.

With this knowledge, we begin our search for the bastard. We only have today, and then our time runs out.

We ask around. I hang behind Marco and Buddy as they question people. Strangers haven't seemed to like me, lately. Many people know my face, or Micah's face. I hide my face in scarves and a hood.

We walk all through the southern roach sector of the city, weaving through streets and alleyways. Everyone knows his name. It's been all people have talked about since it happened. Lots of roaches are murdered, but rarely is a Privy.

A few people say he fled his Privy address after she was murdered in the hospital, so his location is a mystery to many. Some say he's hiding away in the roach district somewhere. The Wardens or Binocs can't do anything to stop him either. He's a Privy. He can get away with murder. No one story is alike. Some speak of a roach and a Privy murdering the woman together, and some speak of just the Privy.

We wander the city. It's beginning to grow dark as the lemon drop sun dips lower into the skin, casting the world in a gray haze.

Chants and screams erupt from further down the street. The roaches around us go frantic, as though their little roach heads were chopped off. They all go running, scurrying in every direction and trying their damn best to get away from the riot as quickly as possible.

Any roach caught in the mob will be tossed to the suburbs.

Marco dashes ahead and I sprint after him, watching as the scene unfolds before us.

A thousand people crowd the street in front of a red-bricked house, which is caught in a massive inferno. Fiery tendrils reach far into the sky, hungry for more to burn.

People pass pieces of wood across the crowd until they're thrown into the fire, making it burn and burn and burn. Roaches in their green-striped jackets and Privies stand together, chanting together, burning together. Some are destroying the shops nearby. They smash the windows and cheer when a flaming torch is thrown into the looted shop and it catches ablaze. A car is also destroyed simultaneously, the same fate as the shop enacted on it. The world is on fire, and we're in the center of it.

The crowd screams two words over and over again:

"Murderer!"

"Rapist!"

Marco has disappeared and I look behind me and Buddy is gone and I'm alone and pulled into the crowd and people press on me from all sides—I CAN'T SEE—where's Buddy? Marco?—WHERE AM I?—

But the blaze roars on and the frenzy continues and I see a glimpse of Marco's bald head wavering in the crowd ahead and he's grabbing a Privy by the shoulders and talking with him and the Privy is confused but he listens, goddammit, he listens!

Privies don't usually listen to roaches, especially roaches that were once Privies. I guess Marco is different.

The blaze rages on and the fiery tendrils reach toward the crowd with uninhibited ambition. The crowd pushes back, watching as the blaze spreads to the surrounding buildings until it's one massive fire destroying the world that the colonists are waiting to live in. I lose sight of Marco. He's consumed by the crowd, the relentless mass of people cheering for the destruction of tyranny.

"Rapist!"

"Murderer!"

Marco spots me, his bald heading finding me in the crowd somehow and he takes my arms and tries to pull me away but the crowd ensnares us and we can't move—WHERE'S BUDDY?—

I huddle into my roach jacket as the autumn chill races through the mass of people and I can't see and the crowd doesn't seem to notice and the fire crackles and echoes against the burning walls and cars honk and people scream and SCREAM—

But somehow, through it all, Marco finds a chance to tell me the story. His disjointed screams create a story of a crowd coming to bring Micah to justice but there was only a building there and he had fled and he's not here, he's not here.

The sky grows darker and, oh god, Marco has vanished and his bald head isn't reflecting the moonlight because he's gone and I can't see—I CAN'T SEE—where am I?—

The light has nearly disappeared from the sky and I hear the whine of a grenade and the mob shudders as an explosion rocks through our eyes and a cheer races across the crowd and more fire, never-ending fire, and only a few slivers of dying sunlight break through the hell.

"RAPIST!"

"MURDERER!"

"BURN IT DOWN! BURN IT DOWN!"

Gunshots erupt. Screams shatter the illusion. Faces press against mine, full of terror, their eyes wide as the fire crackles on, reaching further and further into the black sky. The bodies surround me and I can't see anything, not even the fire, but only the smell of death and horror and the noise of an engine spinning around, silent as a mouse. I hold myself up from the ground as a body slams on me and I'm flattened to the asphalt and rubble digs into my cheek.

Then more people scream as a haze floats across the sky. Fingers point at the clouds above. Tiny flecks swirl in a cloud like the plague descending to exterminate us all.

"Snow?" I whisper to myself.

"It's Ash," the person on top of me whispers. "It's here."

MIRA

Twenty-four hours ago, I was in an empty room where I thought Rollin would be and now I'm on a truck away from the city, headed to hell. We are packed in here like sardines with the scent of death fermenting in the air. Coughs echo endlessly and death spreads its pale glory across our skin. Some cry. Some beg. Some plead for mercy. I only think.

I don't know how it happened. I don't know when it happened. It seems as though I blinked my eyes and now I'm here, miles away from where I was yesterday.

I remember being in the room, falling to the floor and crying and the tears wouldn't stop, they wouldn't stop and John came over and tried to comfort me but I wouldn't have any of it. I fell into myself and I wouldn't uncurl and I sat there, staring at the empty room and the roaches crawling across the floorboards and the smell of booze and Clam and vomit curling through the air and the feel of *almost* slipping through my fingers and the sound of my sobs and the cars going by and by and silence and suddenly, suddenly I couldn't take it anymore.

I smelled fire.

The smoke starting streaming through the room, through the floorboards, into the room and invading my lungs. I couldn't speak. John found my hand and pulled me over his shoulders like those firemen I used to read about and I saw the twirl of his lighter fall from his pocket, the one he didn't like to talk too much about.

The world spun into a world of red and orange and gray and my mind thought only of Rollin and that *almost* slipping through my fingers. Soot covers my face and tears away the soft flesh of my lungs and I cough and cough and cough but nothing comes up.

I hear John cursing and the heat of the fire on my back and legs and

175

calves and John curse some more and feel beads of sweet drip from my forehead and the world is all red, consumed by fire, consumed by hell.

We tumbled through the door and down those cracked cement steps and onto the sidewalk and suddenly, there was a crowd in front of me, all chanting those words on the sidewalk that I didn't believe but suddenly, I did.

Rapist

Murderer

We're all going to hell.

Things happened so fast and it was hard to distinguish left from right or up from down and everything was in a blur from when I stepped into that room until right now, when I'm sitting in a truck heading to the worst damn place in the world with John right beside me, bloody and broken and goddamn, I don't know how if he's even alive.

The mob grew. People asked who started the fire and no one seemed to know. *No one seemed to know.* Someone did it. I watched the steps that I had sat on only earlier that day. I sat on those steps and couldn't believe my eyes when I read those words in the sidewalk. *No, they could never be right. No, he's not any of those things. Rollin would never do that.*

When I walked in the room and saw the emptiness that I expected to be so full, I didn't quite know what to believe.

Was Rollin really a rapist? A murderer? Did he rape that woman and then kill her while she recovered from his attack? How could he do that? I don't know. I didn't know. So when it burned it down, I joined the chant because my hope had burned down with it.

"BURN IT DOWN! BURN IT DOWN!"

We did. We burned it down.

I joined the crowd. My roach jacket fell off me and I drank someone's Clam and I lost John in the mob but it didn't matter because my mind stopped working and it was like before I left Jax and his house and the sex and a bed and the food and I know it was wrong but at least I could blank it all out and float along empty and numb, empty and numb—

At least I could survive.

Now, this...this confusion and Rollin was supposed to come but he didn't, he *didn't*, and then he came and fucked everything up and changed into an entirely different man than who I left in New York, but I guess I changed too.

I've lost a lot more than my virginity since then.

The crowd was hot and pressing and I was in the middle of it, chanting with them as they threw people into the air, watching the building burn and burn and it was so hot, so damn hot, people started taking off their shirts and if only my mom could have seen all the shirtless men.

She would've damned me to two hells for allowing me to see such evil.

One hell for Mirabelle the Maid, and one hell for Mirabelle the Mad.

"MURDERER!"

"RAPIST!"

"BURN IT DOWN! BURN IT DOWN!"

Things blurred and sirens wailed and still we pressed on with the fire, crackling and burning and we all screamed and chanted because Rollin was everything that the people said he would be. If he wasn't, then why did he run?

Everything stopped for a second. Fingers pointed to the sky and everyone screamed and the voices died away, only for a second, the briefest second. Ash fell from the sky, still as snowflakes.

I'd never seen it before. I mean, I'd seen snow a couple of times back in the colonies when I was younger, but that was snow and it was happy and Charlotte giggled and we rolled and smiled and laughed and no one cared. There was snow with Rollin in New York too, when we made a fort and snuck inside and we were in our own little world and that's when he leaned in and our lips met for the first time.

That was snow and winter and the Rollin I used to know. This is Ash, when ash falls and the roaches crawl to their corners to die and Rollin is a rapist and a murderer.

Yorry told me about it on a slow Sunday at Jax's. It was near the end of our stay there. The sky grew dark that day and it made Yorry nervous, so nervous she could barely concentrate on her work. Sweat beaded on her brow the entire day and her fingernails curled into her skin.

"Ash is coming," she whispered to me after her first customer had left and she didn't say any more, only went upstairs and slept for fourteen hours.

Of course, she had to explain it to me and I understood, barely, but I did. Ash never did fall that day, but now it is. Ash fell from the sky and my thoughts turned to Yorry and that dark day and then they turned to Yorry and yesterday's dark day. Yorry must think I'm up there, floating down with the ash.

As she told me, the roaches that don't make it in the suburbs get burned and their bodies, their ashes, are blown from the incinerators and into the sky, where they float down and collect on the ground like they collected when they first died.

They do it to scare the other roaches, Yorry said. They scare them into shape. No roach wants to be ash. No Privy wants to, either.

When we die, we're all one. We're all privileged oddities and odd privileges.

Meat is meat in the end.

Of course, these thoughts make me sweat now as we embark on the ride to hell, to the incinerators. The truck hits bumps and wind rattles its sides, sending us roaches shaking. Ash bombards the thin walls. The suburbs are coming closer and closer and us roaches grow thinner and thinner. If we die along the trip, we turn to ash. If we die in the suburbs, we turn to ash.

In the end, we all fly one last time.

I was in the crowd when they caught me. I didn't care. I wanted to go. My Rollin was gone, replaced by a demon named Micah. There wasn't anything left for me anymore.

Ash started falling and still we raged, watching the fire twist dark tendrils into the night. The sky grew dark as night, causing the flames to cast shadows on the world. Rain began to fall with the ash until it all fell together as soot on the world. Clumps fell from the air and slammed into the earth and whatever was standing in the way. All of us soon looked like shadows in the night, walking nightmares in a living hell.

The soot put the fire out within minutes. The reds and oranges left black behind, the smoke twisting into the air and leaving a dark world in its wake. That's when the Wardens arrived.

They dismissed most of the Privies and let them return to their little Privy world where the grass was green and soot didn't fall down on them and they could go hop in the shower and wash away the darkness and be bright as day.

But not the roaches. We were thrown into the trucks, into darkness different than the kind that was outside. The difference is minimal. Us roaches are accustomed to darkness. Wouldn't it be cruel of the Wardens to take that away?

The Privies fled and there we were, in the open darkness as the Wardens closed in on us. We were goners, we knew. They had the area surrounded.

It was the roaches' fault, not the Privies. Us roaches had to have manipulated the Privies into mobbing and chanting and being horrible citizens because the Privies would never do anything of the sort unprovoked.

Never.

We were herded into giant trucks and that's where I have been ever since. They drove us somewhere for a while and then parked for a while longer. We sat there, covered in soot, wet, hungry, tired, and in the need of using the bathroom.

Some of us have died. We stacked the bodies by the door of the truck and moved as far as we could away from them. That's where we go to the bathroom as well. Filth rots well with other filth.

We're all hungry. I don't know where John is. He's not in here. He would have heard me. I'm the one who came up with the idea of where to put the filth. I have been the only one to speak since we were captured. Everyone else is too afraid of the imminent death. It's coming, and we all know it. Soon, we'll all be ash. Some hope we'll go to the production lines instead, but I know better. Ash brought us here, and Ash will be at the end.

I find another disgraced Warden within the truck. He is the only one who would talk to me. Everyone else huddles against the walls, not looking, not speaking, only scraping off as much ash as they can off their body. I talk to the Warden. He tells me what happened.

"They took the rapist to the suburbs. Everyone in the city was searching for his head, so they decided to take him there until it was safe to send him back down south."

Rollin. He's there, in the suburbs, where I'm going. I might see him. I might find him.

Did the League take him away from Chicago? Did they send him to the suburbs until it was safe to take him back to New York? Or has he gone off the deep end, like these people have said?

I don't know. I just don't know.

I couldn't say how long we spent stopped in the truck before it began moving again. We've been driving for a while now. Ash still hits the roof of the truck with massive *thuds*. It must still be raining. It must still be coming down as soot.

The truck screeches as it stops. We jolt forward collectively. I nearly vomit. From the motion sickness to the stench of rotting bodies and human waste, I'm surprised I haven't yet. Well, there wouldn't be anything to come up if I did. I haven't eaten in more than a day.

I hear the truck doors slam. The truck bed falls in a deathly silence as footsteps sound from all around us. We all know what it means. We all know where we are. We're all not sure if we want to leave the truck at all. Maybe it'd be better to die in here than out there, in the suburbs.

Welcome to hell.

We're here.

ROLLIN

We're here.

The truck doors open and the light pours in. We shield our eyes and hide under our arms, the light too bright, the air too fresh and clean and none of us are used to it. Not after being locked inside for so long. Not after smelling the stench of human disparity for so long. The ash still falls methodically like a curse.

Marco huddles beside me, shielding himself as I am, away from the clean, crisp air that's already filthied by the ash streaming and falling and twirling from the sky. We lock eyes, our faces black as night with the soot that still covers them from last night. Automatically, we look for Buddy, expecting to see him beside us as he has been for weeks now, but he's not there. Marco lowers his head.

It was only twenty-four hours ago when this began.

We knew once we came here, once they trapped us between walls and began our journey from Chicago to the suburbs, we wouldn't come back. We wouldn't see the massive skyscrapers, glowering and glaring. The giants hated the sight of us befouling their city. They despised it.

Suddenly, I'm back there, back in Chicago, before the burning building and before they took us into the trucks. We heard it before we saw it. More gunshots were exploding, echoing to us vaguely, muffled through the mass of bodies around us. Screams filled the skies more than the ash did.

The Wardens had come to take the roaches away. They shot us, prodded us into massive trucks with Tasers and even when I wanted to get away, I couldn't. The bodies were thick and my arms were too weak to push away. I had been part of the damned, and now I was going to hell.

The area was quarantined and nobody could get out. It was only us roaches, crying with our heads cut off, rolling on the floor as the

180

exterminators collected our bodies. At that point, I had lost everyone. Marco was gone once more and Buddy, well, I can only assume he fled long ago.

He had had that look on his face the last second I saw him, like he'd do anything to repent those goddamn sins that had messed up his life so much.

"Yuh can't repent a dark heart, Rollin," he had told me days ago, when he contemplated suicide. "God don't want me no more."

But when I was there, thrown into trucks that would take me to the suburbs and death was imminent and Mira was gone and I didn't make it out alive and I was so close, so goddamn close. I couldn't help but feeling the red-hot brand of abandonment.

I pushed forward, one foot in front of the other because if I didn't, the Warden would see and he would shoot me and I would be like those underneath me, whose groans I heard and I had to step on them, I had to, because there was nowhere else for me to go.

I glanced to the right and even though the ash and soot and everything was hitting me so fast I could barely see or stand, there it was, a smoldering, half-demolished building. The embers crackled as soot fell and fell. Bricks were shook loose from the mortar and rained onto the crowd below. Roaches screeched, some of them knocked in the head, but they still struggled on.

Roaches can survive without their head for some time.

Dozens of Wardens were shoving roaches into trucks. Once one was filled, another was brought in as the other backed out of the narrow street. The cat always catches the mouse, no matter how fast the mouse is. The food chain is the one predictable thing in this world.

A pregnant roach was thrown on the ground in front of me, her legs shredded apart from bullets and pellets and the crowbars some of the Wardens fancied. Some of the Wardens were sick. They liked the blood, the cries, the screams, the pleas.

Gas cans were thrown into the cars, throwing gray haze into the air as ash fell and the world was a bleak mess of ash and soot bleeding the color from the world and finally, a Warden noticed me. He marched over, kicking a crying man holding a bleeding stomach along the way. He raised his crowbar in the air and I threw up my hands.

I sunk to the ground and let the tears come, but still the crowbar fell. The Warden let it land on my body, bruising me past recognition and the pain—I could barely walk. All my previous wounds returned with the strength of a million knives.

It seemed as though there wasn't a minute in Chicago when I wasn't beaten or broken in some way. From a slither poisoning to the attack outside the hospital to the brutal assault by the Warden, I'm surprised the thin threads that have held my body together haven't broken.

Weakly, I heard some in the crowd shouting, still, even through all the madness.

"Rapist!"

"Murderer!"

The Warden paused his assault on me for only a moment. He looked at those around him and then at the Wardens around him and soon the bullets rained and the pellets fell and crowbars upon crowbars rose and fell in a steady motion, a mad crowd bobbing to the violence.

It was around this time that my mind went dark. My vision fell, clouded by gray haze and black soot and the blood spilled all around. When I felt my eyelashes brush my skin, I knew my eyes were open, but there wasn't any other way I could tell. The world was pitch black and the stench was unbearable.

I was huddled in a corner of the truck, my clothes stuck to me with an interesting formula of soot and blood. The ash that covered my skin had crusted over, leaving a thick, impenetrable layer coating my body. There wasn't a place on my body that soot wasn't.

Arms and legs and some body parts that I couldn't identify by the touch were crowded about. Those of us that survived the mob and the assault by the Wardens were packed inside with barely enough room to pull our elbows from our sides.

There were those that made it to the truck, but not through the ride. I was stepping on a body, I could feel it. The flesh was soft underneath, squishing each time I adjusted my position, and the stench, well, the stench of rotting flesh isn't hard to distinguish and even harder to forget.

People screamed and sobbed and cried out in pain and no one knew who was next to us or where exactly we were, but everyone knew the destination. The suburbs could be the only place, and while the hopefuls thought of the production lines, I knew better. There were dead on this truck, and there was only one place they would go.

More people fell. Bodies piled underneath us, but those who survived endured it. Our own waste soiled our already soiled clothes. The stench was a mixture of human waste, corpses, blood and soot.

The air was thick with the stench, so thick I almost couldn't breathe. Some, in fact, couldn't. There were so many bodies around, it was hard to distinguish through the living and the dead. Some lay with the dead and soon became one of them.

The truck drove for about fifteen minutes before it stopped. A night passed before the truck began again. Soot bombarded the walls and consciousness was something I couldn't be confident in. I heard a men scream out and another yell "slither!" There weren't many voices outside after that, but the screams were never-ending.

When the truck began again at what I assumed was morning, I heard a familiar chuckle drifting toward me. It grew louder as the person squeezed through people, their complaints evidence of it. Others would have identified his laugh as one of madness, but I knew better.

"Marco?" I whispered.

Another laugh. "So you made it, did you, roach?"

That was all we said. The others around us began to push and shove and it was all we could do to stay upright. If we fell, it wouldn't be long until we were similar to those we lied with. We drove for hours, or what I assumed was so. Time can be wearisome when there's nothing to compare it to.

So that brings us to now, with the doors cracked open, revealing to us roaches of the horrific conditions we've been enduring for the past twenty-four hours, and giving us the saintly gift of fresh air, even if ash filthies it. The air tastes so sweet and pure compared to what I have breathed that tears well up in my eyes, cleaning some of the muck out of them.

Those who opened the doors are heard coughing, cussing at the stench and sight of us. Those of us inside don't move or speak, we only savor the fleeting moments of sunshine and clean air, ones that will soon pass.

They begin herding us from the truck. It takes a long while, for we have grown weak from standing and struggle at moving our legs over the bodies piled below us. Those of us who make it outside the truck collapse onto the ground immediately, only to be kicked by those who opened the doors.

We are promised bread soon by a guard if we cooperate, and the sound of food makes my mouth water so much I can't dare to refuse.

Marco and I are the last to exit the truck. Bodies upon bodies rot before us, so filthy with soot and blood and human waste, it's hard to distinguish between genders or races or anything really. They're bodies now. Nothing more than that. We're all the same once we die.

Once our feet land on soil, real actual soil and earth instead of rotting flesh, it takes all the strength remaining to keep myself standing. Marco's knees buckle beside me, but he stands tall. Neither of us speaks a word. Neither of us can.

Only a dozen of us remain from the fifty of us who came with the truck. The ones who did not make it are being cleared from the truck and piled into a different one. I can only suspect they'll be taken to the incinerators to burn into what killed them.

There are a couple more trucks parked beside ours, but no people or bodies stand near them. I turn away from them, close my eyes, and lift my face into the air. A gust of cold wind hits us, but I don't shiver. It's the closest I've come to a shower in weeks.

The wind peels flecks of ash away from my skin, but it is selfish in its courtesies. Soon, the wind has disappeared and the dozen of us march on.

A town appears before us. Mudded dirt is squished between crudely built buildings. Even cruder bridges connect the buildings together, and it continues like this for miles and miles. Barely a soul walks about, and those that we do see quickly hide their face and scurry along faster. In the distance, a massive building wider than any in Chicago stands, two chimneys reaching from the roof and into the sky. Ash cascades from the chimneys and falls to the earth. Some of it is caught into the wind and flies behind us, toward Chicago, but most of it falls right here. Goddamn.

It's like the sky is falling all over again.

MIRA

We've spent only two hours in the suburbs. I already watch the fires dance in the incinerators, licking up the corpses of the dead, and contemplate how painful it would be to lie there with them.

Don't try to question my sanity. Trust me, I already have.

We were released from the truck two hours prior. Now...now we're doing what the rumors had said we'd do. We're burning the bodies.

We were navigated through the suburbs and to the incinerators at the center. We pulled our bodies through the feet of ash below us, all the while dragging all those who didn't make it through the walk behind us. Once one fell, it was plain to see that many would soon fall as well.

My brain shut off. I couldn't think. The world was an empty, gray place and my feet were moving, one in front of the other, right then left, right then left, and if I fell, I wouldn't make it and I wouldn't find Rollin or whoever the hell he is now and all the suffering, all of it, would be for nothing.

My mouth watered and my stomach knotted itself as it searched and dammit, it searched for food but there was nothing there but a gnawing emptiness and they promised us bread. They promised us bread, but they lied. I'm not surprised, but I still hoped.

The truck grumbled in front of us, sending fumes from the exhaust into our eyes as it led the way to the incinerators. Bodies upon bodies were nearly pouring from the bed of the truck. Arms, legs, and heads occasionally rolled off, tumbling into the ash. They were hidden from us, buried in the ash, and it turned into a lottery. Who would win the body part? The scream usually gave it away.

There was a tiny child, no more than ten, beside me. Her hair was a tangled bird's nest on top of her head, her eyes like sunken ships in her skull and her skin pulled taut across her bones like a dress three sizes too small. At one point, the twigs underneath her couldn't handle it anymore and she collapsed, right beside me.

Since I was the closest to her, I had to drag her behind me as we made our way through the ash. Always the ash. The truck wouldn't stop to let us load the bodies in. It took too much time, they said. Might as well just drag 'em. Soon, she got so muddy from being dragged across the ground and through the ash, she didn't even look human anymore. She was a monster.

We kept going though, and soon, every one of those who kept walking was carrying a body behind them by the end. Some of the dead had fallen from exhaustion. Others were pried from the slithers and had their throats slit to stop the screaming. Only eight of us remained alive by the time we reached the incinerator.

The ash was a never-ending assault. It fell in massive torrents about us, blowing us backward and forward and I stumbled but I never fell. I never fell. If I did, I knew those that looked over us would not allow us the chance to stand back up again. Once you fall, you're dragged until you're dead. Only the strong make it to the incinerator alive and on their feet. All those that fall are corpses when they come here.

The building is a massive giant, similar to all those skyscrapers that stared down at me in Chicago, but this one is different. Death leaks from the shiny gray metal in the dim daylight, the only escape from one, tiny pair of doors in front of us. There is only one way in, but there are two ways out. One for the living, and one for the dead. This is where the work begins.

A man dark in features and in skin steps from the incinerator and in front of us. He pulls a key ring from his pocket, jingling them around until he finds the key that unlocks the doors. He growls the entire time, shooting me a scowl when my legs buckle for a moment, the weight of my body almost too much for the toothpicks underneath me.

The doors clatter against the walls when they are thrown open, and the leader screams at us to go inside. We oblige, tugging hopelessly on the bodies behind us. I think I see mine twitch, the tiny girl, but my body is so weak and the world spins and the stench, oh god, that stench hits us—

—right and left, right and left, right and LEFT—

—none of it works, none of it works anymore CAN YOU HEAR ME—

—skinny gray corridor with fires crackling—massive machines and a scream ripping through my sanity and dark laughter, echoing against the walls—

—IGNORE IT, PUSH FORWARD—

—her ankles drop from my hand and she falls just as she did before and—

—the leader is screaming, hitting, punching and my cheek—MY ANKLE—pain splitting through everything but I stand—GODDAMMIT, STAND—I'm not going to fall—

—soot and filth, soot and filth—is there a body underneath all of this and—

—my legs, oh god, my legs—how do they work anymore?—

—mind blurs everything and nothing works—my eyes look but don't see—my fingers touch but don't feel—my ears hear but don't listen—my mind is mechanical and I throw people in—*ow*—I stick my red skin into my mouth—I gag at the taste—nothing works—fire swallows corpses up, burning burning BURNING—ash shooting up the chimneys as it falls and FALLS—NOTHING WORKS—

Water.

My brain whirls and the leader, he's leaving!—we're here and people like us—dirty and tired and broken—so broken...—a scream scratches my throat, burning BURNING—pain twists my bones to dust and help, HELP—

Water.

There, on my body—no clothes—only soot, like a second layer of skin... falling off... swirling in the mud...washing away...only skin, stained gray and cracked and raw.

Bare people are all around.

Water—running down my throat and clearing the ash and dirt and taste of death from my mouth and bread, oh sweet bread and I'm crying, tears rolling down my face, taking the last of the black soot away and finally. Finally.

Clothes are thrown at me and I pull them on, noticing they're gray jumpsuits like other people wore in the incinerator but they're somewhat clean and not too full of ash and I collapse on the floor, wherever we are, and sleep or die. I'm not quite sure which, and I'm not sure I care.

MICAH

I'm going to hell.

Do I care?

No, not really.

It must be like this, where skin turns crisp as bacon, roasting in the rich fires as the eyeballs disintegrate. The world is cast in red and black and it dances against the wall.

I have my own balcony that hangs over the main hall where the little roaches, the bad ones that I spit on in the city and called the Wardens on when they annoyed me, scurry about. They drag bodies behind them twice the size of what they are and struggling to dump them into the fire where they burn, and burn.

Technically, this balcony is for the leaders of the incinerators. They told me I was only a Privy and was moving back to the south soon enough. They said I wasn't going to be here long, just long enough to guarantee safe passage. They said I shouldn't get comfortable. I put a knife through the throat of the man who said that, and the men behind him weren't quick to support the dead man's words.

Fiery tendrils lick up their vulnerable bodies, tearing the ash that embedded itself in their skin away. For a moment, just a moment, their skin is clean for the first time in their lives. The fire takes on the strands of hair and there's a moment, right before it hits the scalp, when the bodies look like fire children. The effect looks better on women, but unfortunately, more men are being thrown in.

There isn't any other part afterward, only burning and scalding and black corpses that crumple into ash. It's blasted upward with a thick shot of air. The ash clouds the hall but pushes much of it outside, up into the air, where it falls on the earth like a broken cloud.

I prop my feet on the glass wall and press against it. Maybe it will crack and fall and collapse onto of the roaches. I'll hear their screams echo against the halls and the stench will hit me and a smile will grow across my face. It's a burning fire in my chest and I want the smell.

If that bitch sent me here, I might as well experience it all.

"Nova," I growl under my breath, feeling the name bite my tongue and I spit, attempting to get the filth out of my mouth. It doesn't work. Only the thought of her dead does.

I knew I shouldn't have ever gotten involved with her, but she was so…*easy*. It seemed a crime to leave her like she was. Her mind was open and her legs opened farther.

I twirl around the toothpick that hangs from my mouth. An empty plate, one that was filled with roast lamb and carrot puree, sits before me. I laugh when I see it, thinking of the caved-in stomachs of those beneath me, pulling bodies, burning bodies, being a body. I watch their business, their burning, their exhaustion and eventual defeat. It makes my experience less painful. Watching others suffer makes your own hell less apparent.

"Nova," I spit, taking the plate and watching it shatter against the glass. Some of the roaches below look upward, but soon get back to their burning when their master snaps at them.

If only the bitch had given me what I wanted that night. If she would only have acted normal and if only that bitch had listened. That mob would never had attacked my house and everything would be fine. The mobs wouldn't have torched my hideout in the roach sector. They wouldn't have burnt my car. The smoke wouldn't have twisted through the night. They would have never dragged me from that place and stuck me here to wait. This hell wouldn't be my life and the south wouldn't be my destination.

I'm leaving in two days' time and the bodies will stop burning and my heart will stop burning with it and the flame will die. I'm going to miss my glass case. I'm going to miss watching the bodies burn and the skin like black bacon and the smell. Goddamn, that smell.

The door squeaks open behind me. One of the roaches that's been serving me in this hell-hole appears through the door, shaking like a damn leaf in the wind. My hand clenches and my fist swings back and it's shooting forward when—

"Sir?"

I don't answer, only watch the bodies burn. I imagine the guy behind me was one of the bodies in the fire, twisting ash and death into the air, a potion, a delicious potion.

"You got any Clam?" I ask him, twirling that toothpick through my teeth.

I hear the ruffling of his jacket and he procures the tiny little bottle. He tosses it to me gently. I snatch it from the air, tear the cap open and down the contents. It's the first bottle they've gotten for me since I left Chicago and it rushes through my veins and my nerves light on fire and everything…everything is burning.

I almost don't want to take it, but it tastes almost as good as Nova's cunt the day I raped her. I know soon, I'll be far away from this hell, but it's a nice hell. If there were ever a hell I would choose, it'd be this one, right here, watching bodies burn and roaches slave away on the floor until they fall themselves. Still, they'll keep going, keep working, because they're roaches and that's what they do.

I feel all the bad emotions—pity for these roaches, guilt from killing that man earlier—and I sit there, feeling the darkness grow inside, feeling the heat burn like a thousand suns and I smile. Hell burns within me, twisting a smile onto my face and burning a scowl onto the roach's.

The soft red of my heart burns black as I burn with the bodies. I take a piece of the broken plate, feeling the rush of Clam go through my veins. I turn toward the roach that is serving me tonight. I take that piece of the plate and drive it through his neck. I feel the warmth of blood twist down my arms and his screams, twisting through the room and driving into my eardrums and—

Goddamn, I missed Clam. I hated all these bad feelings stirring inside me, all these emotions like I'm some sappy little roach that cares too damn much about his mom that he sacrifices himself to go to the suburbs.

The roach's blood runs through my fingers and the warmth brings icy heat to my heart, chilling it stone cold. His eyes glare up at me, vacant, empty, but not surprised. No, these roaches are getting too damn smart, if you ask me.

The body falls limp in my hand and I throw it to the side, yelling to the roaches that are most likely waiting in the hall. I collapse back in my chair, twirl my toothpick in my mouth and watch the world burn as I sit in my chair of fire. The slow, ruffle of clothing whispers through the air as the body is dragged away.

"Make him burn," I smile, hearing the soft *click* of the door behind me.

MIRA

My first day of work begins. I woke up in the mess hall with a hundred other roaches like me. All of us were wearing the same gray jumpsuit, all of us were hungry, and all of us won't get food. Our limbs were stiff from sleeping on the floor, but we were grateful for any type of sleep we could get.

It has been a long couple of days. The day on the truck was the longest I've ever known. I don't know if I could make it another trip on that truck.

We don't have long before we are ushered away from the mess hall and into the muddy, ash-filled fields. Our leaders give us a dull congratulatory speech for making it longer than the hundreds that have died in the past few days. They hope we'll make it a while longer, for their sake more than ours.

They lead us to the incinerator room. The bodies that the truck dropped off yesterday are now gone, most likely part of the ash that sticks to my legs. The stench still lingers in the air like a haunting ghost.

We don't question the leaders as they bring us through the hallway. The last person to question them was thrown into the incinerator alive. His screams scratched against the walls and our sanity. After that, we scarcely have spoken. Silence is a sacred virtue here.

My limbs are weak, the bones gone from my body and my muscles receding underneath my skin. My breath comes out faint and distant, my stomach has shrunk to half its original size and I doubt it'll ever fully return. My hair is lackluster. My eyes are dull and vacant. My smile has vanished, leaving only a pair of lips and yellowing teeth. I've lost myself and I don't know whether I will return.

The leaders are talking to us, and I really should be listening, but my brain is falling short and I can't remember why I'm here or why I would ever want to be in this hell hole when–

"Roach!" a scream flies in my direction as a palm is pressed against my cheek and I fall on the ground, my nose bleeding but no, no, I can't lose any more blood—

"Next time you stop paying attention, those fires over there will be greeting you."

No one offers a hand to help me to my feet. They only shuffle away. They won't be standing by me for a long time, I suspect. Someone else was punished similarly yesterday and we've all stayed away from him, as though his insubordination would spread to us like a plague and we'd all die.

We'd all die.

I snap my attention into focus and listen as the leaders explain to us how to do our job. It's simple. We take the bodies that other roaches bring in from the outside, throw them into the fires between two of us, and make sure no body parts fly out. I don't quite understand how that last part happens, but I don't dare to ask a question.

We begin the work slowly, afraid of doing something wrong, but the leaders soon leave and we're left with only each other and the bodies. Neither provides good company.

I work with an elderly man. I'm surprised he has made it this far, but there's determination in his eyes that I can't see in anyone else's. He picks the people by the feet and I pick them up by their armpits. My arms are burning by the tenth body, but I keep going. If they even sense weakness, I'll be the next body to go into the fire, and this old man will be the one throwing me into it.

My arms go numb, and I'm almost thankful. If they go numb, the pain won't shoot up them and I can let my mind drift away from this hell. The scent of burning flesh is so horrific, I almost wish I had lost my sense of smell so I would never have to experience anything like it again.

I turn my mind to Rollin, my Rollin. Could he be here? Could he have found his way here? No, he has to be here. I can't believe that he is a rapist and murderer like the others. I *can't* if I still hope to find him. Even if it means that he really is all those things, if he's the worst person and he rots here like the rest of us, then at least I know. At least the answers will be given.

I think of his black-brown hair, how it would sometimes grow too long and I'd have to cut it for him. Otherwise, it'd go in his face and he could scarcely see…and those eyes! Eyes like emeralds in a royal crown, so dark and beautiful, full of specks of different shades and every day, every day they seemed like an entirely different color.

The leaders come over to us and offer us a quick five-minute break. They give us a jug of water to share. It disappears in seconds. I barely have a mouthful. Each of us gets a small scrap of bread as well. I devour it greedily and look for more. Of course, there is none.

I glance around at this incinerator I'm in, sweat rolling down my forehead as my clothes stick to me. I eye a balcony jutting from the metal wall, the glass crystal clear as the observer stares down at us, a toothpick hanging lazily from his mouth—

It's him. It's Rollin, my Rollin. He stands and walks to the glass, his eyes set on the incinerator in the middle where bodies burn and burn and I swear, I swear he, he—

He smiles, but doesn't look at me, only at those bodies burning and burning.

It's him.

ROLLIN

Another day shakes me from my sleep and smacks the sense out of me. It's a feeling I've gotten used to in the little time I've been here. We've been bringing bodies to the incinerators and watching them burn and burn. Marco is close at times. I can see him, slaving away next to me, but neither of us can speak.

It's almost like the League, when nobody could talk to each other or be friends or doing anything at all that would make you more than acquaintances, but there, the rules could be broken and nothing would go too wrong but here, here…you die if you break *any* rule.

So we don't talk to each other. We share glances every now and then, making sure the other one hasn't fallen like the others yet, making sure the other is still there, making sure we're surviving, even if it doesn't seem so.

Buddy's words twist through my head: *"Yuh can't repent a dark heart, Rollin. God don't want me no more."*

He doesn't want any of us anymore.

I was walking toward our mess hall when I saw an old necklace, like the one Buddy wore religiously. The cross was pressed into the mud before me. The gold was scratched and dull, but soon ash swept over the necklace and it vanished.

Marco was marching ahead, his shoulders stooped and his spirit nearly broken. Not a word of complaint has slipped from his mouth. I don't know if it's because the leaders would throw him in the incinerators for it, or because he knew that neither of us meant to come here.

We never expected this. I think of Buddy, in Chicago, repenting his sins after I created them for him. Not once did he ever ask me for a favor. Not once did he question my motives. It's only now, in hell, that he's left my side. I thought those kinds of people, the kinds that find a stranger in need and help them, were gone from this world. Damn him if he thinks his heart is dark. Damn him if he ever thinks that again.

Our gray jumpsuits crinkle as we march toward the front doors to the incinerator. They gave them to us only yesterday, but they're already caked in dirt and filth and ash and I doubt if I'll ever receive another one again. I'm not going to be here much longer anyway.

We trudge forward, ash falling on us, clumping on our shoulders and destroying our hair. Nothing works, nothing works anymore. My limbs are mechanical, pushing through the motions even though they don't know why.

The threads of my muscles seizure uncontrollably. My eyelids don't have the strength to stay open. My smile has vanished and has left behind a ghost of a mouth. I'm a fading image of my former self. I keep her in mind, my Mira, my Mira shaped so horribly wrong that it led her to delusion so awful she didn't recognize me. She didn't recognize her friend.

I grab a body from the outside doors and throw it across my shoulders. The flesh squishes against me, releasing a scent that makes me gag, but I keep the little food in my stomach down. I don't know when I'll see another piece of bread.

I march with the other men, all of them with bodies on their backs, bringing them to the people outside the fires who will then throw them in. They are the weaker ones, the ones who can't bring bodies in from the outside on their own.

Mira. My Mira.

I'm sorry.

I'm sorry it had to come to this.

I'm sorry you had to die.

I'm sorry you and I ever agreed to become part of the League.

If I knew this is where we'd end up and I had to choose between this or never meeting you, I'd choose the latter. At least then, you'd be safe. You wouldn't be dead. You'd be alive and with your family and damn me if that's a life worse than this.

I let the body fall from my back and hurry back to the pile outside. If I take too long getting back to them, they'll either whip me or burn me. In their minds, it's a sign of either weakness or laziness, and both are equally crippling to the suburbs. That's why so many fall.

I see Marco's head bobbing a couple people in front of me. He's trying to hold it high, but it's taking all his strength to even do so. He grabs a body from the mess and throws it across his shoulders with a groan. He bites his lip and I know, goddamn I know, he's trying not to scream.

I'm barely doing any better. My bruises and wounds and broken bones have barely ebbed off and I've tried so hard not to limp when the leaders are watching, but it's hard, it's so goddamn hard when my damn bones seem to be made of poison.

I grab a body and pull it onto my shoulders, my leg screaming and my vision falling in black and no, NO GODDAMMIT NO—

—I grit my teeth, pulling against the blackness and—GODDAMNIT—

—the body slips from my shoulders and I can't hold it, I CAN'T HOLD IT—

—I collapse on the ground and—no, PLEASE NO—

But the leaders don't see. One of the other roaches helps me to my feet and tells me to go to the group by the incinerators and I do, I do because maybe then I won't be thrown into the fire—

I look up, expecting someone to be watching, expecting someone to be looking and there is, this man in a balcony with hair like mine and he's there, a toothpick in his mouth grinning at me trying to escape death and goddamn, goddamn me.

It's him. It's Micah.

MICAH

It's nearing the end of the day for the vermin. The bodies for the day have been burned and I watch them, protected by my sheet of glass. The bodies of all the roaches I killed after the first lay around me and I laugh because goddamn, I didn't know how *wonderful* this place is, how goddamn *wonderful*.

Bottles upon tiny bottles are littered around me, the Clam gone from them and in my stomach. The magical effect it once had on me has vanished. I don't pass out. A certain resistance must have built up to it and when I take it, goddamn, when I take it, there isn't a damn thing in this place that could touch me.

I have another bottle in my hand and it's down my throat before the incinerators begins their pulsing alarm to signify the fires turning off for the day. The ash will settle outside and the roaches will settle as well. The workers will go to the mess halls and collapse on the cement floors and in a few hours, they'll be at it again. There's never a shortage of bodies to burn.

I leave the balcony. The stench of the blood and the bodies rushes to my face and I breathe it in, let it collect in my lungs as I gallop down the set of stairs, laughing still at the thought of some roach finding the bodies upstairs. Eh, it won't do him much harm. He might be blamed for it, but at least he'll be thrown in the incinerator along with his buddies.

I walk to the main doors, a trail of gray-clad roaches following close behind me. They don't speak, only wobble on behind me, silent as a pack of mourners. I mean, they are mourning for their own lives. I heard the leaders talking about how a roach doesn't last a week around here, and they're always getting a couple truckloads in daily.

They're never-ending, apparently. They pick up a lot of stragglers. The trucks pass by people along the outskirts of the city. They don't stop for them. They either die from starvation, dehydration, or the slithers get them.

The doorway is opened in front of me, and a rectangle of late daylight cascades through the dark hallway. I hear a few surprised gasps behind me, many of the roaches unaccustomed to the light. I laugh under my breath. I turn to the right, down a long, twisting hallway that will take me to my room.

The smell of burning flesh drifts in from the incinerator. I close my eyes and take the stench it. Another good day. I laugh, remembering the image of them wobbling around in the room, barely staying on their feet, knowing that if they fall, they'll be the next body to be thrown in.

Fingers brush my shoulders and I turn around, my brows furrowed because no roach, no roach with any sense would touch me, not when they know it'd be their death and damn this roach—

But I turn and it's not a roach it's…shit…it's—

"Rollin," she whispers and shock has clutched my body and it won't let go, it won't–

It's Nova. It's fucking Nova, back from the dead like a ghost.

I barely recognize her at first. Her hair has been chopped short and her face is covered with ash and soot and dirt and she looks absolutely disgusting, but it's her. It's Nova. I grab her shoulders, squeezing into her with my nails and she's just like I remember her, all hating and crying out at—oh, that cry. It sends shivers down my spine. I smile at her.

"What the hell are you doing here?" I growl. "You're supposed to be dead."

She cries out more as I press my nails into her, feeling the flood of warmth on my skin and— "Rollin what are you doing? It's me…Mira…Rollin!"

She thrashes against me, pushing her arms at me and oh, how I love the fight. The blood rushes up my veins and I pull my fist back and feel the sweet crunch as it hits her face. She falls, the bitch, crying her eyes out to the world.

She's babbling some shit I don't understand and I stop listening, only pulling her up by her hair until spots of blood appear on her skull and I laugh, throwing her onto the ground. The other roaches stand around and gawk, staring at me with their beady eyes as I pull my fist back again and again, watching her squirm and scream.

"What the hell are you doing?" I yell at them, spit flying out of my mouth as anger races through my veins, amplified by the Clam, feeling the beautiful anger, and I can't see because everything is red and burning, burning, BURNING–

The roaches scram and sprint from the exit, the door slamming shut and casting us into darkness, the only light coming from the incinerator's dying fire. The red and orange flicker against the wall, making the blood splattered on the floor even darker.

It's beautiful.

The leaders won't question where she is. They won't even notice, the damn worthless thing. I pick her up by her hair again and she screams out, begging for me to kill her. Oh, I will.

I won't make that mistake again.

MIRA

It started innocently enough. I hoped so badly, so goddamn badly that it was the Rollin I left back in New York, the Rollin whose eyes watered when he refused to cry. He was always the macho man, trying to be tough and strong even when he didn't want to or couldn't be.

The day had ended. I had seen him up in the balcony, watching us with that smug grin on his face. He never saw me. He only watched the bodies burning and burning in the incinerator. Every time we threw a body into the fire, I swear the corners of his lips twitched as the fire consumed the poor soul.

The alarm sounded. The day was done. My bones were sore and my muscles fatigued to the point of ripping apart, my mind was dying, my senses were fading, my every movement was a struggle in itself but still, I pushed on. I knew what I had to do.

I wouldn't make it another day doing this. They give us barely any sleep or water or food and my body is failing, I can tell. The little fat I had built up over the years has been sucked away, leaving only a skeleton protected by a sheet of skin.

The other roaches and I were gathered together, making sure the area was somewhat clean, making sure the bodies that were in the incinerator were burnt. The bodies were disgusting. I stopped watching after a while because the mere sight of them, brunt and black and gone from this world so easily, their lives vanquished and gone and that could be me next and it was too much because my eyes started watering and if we even dropped a tear, they'd see the weakness and surely, we'd be in there next.

I would make it. I would do it.

My legs were failing me, I knew it, but still I ran, pushing through the crowd because I saw the balcony light had died away as the fires in the incinerators had and I knew, I knew he'd be leaving with the rest of us and I could get to him and the leaders weren't there so they couldn't stop me and it'd be only me and him and the rest of the roaches—

So I pushed and shoved and made sure I would be able to get there but my limbs were failing and the concrete hit my knees and I cried out in pain and I wouldn't be able to make it and the other roaches kicked and stepped on me and I saw darkness bleed into my vision—

I pushed my way to my feet because there was Rollin's head, drifting away from me and that was my only chance to get him, my only chance to find him like I've been searching for all this time—

I kept running and soon the other roaches got out of my way. I turned down a hallway and sprinted after him, taking turn after turn, and I kept going and he was steps before me and my hand fell on his shoulder and he turned around, a glare in his eyes that wouldn't relent—

That's when it began. It wasn't my Rollin. My Rollin was gone, replaced by this demon that kept calling me Nova and kicking and punching and he won't stop, he won't stop the assault and that's where I am now.

He's still above me, brutalizing me, making sure I feel every inch of pain hitting me and yelling and screaming and calling me names and he tells me, he says he'll make sure I die and I can't, it's too much—

"You were the only one who mattered," I whisper, but a punch lands in my stomach and everything that was in my stomach—which wasn't much—comes up and tears stream down my cheeks.

"Shut up, whore," he growls, fire and evil and rotten life burning away in his eyes and he doesn't see, he doesn't see me.

"I never wanted to leave you," I mutter, through the blood in my mouth through everything.

"You worthless piece of shit!"

I feel it, the darkness coming but still Rollin, my...Rollin...he hurts me and kicks me and nothing matters anymore except the fact that here I am and there he is and there couldn't be a distance in the universe larger than what's between us right now.

"I was yours," I murmur, my voice a breath, so quiet I doubt he can hear me, "and I hoped..."

My eyelids flutter close as the punches fall and clumps of my hair are strewn across the floor and the flickering light from the incinerator fire growing fainter and fainter, the orange and red a shadow against the wall as my blood leeches from me like a dark river, twirling and twisting away...

The black night attacks me, pulling me away from the pain and the hunger and the tears pouring and pouring. His punches and kicks and scorching touch aren't painful.

It's all those words that are killing me.

Goodbye, my love. I'm sorry I never found you.

ROLLIN

I—I don't know what to do. Please, someone tell me what to do because my legs are shaking and my bones are breaking and my sanity is falling through the earth and I can't bear to watch any more of this madness.

The alarm rang earlier, the huge *clang...clang...clang...*that never seemed to cease and it vibrated throughout my head and I couldn't get it out—it wouldn't get out—until I was on the floor grasping my head and the ringing wouldn't stop—IT WOULDN'T STOP—

—it only kept going and going, ringing and ringing and I felt hands on me, weak hands, trying to pull me up because they understood, they got it, the madness that was wrapping around my brain and pulling me under a thick sheet of water and help, HELP—

—I couldn't tell you what was happening, only that I heard a scream and then there were no more hands and yelling and cries and screaming but I only sat there, rocking back and forth, back and forth until I thought I would die, lying there, not moving, holding my forehead because if I didn't, my brain would fall out and I would die—

—but then I heard the voice, the smallest whisper, reach to me through the darkness and pull me from my grave and my eyes flickered open and for a moment, for a moment all I could see was black.

Pain stretched across my limbs like an old friend, stealing my strength, my everything, until I was lying there, unsure of the world and what was happening and why I was chosen to wake up from my grave and how did my sanity come back to me and—

There it was.

The voice.

Coming back to me.

Bringing me back.

Oh, oh god.

It's—

But the pain returns and stabs and steals and I am slipping away and I try to reach for the voice but it's gone—it's gone.

It comes and goes and I can't remember if it's a memory or reality because the darkness is rushing back but I'm fighting it, I'm fighting and oh, god please don't let me fall—please—HELP—HELP—

There's the voice again, drifting, coming—

There it is.

But it's less of a voice and more of a scream that rips through the night and tears my senses away until my eyes flutter open despite the pain and the horror and the black everywhere and why is it so goddamn dark? WHY?

The fires from the incinerator flicker and flutter and hit against the sharp metal wall until the darkness ebbs away a little and I feel it, the handle of the knife I stole off a body earlier—I'm sorry—I'm so sorry....

Then it rips through the night.

ROLLIN!

—and the pain falls away and I'm on my feet and running and sprinting and the pain is gone, taken away because my legs are moving back and forth and my mind is racing and racing but it doesn't think because that voice, the voice that brought me back—

Mira. It's my Mira.

—and in the back of my mind the doubt is there, that I'm already dead and I'm running toward an angel who will take me to heaven, but I know it can't be because the Mira that died in my arms didn't know my name but she kept calling me Micah—

—but she isn't saying that. She's saying my name, my real name, the name she called me in the night and the name she whispered when she was afraid and the name she said when she laughed and oh, that laugh!—

—one foot in front of the other, in front of the other—

—keep going, dammit—

—and I turn the corner and she's there and on the ground and Micah is above her, the bastard who raped and killed Mira but it wasn't Mira back there, it can't be because there she is on the ground being beaten and bloody and looking like she's barely holding on, but she's talking.

Goddammit, she's talking.

"Goodbye, my love," she whispers and it's her, goddammit, it's her.

It's Mira.

Things stall and time stops until we're all spinning in slow motion, all around Mira because she's here and the pain I was feeling—what pain?

My Mira is here. She's alive.

The knife is still in my hand, the black of the steel rising into the air and my feet leave the ground and that goddamn son of a bitch is looking up and it's only then he sees me, flying through the air and the knife comes down and—

—and—

—it falls, slowly, horridly, and the look comes on his face—

—the look of oncoming death and—

—the knife handle shudders as it plunges into his neck—

—blood, oh god, the blood—

—dark night splatters all over me and into my mouth and—

—goddammit it scratches at my throat and I can't see—

—we're falling, twisting through the air—

—my knife in his throat—

—and our bodies collapse on the ground and the air is knocked out of me and the pain rushes back and I'm not seeing or feeling but only there, looking at this son of bitch that—

"Rollin," a whisper, the tiniest whisper and I turn to her—

—the knife handle disappears from my hand—

—and in its place is her face, her porcelain face. The most beautiful face in the world.

She looks up at me, her eyes blinking, unknowing, unyielding and they barely see me, those depths of blue beauty barely see me. Tears prick at her eyes through the blood that's crusted on her face but I've never seen someone more beautiful in my life.

"Mira," I say and pull her to me, holding her close and listening as the last breath falls from the bastard's mouth and I see her watching him, her eyes wide and empty and I hold her, hold her so close that no one will ever take her away from me again.

"You…" she coughs in my ear but she can't finish and warmth hits my throat and I know its her blood but I stop caring because she's here, with me, right now, and that's all that matters.

Everything else is useless.

Her fingers squeeze my shirt with all her might and I don't know what to think or do because she *died*, she died in my arms and Buddy put a knife through her but suddenly she's here, before me, her hair short and her face bloodied and bruised and ash covers her and me but she's *here*.

She's here.

I found her.

She's breathing heavy and blood is still coming from all sorts of places and she's so *small*, so goddamn small, like a child in my arms. I hold her arms but there isn't much to hold and there's nothing to her, nothing at all and—

The world blurs as I look down at her. She's so beautiful, so I tell her that. I tell her how beautiful she is and—and, the words fall from my lips and—

"I'm sorry," I mutter, holding her and pulling my fingers through the hair that's still on her head and not on the ground—

Sobs choke the life from her and she only clutches me, her fingers pulling at my shirt as though she'll fall away if she lets go.

"I…I don't think…"

I only hush, blinking away the tears because I can't hear it. I won't. Not now.

She's in my arms and her grip is loosening and the blood is still coming but I hold her and I'm not letting her go and I can't let her go and so I hold her tight and I rock and my voice is stolen and nothing works. Nothing works anymore.

She coughs and blood splatters on my neck once more.

"I guess…my mom…was right," she laughs weakly.

"She always said the moment you saw a man without a shirt would be the moment your life would fall apart," I whisper, remembering the words she told me when we were in our snow fort and our lips glistened with the remnants of our kiss.

She laughs again, weakly, blinking tears away as I watch her, her beautiful smile. "I was a whore…I thought you would come but—"

"I tried," I whisper. "I tried to find you. The commanders didn't tell me anything, only that you stopped communicating with them and—"

A weak chuckle escapes her. "The commanders didn't…give me a way to… communicate with them."

We're both silent for a moment, holding each other, realizing the sickening truth of it all but it's okay because she's here now and—

My limbs are growing weaker and weaker and I won't be able to hold on much longer and I'm sorry, I'm so sorry and pain races through my veins and I scream out because nothing works…nothing works anymore. We're all damned.

She's slipping from my arms and she's trying to hold on, her weak fingers clutching onto my jumpsuit but we're both falling and my head hits the concrete and I hear her whisper, her voice call to me—

But I can't answer. My voice falls and the world falls to darkness and I feel her, in my arms, her soft hair brushing against my cheek and we both are falling now, twirling in the black night and we fall and fall but it's okay. The pain is gone.

Memories float back to me, memories of my life, of before I came to the League and after I left until now, right now, when I lie inside an incinerator in the suburbs with the woman, my Mira, that I came here for.

I found her.

I think of when the elderly lady who took care of me when I was little would come back with her basket of juniper berries and I'd help her boil them and pull them through her hair and she was always so happy after her hair was dyed because it was the one goddamn thing in this world that made her happy.

Now I'm here twisting and falling with my juniper berry who has turned to ash, twirling through the darkness and the ash melts away, leaving only a memory, the faintest memory and even the memory floats away until it's only us, falling and falling but then she slips away too and it's only me...

...

I'm alone.

...

The memories still come, fleet and forgiving, good memories, ones of Mira and me in the League and Mira and me just moments before when I found her and she wasn't dead and it didn't matter that her existence didn't make sense or that I had finally killed the bastard. Because she was there...

Goddammit, she was there.

...

The black night is all around me. Not even the light from the incinerator furnace shines in. I still feel her in my arms, a brush of an angel protecting me from the demons around...

...

...the world grows darker...

...

...it presses on me...

...

...on us...

...

...it creeps into my mind...

...

...I can't feel her touch anymore...

...

...am I afraid?...

...

...

...no... I don't think so...

...

...

...I've seen too much of hell to be afraid of it any more...

...

...

...

...it's okay...

...

...

...

... Mira, my Mira...

....

...

...

...Yuh can't repent a dark heart, Rollin...

...

...

...

...

...

...my juniper berry...

...

...

...

...

...he repented his sins, and I created them...

...

...

...

...

...

...

...

...

...she's a friend, nothing more...

...

...

...

...

...

...

...

...

...

...

...let's meet in the library...

...

...

...

...

...

...my juniper ash...

It is complete.

I'm inside the incinerator building that my subjects spent their last days in. I stare down at the three bodies, broken and bleeding onto the floor, and a pang of guilt rings in my chest. I can't help it, even if they aren't real.

Their stares are blank. Their world is gone. Their bodies have been broken.

Outside, clones are falling faster than the ash from the sky. If only they knew...

The world is a damn cruel place.

I look down at the three people again, the light from the doors cascading on their pale faces. I see the man I spent so many weeks with. His black-brown hair flutters in the dull breeze coming from the open doorway. His eyes are closed, lying in an eternal sleep. It is painful to see him gone. He was one of the few clones I liked.

Beside him is his love, the redhead girl that caused him so much grief over these past few months. Her eyes are still open, seeing, watching, and waiting. The blue ice glares at me, seeing the lies burned into my skin.

At moments like this, I have to remind myself that they were clones. I did this for humanity. I did this for the colonies. I did this for the new world.

Beside the pair, curled together like lovers gone to sleep, is the second clone of the male figure. He was the...experimental one. He went a little wilder than we expected, but the results proved effective.

I'll have to put this all in the report later, the entire story. It's been a long journey, traveling through the cities, introducing the clone poison we dubbed Calamity, a fitting name for its effect on the clones. Damn, it's a beautiful drug though.

They created it in the colonies. Its effects are similar on humans as they are on clones, but it is not lethal to humans. In the clones, they twisted a few strands of their DNA to make the clones genetically distinguishable from the humans. It was with this identification that they were able to create the drug to kill the clones exclusively.

This is the last stop on my journey. I was assigned the former region of Illinois and other cities close in the region to infiltrate and Chicago proved to be a massive issue. Many of the smaller cities within the state were easy to infiltrate and have the clones grow addicted to the drug.

If a clone were to stay off the drug for an extended period of time, insanity, depression, or suicide would curse them instead. Either way, death would be inevitable from the first drop.

When we fabricated the false organization of clones, the "League," we knew what we were setting ourselves up to do. Each clone had false memories, false preconceptions, and false knowledge. They believed their fabricated lives wholeheartedly, and thought they were the real people from the colonies.

Instead, they were social experiments.

The Minister of the colonies decided social experimentation would be beneficial scientific research. He assigned a group of scientists, myself included, to study the effects of a degenerating world on the clones. He was certain the results would be beneficial to the colonists coming to America. These social experiments were secondary to the clones being exterminated, we knew, but the information would still be useful.

The clones in the so-called "League" were told *they* would be the ones to infiltrate the clone societies and dispose of the clones. Each scientist devised a different experiment from their tests subjects, actual clones of people from the colonies, and each was assigned a different region. My experiment was seeing the effects of fear and love on a couple when the conditions were driving them apart.

To encourage doubts about the clone societies and create paranoia in the subjects, I had two copies made of each colonist and twisted their DNA to make each copy a bit different from the other. I created a society where Calamity was unbearably tempting and an imposing "Exterminator" ruled over them all. There never was an Exterminator, but the councilors of Privileges, Oddities, Binocs, Wardens, etc., was real. A group of novices I was tasked to have shadow me were assigned various leadership roles to keep the city functioning. One of their names I remember...he was especially unpredictable. His name was Max...or was it Jax? It matters little.

The Oddities and Privileges was one of the novice's ideas. He wanted to observe caste systems in the new world, and since his experiment didn't largely interfere with my own, I allowed it. The only unexpected curveball in the game was the slither poisoning Rollin. It was out of our control, and it made little difference. We could hardly control the animals that the clones had become when they revolted. How could we expect to control the wild creatures?

The story was fabricated. The ball was sent rolling. Their pseudo-world became real. There was some truth to the lies. The colonies, the clone revolts, the memory wipe of the clones…only their lives were fake. The rest of the world was very real.

This saga was interesting and will provide research that is hopefully beneficial to the Minister. He will be able to use the research to better the conditions of his subjects and create the best new world possible.

I call six clones into the cavern. Their faces are sunken in, driven mad by the withdrawal from Calamity as well as from starvation, dehydration, and exhaustion. It matters little. They're dying more from Calamity withdrawal than anything.

We've slowly been bringing more and more roaches from the city to the suburbs, where they eventually die of withdrawal or exhaustion and can be easily disposed of by the incinerators.

I predict I'll have the whole city cleared by the end of the winter. I expect the Minister will be pleased with my work. Almost the entire former state of Illinois, as well as the close region around it, has been cleared. I know not of the others' work in the rest of the country. Soon, the clones will be gone from the country and the colonists can begin a new world in a rebuilt empire.

The clones I summoned from outside take the three bodies between the six of them and follow me to the incinerator. I flip the switch on for the main gas lines and the fire roars back to life. Sweat beads from my forehead, but I ignore it. I watch as the clones bring my dead subjects to the fires and toss them in. I dismiss them. They scramble out of the hall, surely curious about me, but it matters little.

They'll be dead by tomorrow.

Calamity is a beautiful poison. The clones should be happy it was created just for them.

I force myself to stay, to watch my guinea pigs burn and blacken, watch their lives burn away to ash. Soon they'll be floating through the air like the rest of them.

Once they're blackened like fish, I leave the incinerator hall. I flip the gas lines off and watch as the fire dies away. The orange and black flicker against the wall until it fades to black and then, only then, do I walk away.

My name is Buddy Gavins, and I was not the angel Rollin thought I was.

ABOUT THE AUTHOR

A. E. OGLESBY is the author of five novels. At only fourteen, she penned her first novel about a polar bear named Soul. She lives with her family and two dogs in the suburbs of Chicago. For more information, visit aeoglesby.com.

26993393R00122

Made in the USA
San Bernardino, CA
07 December 2015